Doctor Zay

Doctor Zay

Elizabeth Stuart Phelps

Afterword by Michael Sartisky

The Feminist Press
at The City University of New York
New York

Library of Congress Cataloging-in-Publication Data

Phelps, Elizabeth Stuart, 1844–1911.
  Doctor Zay.

  Reprint. Originally published: Boston: Houghton,
Mifflin, 1882.
  I. Title.
PS3142.D63   1987   813'.4   87-48
ISBN 0-935312-72-2 (pbk.)

Cover design: Paula J. Martinac
Cover art: Detail of *Self-Portrait* by Cecilia Beaux,
National Academy of Design, New York

Doctor Zay

DOCTOR ZAY.

I.

"To my nephew, Waldo Yorke, of Beacon Street, Boston, Massachusetts, all such properties of mine as are vested in shipping, timber, or lumber, in the town of Sherman, in this State."

This was vague, but the more stimulating. What can compare with the bewitchment of arduous pursuit for uncertain privilege? There is an Orphean power well known to reside in testamentary documents, whereby the most insignificant legacy will draw the most imposing fortune to dance attendance upon its possession. But it is doubtful if Waldo Yorke, of Beacon Street, Boston, Massachusetts, would have found himself inspired to a personal investigation of his departed relative's kind intentions concerning himself, but for a certain constitutional sensitiveness to this allurement attending the pursuit of unknown results.

"Send a lawyer, Waldo." His mother had said this over the coffee for which she delicately prescribed the proper Yorke admixture from the Sèvres creamer. She spoke with the slightly peremptory accent which certain mothers retain, either from force of habit or from intrinsic delight in the sound, long after the expectation of filial submission has become a myth of the Golden Age. Mrs. Yorke was a handsome woman, who wore *point appliqué.* She was lame.

Her son had reminded her that in sending Waldo Yorke he really was not far from doing the precise, if remarkable, thing of which she spoke.

"Quite true," said the lady. "I had forgotten. Your having a profession so seldom occurs to one, Waldo. And cousin Don would have been glad to go, now the season is over at the Club. He has nothing else to do."

"I am somewhat overborne with that calamity myself, mother," the young man had said, coloring slightly. "I don't think we will discuss the thing; I am going to hunt up Uncle Jed's legacy."

Mrs. Yorke had not discussed the thing. Although not even indulgently talked of as "rising" in his profession, this idle, strong-limbed, restless son of hers had incisive preferences, with which she was familiar, as well as with his somewhat sturdy methods of executing them. And although they had only each other to be " beholden to " in all the world, — that is to say, in Beacon Street, — they were accustomed to yield one another the large liberty of assured affection. A summer of separation was to be expected, when one was the lame old mother of a nervous young man. Mrs. Yorke had kissed her son good-by royally, and here he was.

Here he was, lazily riding at the laziest hour of the sleepy noon, — he and the sensitive horse he had been so fortunate as to find in Bangor for the trip. He had been alone with the pony and his own thoughts, through the magnificent Maine wilderness, for now two long, memorable days. An older traveler than young Yorke would have found them valuable days. He had chosen the land route, seventy-two miles from Bangor. He had a certain kind of thirst for solitude, which comes only to the city born and bred ; most keenly to the young, and most passionately to the overtasked. Waldo Yorke had never been overtasked in his life. He leaned to the splendors through which he journeyed, enthusiastically, but criticised Nature, like an amateur, while he drank.

He had chosen the land route partly, perhaps, in deference to faint associations with wild tales

of it, told him years ago by that myth of a dead
uncle, in course of the only appearance he ever
made in Beacon Street, — Uncle Jed, whom his
mother, somehow, never urged the child's going
to visit, while never distinctly discountenancing
it, either.   Poor Uncle Jed was a good man, but
had never had papa's advantages, my son.   But
my son had conceived a passing chivalrous fancy
for an uncle at a disadvantage, and remembered
sitting in his lap, and stroking his grizzled cheek
with the soft pink palm of first one little hand,
and then the other, and asking him why he had
n't any little boys, and if God left them in heaven,
or forgot to send them down.   Poor Uncle Jed
was a bachelor, as well as a myth.

So this was the wilderness where the good old
myth had lived, loved — did he ever love ? his
nephew wondered.   Lived, loved, died.   No :
lived, loved, got rich, and died ; or lived, got rich,
and died, as you choose to put it.   What a place
to live and die in !   Or to get rich in.   Or to
love in, either, for that matter.

The young man leaned against the cushions of
the covered buggy, which seemed to arouse as
much bewildered effort of the perceptive faculties
in the stray natives whom he met as if it had been
a covered mill-pond, and indulged in that hazy

reverie which is possible only to ease and youth. What were his visions? What *are* the thoughts of a distinguished-looking young man, with one foot swinging for very luxury of idleness over the buggy's edge against the step, the reins thrown across one muscular arm, and both gloved hands clasped behind a rather well-shaped head. A young man with well-born eyes, and well-bred mouth; and he scorns to stoop to vices who carries just such a fashion of the nostril and the chin.

The route that young Yorke had chosen led him into the unparalleled deserts and glories of the wild Maine coast. Sudden reserves and allurements of horizon succeeded each other. They were finely-contrasted, like the moods of a woman as strong as she is sweet, and as sincere as she is either. Forest and sea vied to win his fancy. At the turning of a rein he plunged into an impenetrable green solitude. He became, perforce, a worshiper in Nature's cathedrals. Arch beyond arch, they lifted stately heads. Density within density, hung shadows in which it seemed no midday light could see to find a target. Welcome chills came from these shadows and struck upon the feverish cheek. Across them fled dry, unrecognized perfumes, clean and fine. Above, the dome of ether quivered with the faint, uncertain motion of hot

air upon a summer noon. Drops of light fell
through, upon the neutral-tinted shade that broke
the sienna color of the winding road. As far as
eye could see, the forest locked mighty arms before the traveler, as if to hold him to its heart forever.

Then swiftly at the tripping of a cypress, at
the surrender of an oak, at the fleeing of a rank
of pines, at the shaking of a ghostly beard of
moss, behold ! the solemn barricade has given
way. You have but turned a corner, yet the forest lets you go angrily, desperately, and yields
you to the sea.

Now the straight noon sunshine palpitates before, behind, about you. The road sweeps, yellow
and lonely, past a dreary little hut, a solitary
farm. The ruts worn by the daily stage, passed
an hour before you, begin to grow distinct in the
white heat. Rocks loom, a mass of wealthy outline against unbroken sky, and curved and curious
beaches kneel to wet their lonely foreheads in the
sea.

Your cathedral has turned you out-of-doors utterly. Galleries of wonder beckon you on. Irregular sculpture starts, half-moulded, from the
wild, gray cliffs. Sketches which Nature seems
to have begun, but never cared to finish, unfold

before you, vast, imperfectly interpreted, evanescent. Music, sweet from the now unseen birds in the deserted forest, sad from the waves upon the untrodden beaches, pulsates through the vivid air. It seems to the rider that the butterflies keep time to it; that the daisies in the gentle fields are nodding to it. Motionless cattle in the pastures, stray, solitary children on the fences, idle smoke from desolate chimneys, pass him by rhythmically. His thoughts, still busy with the forest, receive from all these things little else than a vague consciousness of the presence of life and light.

Life and light! The words have a familiar and a solemn sound.

Are they snatches from some forgotten sentiment of Holy Writ? John, perhaps? John, the golden-lipped, happy-hearted young enthusiast? What a poet that fisherman was! No wonder that modern dispute centres battling about the authenticity of the Fourth Gospel. *Life and light!* In all the universe, those only were the two words that could interpret the summer-noon meaning of this virgin State of Maine.

In all the universe —

Nonsense!

Yorke remembered that he was hungry, and

would have his dinner. In all the universe, —
what then? Heaven knows! It was some mad
fancy about womanhood, or youth, — love, perhaps, if the truth must out; how a woman sometimes came to a man's life — he had heard of such
women — suddenly, thoroughly, as upon the reserve of the forest had flashed the glory of the sea.
Meanwhile, a man must have his dinner ; a matter
not to be ignored in dealing with ideal wilderness
or ideal woman. He pulled the rein smartly over
the nervous pony, reflecting, with the hardened
cynicism of a bachelor of twenty-eight, that he
would like to see the woman who would be Life
and Light to him! I think, though, if we stop
to look at it, that the young fellow preserved, after
all, for his sacred metaphor something of the reverence which is native to all delicate natures; and
that in the innermost of all consciousness, which
we hide even from ourselves, the words held under
covert of a sneer the fugitive of a prayer.

With the fall from heaven to earth, discovering
that he was hungry, the young man cherished a
mild suspicion that he had strayed a little out of
his way. Surely, the last reduced but hopeful
sign-board had explicitly " arisen to explain " that
it was six miles and a half to the town of Sherman. If he had traveled six miles and a half he

had traveled ten since then, and of other guide-boards, those *ignes fatui* in which he confided with the touching faith of youth and inexperience, there were none to be seen. Two, indeed, he had passed, valorously guarding a cart-path, but wind, weather, or fate had long since decapitated them. Over against their corpses one patient fellow stood on duty in a whortleberry thicket, for what concrete or abstract purpose no mortal could divine, with his head, from which all recognizable features were successfully washed away, held rakishly under his arm. Another, apparently a drunken, disorderly officer, seemed to have gone upon a spree, and tumbled face-down into a brook. But neither of these sources of Maine enlightenment had directed the dense Massachusetts mind to the town of Sherman.

Bringing the entire force of the Massachusetts mind now to bear upon the non-appearance of any visible means of dining, a process in which the Maine pony showed a sympathy above all provincialism, the traveler accosted the first native he happened to meet, and something like the following conversation took place : —

Yorke : " Can you tell me how far it is to Sherman, sir ? "

Native : " Hey ? "

Yorke : " Would you oblige me by saying **how** near I am to the town of Sherman ? "

Native, interrogatively : " Sherman ? "

Yorke, decidedly : " Yes ; Sherman."

Native, reflectively : " Sherm-an."

A pause.

" Travelin' fur? "

" From Bangor to Sherman."

" Oh ! "

" I fear I have got out of my way. I hope you can direct me."

" Wall. You said Sherman ? "

Yorke, emphatically : " I certainly did ! "

Native, cheerfully : " Wall. If it 's *Sherman* you 're goin' fur, I sh'd ventur' it might be a matter of eight mile — to *Sherman.* Hancock's nigher. So 's Cherrytown."

Yorke, explosively : " But I do not *wish* to visit Hancock or Cherrytown ! "

" Oh, you don't. Wall."

Native's wife, coming to the door, and standing with heavy hand raised, gaunt forefinger stretching down the road : " That 's the way to Sherman : down that there gully, and take your second left and your fust right, and then foller the wind. But it ain't no eight mile."

Yorke, lost in thinking how much she looks

like a Maine sign-post: "Thank you, madam. How far do *you* call it to Sherman?"

"It ain't a peg over six, — Sherman ain't."

Native's boy, pushing between his parents, and appearing vivaciously in the foreground: "It's three mile 'n' a half, mister! And you don't take your second left. You jest foller your nose, an' you 'll make it. Folks hain't been thar sence the old hoss died. *I* went one winter. *I* belong to the Sherman Brass Band."

"It's true," said the woman, apologetically, "me and Mr. Bailey don't get to Sherman very often. But Bob, — he don't know a mile from a close-pin."

A prolonged pause.

"Is there a hotel in this — this metropolis?" asked Yorke, looking vaguely about the beautiful wilderness.

"Sir?"

"Is there a tavern in this village?"

"No, sir."

"Do you ever accommodate hungry travelers with a dinner in your own family?"

"Wall, no; we never hev. They mostly go to Nahum Smithses."

"Can I get anything to eat, in this desert, of Mr. Smith or any other citizen of your acquaintance?"

" Wall, mebbe you might. Might ask. Nahum Smith is a gentleman as puts up."

Yorke, reviving : " A gentleman that puts up ? That sounds hopeful. How far is it to this gentleman's ? "

Native : " Two miles.

Native's wife : " It 's two 'n' a quarter."

Native's boy, disrespectfully and musically : " 'T ain't a mi-i-ile ! "

Yorke turned away with such gratitude towards this enlightened family as he could muster into expression, and set out grimly in search of the gentleman that put up.

The woman ran after him for some distance through the dusty, blazing, blinding noon. He reined up, and she called kindly, gesticulating with her lean arms, " If you come acrost a woman ridin' in a little frisky wagin with an amberel atop, just you ask her. *She* 'll know ! "

It was one of those coincidences which make, according to one's temperament, either the poetry or the superstition of life, that young Yorke, in the course of twenty minutes' savage and unsuccessful pursuit of the gentleman that put up, coming sharply to the top of a glaring hill, saw at the foot of it, dimly through the dust, a sight as foreign to the Maine wilderness as a sleigh to Florida or a barouche to Sahara. It was a pony phaeton. It stood before a gray old farm-house door, and the clean-cut, slender gray mare who drew it was tied to the crumbling fence. It was a basket phaeton, with a movable top of a buff color, — a lady's phaeton, evidently.

Yorke was as yet too inexperienced a traveler across country to know that in three cases out of five it is from a woman one will get most accurate geographical directions. He might have passed the pony phaeton with scarcely a serious remembrance of the advice he had received, but just before he reached the farm-house the owner of the carriage came suddenly out.

She came suddenly out and down the grass-grown walk, with the nervous step natural to a person in habitual haste ; but a healthy step, even and springing. Yorke noticed as much as this in the instant that he balanced in his mind the advisability of addressing the lady.

For it was unmistakably, a lady.

The young man — being a young man — took in with subtle swiftness a sense of her youth, for she was young ; of her motions, which were lithe. Of her face his impressions were hazy. It might have been fine, or not. He seldom suffered himself to acquire an opinion of a woman's face at first sight; he had so often learned to hold such impressions as frauds on his intelligence. Her dress, he thought, was blue, or black, or blue-black, or black-and-blue. What did it matter? She was already escaping him, and with her, apparently, his only mortal hope of dinner. What superhuman power could do for a man even in the Maine wilderness he would not dogmatically decide, but his confidence in human assistance was at that faint ebb produced by prospective starvation; and Mr. Nahum Smith, or any other gentleman that put up, he had begun to locate with other interesting and amusing myths with which his education had made him familiar.

The young lady had untied her horse (with the quickness of a practiced driver), had swept into the phaeton, had gathered the reins, and was off. If she had noticed him at all, it was in a busy fashion, with the single quick, abstracted glance usual to strangers in a crowd, in vivid contrast to the Down-East stare. Yorke felt that it was becoming a desperate case. He reined in the Bangor pony.

"I beg pardon, madam!"

The basket phaeton, just whirling away, came to a pause unconcernedly.

"I beg pardon for the liberty, but *will* you direct me to the town of Sherman?"

Something in Yorke's accent of desperation *was* funny. The young lady's eyes twinkled for an instant. She looked as if she would have laughed if she had dared. But she answered him with grave politeness.

"It is four miles to Sherman."

"Thank you." The young man sat, with his hat raised, hesitating. "I ought to apologize for troubling a lady. But I have met nothing but dislocated sign-posts and admiring natives for ten miles. One gave me as correct information as another. Is Sherman the nearest place where I can get a dinner?"

"I think it is," said the young lady. "Yes, I know it is. If you take your first left below here, you will find it an easy four miles." She spoke with the unconscious ease with which, perhaps, only an American lady could have addressed a stranger met upon an unknown errand on a solitary road; but she gathered her reins as she spoke.

"I am extremely obliged to you," persisted Yorke. "You said the second left?"

"I said the first left. I am going to Sherman. If your horse is not too tired to keep distantly in sight, my phaeton will direct you without further trouble."

She spoke as simply as one gentleman might
have spoken to another. Yorke, too profoundly
grateful to her to notice this at first, remembered
it as the gray mare sped away through the hollow.

How exquisitely it was done! The Beacon
Street gentleman felt a glow of appreciation of
the little scene, viewed purely as a specimen of
the religion of good manners. He would have
liked his mother to see it. It was the sort of thing
she could estimate at its worth.

"Going to Sherman," what a divine Christian
recognition of the fact that he was a stranger, and
the Maine wilderness had taken him in! Even
that though a man, he might yet be a gentleman,
out of his way, misdirected, tired, perplexed, and
hungry. "If his horse were not too tired," —
what a delicate fashion of comparing the exhausted and now abject-looking Bangor pony with her
own sturdy little steed! "Distantly in sight," —
could language more? Faint, swift, maidenly
afterthought to the kindly impulse! Yorke had
wrought himself into rather a glow, perhaps, by
dint of present gratitude and promised dinner,
but that simple little speech certainly seemed to
him, as he thought of it, a classic in its way.

Meanwhile, the "frisky wagin" had tripped
along over knoll and hollow, and the bright "am-

berel atop" had turned into the thickly-wooded
road and disappeared from view. Waldo Yorke
whipped up and hurried on.

Distantly in sight, indeed! Was there an innocent sarcasm in that womanly thrust? The
gray mare could make her eleven miles an hour
easily, if put to it. The Bangor pony begged
piteously now at six. The basket phaeton flew
to Sherman. The buggy struggled after. The
mare put her head down, and trotted straight and
stiff, — a steady roadster. The buggy followed by
the fits and starts, the turns of elation and depression, the jerks of hope and lurches of despair,
familiar to drivers of nervous ponies at the end of
a steady pull. Distantly in sight! He should do
well, indeed, if he kept a mirage of her in sight.

They had turned now quite away from the
coast-line. The scattering farms, the tiny huts
with enormous barns attached, the intelligent natives, the heavy stage-track, the dust, the glare,
the cliffs, the sea, had vanished. The forest
opened its arms again to the travelers, and the
world grew green and cool.

Off the stage-road here, the density seemed
deeper, the shadow more abandoned. Through
the impressive solitude the gay little phaeton
cover danced along; through it the solemn black

buggy-top lumbered and climbed. The figure of the dainty driver in the phaeton, erect, slender, and blue, sat motionless as a caryatid out of employment. The eyes of the traveler in the buggy vigilantly pursued it; chiefly, it must be admitted, because he wanted his dinner; possibly, in part because he fancied the pose of the caryatid, — any man would.

The shadow deadened as they rode, but not from the darkening of the day. On either hand the solid serried oaks seemed to step out and press against the narrow drive-way; thickets, whose black hearts relieved the various outlines of wild blackberry, sumach, elder, and grape, netted themselves more tightly, and grew stiff, looking like bronze; the aspens and pallid birches wooed one another across the narrowing road. Vistas of soft gloom stretched on. There was no light now, but flickering needles, fine as those of the pines, and drifting with them, that with difficulty pierced the opaque green heavens of the overreaching trees. One looked twice in the low tone of the place even to see what the roadside flowers were. Yorke had almost passed unnoticed an apple-tree in full blossom, and it was past the first of June. Nothing could have so vividly presented to him a sense of the painful Maine spring, and the frozen, laggard life that looked out from behind it upon a gentler world.

It occurred to him for the first time, as the depth and solitude of the road made themselves fully manifest, to wonder if the young lady felt no hesitation in trusting herself to drive over it alone. Apparently, he had here some society girl, whose whim it was to be unfashionable, and in Maine, at this unusual season. She was a little intoxicated with Nature's grand unconventionality; had no more fear, it seemed, than a butterfly released from a chrysalis.

He wondered if she did him the credit not to take him for a cut-throat. But a grim glance at the widening distance between the phaeton and the buggy strangled this bit of self-satisfaction at its first breath. Plainly, the case involved not so much a high opinion of the man as a low one of the horse.

Those delicate lovers, the birch and aspen, and the more ardent ones, the oak and hickory beyond them, were now making themselves obnoxious, as lovers always do to third parties, and swept a fragrant and defiant arch low across the way. Swift in the passing, the buff umbrella went deftly down. Slow in the following, the buggy-top groaned back.

The blue caryatid was daintily cut now against
the heavy shadow.   Fine pencilings of light fell
on her : she wore, it might be, a straw hat, which
caught them ; they struck her hair too, and her
shoulder.   She stirred but once.   Then she turned
to break some apple-blossoms.   She picked the
flowers at full speed and standing.

Yorke, as he watched her with the half-amused
attention of a traveler who has nothing better to
do than to " follow the duty nearest him," got the
jingle of Lucy Gray into his head : —

> " O'er rough and smooth she trips along
>   And never looks behind."

And now Yorke put his case to the Bangor pony,
and despairingly relinquished it.   The buggy
lagged dead at the foot of the hill.   The phaeton
speeding across the hollow, reached the crossing
of the ways, turned a sudden corner, and was
gone.

" And never looked behind " sighed the young
man, out of temper with the pony, or the jingle,
or what not.

> " And sings a solitary song
>   That whistles in the wind."

When the Bangor pony panted up to the cross-
roads, the phaeton had vanished utterly.   The
caryatid had become a dream, a delusion, a slen-

der and obliging deceiver. Four solitary roads
pierced the forest at four separate green angles.
A dull sign-board stood in the square, and the
traveler hastened gratefully to it. It bore in
faded tints, once red and yellow and inspiring, an
advertisement of Hooflands' German Bitters.

Blue caryatides indeed! In what hues less intellectually respectable was the young woman perhaps portraying him by this time to the summer
people at Sherman, a party of gay girls like herself?

The young man bit his lip somewhat distinctly,
for a Bostonian, and stood for a moment irresolute
in the heart of the cross-roads, uncertain which of
the four narrow wooded ways looked least as if
it ended in a cranberry swamp, or a clearing, or
other abstractly useful but concretely dinnerless
locality.

Suddenly, his eye caught the soft, irregular outline of some small object lying in the dust, a rod
or so down the direct road. He drove up to it.
As he approached it grew pink, as if it blushed.
It was an apple-blossom.

II.

YORKE'S faith in woman rallied. If the cary atid meant it, — and a caryatid might be capable of just such a picturesque procedure, — it was very delicately done. If she did not mean it, at all events he had got scientifically past the cross-roads on his way, and she had got successfully out of it. He picked up the apple-blossom, and drove on. It could not have been ten minutes before his dumb guide brought him abruptly from the forest almost into the heart of the village.

The little town of Sherman slept peacefully in the afternoon sun. No one seemed to be astir. No glimmer of a phaeton cover shone across the hot, still street. The caryatid was gone, — where, it really did not occur to the young man to wonder. He and the Bangor pony forgot her with equal rapidity and success, in the leisurely hospitality of the Sherman Hotel.

SHERMAN, MAINE, *June 5th.*

MY DEAR MOTHER, — I hope you promptly received the letter I mailed from Bangor. Another went, also, from some indefinite locality in the Maine wilderness: they called it a post-office; I believe it was a town-pump — or an undertaker's; but my memory is not precise on this point.

I am just settled and at work. Uncle Jed's affairs are a mesh as fine as that eternal tatting Lucy Garratt used to bring over to our house, when she was a school-girl. My regards to the Garratts, by the way, when you write.

It threatens to be a process of some weeks to unravel my tatting, and I have taken lodgings with Uncle Jed's executor. I stood the Sherman Hotel for twenty-four hours. I've saved one of their doughnuts for a croquet-ball, to complete our imperfect set. Direct your letters, if you please, care Isaiah Butterwell, Esq.

In Isaiah Butterwell I find a genuine "fine old country gentleman," and Uncle Jed's confidential and devoted friend. He is a man of property, influence, and honor in this place. It is kind in them to take me in. Mrs. Isaiah says she is glad of my society. She, by the way, has an eye like a linnet and a tongue like a Jonathan Crook pocketknife, and a receipt for waffles which in itself has reconciled me to Sherman society for indefinite lengths.

I seem to be the only member of the family

besides the united head. It is a huge house, with wings, dead white, and reminds me of a Millerite robed and wondering why he can't fly. We seem to live a good deal at one side of the house, and one of the wings belongs to me. I have not explored as yet beyond my own quarters and the dining-room. Strain the Beacon Street imagination, if you can, up to the level of waffles for tea! She asked me, too, if I would have feathers or hair, and did I prefer *woolen* sheets? The house is perfectly still, and altogether delightful. As I write, a single sound of wheels breaks the deep, sweet country silence. They roll softly up and past my window to the barn ; probably Mr. Butterwell has been to the prayer-meeting, a dissipation to which his good wife endeavored to decoy me. Rather late for a prayer-meeting, too. Mr. Isaiah drives a good horse, I perceive.

Speaking of good horses, I lost my way, coming on, and was piloted through the forest by a cary-atid in a basket phaeton. Remind me to tell you about her when I get home.

To-morrow I drive out about twelve miles along the coast, to see a man who knows another man who has heard of a "widder lady " who stands ready to purchase certain shares of a certain ship which come into poor Uncle Jed's legacy. They launch their ships in salt brooks here, and trustfully tug them out in search of the sea. I shall convert all these wandering investments into cash as soon as possible, at any reasonable sacrifice, for I fancy there can't be more than three or four thousand involved at most. The property is widely scattered, much of it in local loans, like that of most Maine merchants. My share, as you remember, is more concise. Write when you can. Remember me to cousin Don. Don't miss me. It does n't pay. Your affectionate son,

WALDO YORKE.

Waldo Yorke had started in search of the postoffice to mail this letter, when Mrs. Isaiah Butterwell followed her guest to the door, and stood, while he was gathering the reins over the now gayly-recuperated Bangor pony. Mrs. Butterwell was a well-dressed woman, in the Maine sense of the term. She had a homely, independent face, with soft eyes, — not unlike a linnet's, as Yorke had said. She regarded him closely for a moment, and without speaking.

" What a charming day ! " said Yorke, feeling it necessary to be polite even at the expense of originality.

" I 'm too busy to bother with the weather," replied Mrs. Isaiah, briskly. " Can't spare the time for that Down East."

" Indeed ! That is a frugal sentiment, at all events," Yorke ventured.

" There 's no sentiment about it," retorted Mrs. Butterwell. " It 's sense ; as you 'd find out if you lived here. If I 'd spent myself noticing weather, I should have been in my grave ten winters ago. Are you fond of young women ? "

The linnet put this startling question with gentle eyes, in which it was impossible to capture a ray of satire or of fun.

" As I am of the State of Maine, — with reservations," said Yorke guardedly, visions of Sherman " society " presenting themselves at once.

" Are you fond of an early dinner, then ? " pursued Mrs. Butterwell, with the serene air of one who clearly sees the links of her own syllogism.

" Passionately, madam."

"We dine," said the hostess, bowing herself away with a certain dignity, " at half past twelve."

" I will be at my post," said the guest, smiling, " dead or alive ! "

" I would n't say that if I was you," urged Mrs. Isaiah Butterwell, returning to the door-step, and looking gravely at the young man. " I 've always thought, if I'd been God, I'd have been tempted to take people up that way, just for the sake of it. Talk about his tempting folks! Folks throw a terrible lot of temptation in *his* way. But there it is. It just shows he isn't made up like other people, after all. How that horse of yours does fuss!"

The Bangor pony was nervous indeed that morning; highly grained, after the journey, in Mr. Isaiah's generous stable. The buggy sped along the village street with emphasis.

It is doubtful if the caryatid would have offered her services as guide to its occupant that day, through the beautiful heart of the forest, four miles deep.

Waldo Yorke, as he clattered through that pleasant representative Maine town, where the meeting-house, post-office, and "store" were the important features, and impressed him chiefly as reminiscences of American novels which he had tried to read and failed at the third chapter, amused himself by a rapid acquaintance with the business signs.

"Goodsell, Merchant." "Cole and Wood: Lumber Dealers." "Dr. A. Lloyd." "Coffins, cheap for Cash." "Smith and Jones, formerly Jedediah Yorke," — and so on. He got these

things into his head as he had the rhyme of Lucy
Gray, the day before, with that idiocy which asserts itself in this exasperating form, and which
threatens to prove the human intellect more law-
less than the passions or the will. He found himself particularly a victim to the cheerful refrain of
" Coffins, cheap for Cash."

His host overtook him before he had driven far.
Mr. Isaiah Butterwell, as Yorke had observed,
shared the apparently well-spread Maine appreciation of a good horse. He reined up his heavy,
handsome sorrel, and the two men rode abreast
for a mile ; they chatted, across wheels, of horses,
the estate and Uncle Jed, and Maine politics, and
the price of lumber, and horses again. The Boston boy listened deferentially to the gray Maine
merchant ; perceiving in him something of the
same rugged dignity that Uncle Jed had borne in
Beacon Street. Yorke felt that here was a king
in his own country ; he regarded the hard-worked
man with respect, and pleased himself with drawing his points out, and storing them up, so to
speak, with a sense of increasing one's knowledge
of " types."

" I 've got to leave you, to collect some interest," said Mr. Butterwell presently. " That 's
my turn, — the first right. You keep straight on

till you find your man. Drive easy over the
bridges. They 're plaguey rickety, some of 'em.
That pony of yours ain't used to 'em in Bangor. Back to dinner? Hope so. There, now, I
wonder if my wife has told you — whoa! — told
you about — whoa, Zach Chandler! — about —
Whoa!"

"Oh, yes, she told me!" called Yorke politely,
as the two horses nervously parted company. He
looked, laughing, back to watch the old man,
thinking how sacred their dinner hour was to
these two lonely people; how large all little events
must be in lives like theirs. His heart was full of
a gentle feeling, half deference, half compassion.
Mr. Butterwell's gray hair blew in the wind; he
held the reins wound double over his knotted
wrist; he sat with left foot forward. Zach Chandler was a long-stepping horse. Waldo Yorke,
looking over his shoulder, saw and long remembered that he saw these trifling things. Suddenly he felt a thrill in the reins at which his own
horse was tugging steadily and sensibly. He
turned his head, to see the Bangor pony tremble,
rear, and leap; to see the loose yellow boards of
a murderously-laid bridge bound up; to see that
there was no railing; to perceive a narrow streak
of black — water, presumably; and to know that

he was scooped into the overturned buggy-top, and dragged, and torn, and swept away.

The whole thing may have taken three minutes. All that occurred to the young man quite clearly, as he went down, was, " *Coffins, cheap for Cash.*"

Against the blackness of darkness a blur appears; it stirs; it has extension and intension ; it throbs and thrills, and with the eternal wonder of creation moving upon chaos, there is light. After all, how easy a matter it was to die ! And coffins in Maine are cheap for cash. How could a man have believed that a process so abnormally dreaded for nearly thirty years could be, in truth, so normal and so deficient in the extreme elements of agony ? To be sure, there was one crashing blow; a compression of some endurance within narrow limits ; but he had suffered as much from neuralgia, far more from the prospect of death.

How clearly and distinctly, though slowly, vision returns, in this new condition ! There is a handsome old lady in a *point appliqué* cap. Like the child of A 'ah, she " goeth lame and lovely." By the way, will one make the acquaintance of a man like Lamb, in the society to which one is now to be introduced ? Yes; still the old lady in the lace cap. She is sitting by the library grate,

aione; her crutch has fallen to the floor; a yellow
telegraph envelope is on the hearth; she is not
weeping, but her face is bowed; she looks very
old; the lines about her mouth are pinched; she
has a haggard color. It seems easy to speak to
her. How easy! Mother? *Mother!* She does
not lift her head. *Mother!* It is true what we
were told, then. The living do not hear. The
dead may cry forever. A horrible deafness has
fallen upon her. A man would have liked to see
her once, — to say good-by, or to have her sit
by him a few minutes. Yet it seems there is
a woman here. That is a woman's hand which
rather hovers over than holds me. How cool it
is! How delicate! . . . *Ah, no!* Remove your
hand! It does not caress; it tears me. *Remove
your hand!* I am in agony. What in the name
of life and death has happened to me in this
accursed wilderness? Was there anything in
those old-fashioned dogmas after all? Take off
your hand, I say! I know I might have been a
better man, but I 've tried to be clean and honest. I don't say I'm fit for heaven, but I don't
deserve *this.* You torture me. *Remove your hand!*
Am I in —

"You are in your own room, sir," said Mrs.
Isaiah Butterwell, distinctly.

" Ah ! — so I see."

Yorke tried to lift his head ; it fell back heavily, and he felt blood start.

" Madam, you are very good. I must have been troublesome. I thought I was — dead."

" I 'm sorry for you, Mr. Yorke, but I *must say* that I don't approve of your theology," said his hostess, grimly.

" I dare say. I would not have offended you if — Ah, how weak I am ! "

" Yes, sir."

" Am I much hurt ? "

" Some, Mr. Yorke."

" How much ? Answer me. I will have the truth. The blood flows — see ! when I even think that you may be deceiving me. Am I terribly hurt ? "

" I am afraid so, sir."

A heavy silence falls.

" Shall we telegraph for your mother, sir ? "

" My mother is crippled. No."

" For any sister, or anybody ? "

" I have no sister."

" Mr. Butterwell will write."

" Where is the doctor ? I should like to see him first. You have called a doctor ? "

" Oh yes, sir."

" Where is he ? "

" The doctor left about five minutes ago."

" What does he say ? "

" Very little."

" I wish to see the doctor before my mother is written to. Call him back ! — if you please. . . . Call him back, I say ! Why do you hesitate ? I may be a dead man in a few hours. Do as I bid you ! "

" The doctor said, Mr. Yorke " —

" Said what ? "

"Said that — sh, Isaiah ! — he was to be the judge when it was best for you to see your physician. If you asked, I was to say that you will have every possible attention, and I was to say that all depends on your obedience."

" That sounds like a man who understands his business."

" Oh, indeed, sir, *that* is true ! Our doctor " —

" Oh, well ; very well. Let it go. I must obey, I suppose. Never mind. Thank you. Move me a little to the left. I cannot stir. I am unaccountably sleepy. Has the fellow drugged me ? I think perhaps I may — rest " —

He did, indeed, fall into sleep, or a stupor that simulated sleep ; he woke from it at intervals, thinking confusedly, but without keen alarm, of his condition. The thing which worried him most was the probable character of this Down-East doctor upon whose intelligence he had fallen. " The fellow absolutely holds my life in his hands," he said aloud. It was hard to think what advance of science the practitioner undoubtedly represented. Dreamily, between his lapses into unconsciousness, the injured man recalled a fossil, whom he had seen, on his journey from Bangor, lumbering about in a sulky at one of the minor stage stations; a boy, too, just graduated, practicing on the helpless citizens of Cherrytown, — was it? No, but some of those little places. Then he thought of some representatives of the profession whom he had met in the monntains, and at other removes from the centres of society. He understood perfectly that he was a subject for a surgeon. He understood that he was horribly hurt. He thought of his mother. He thought of his mother's doctor, whom he had so often teased her about. In one of his wakeful intervals, another source of trouble occurred to him for the first time. He called to his hostess, and restlessly asked, —

" I suppose there is n't a homœopathist short of Bangor ? "

" Our doctor is homœopathy," said Mrs. Butterwell, instantly on the defensive; "but you need not be uneasy, sir, for a better, kinder" —

"My mother will be so glad!" interrupted the young man, feebly. He gave a sigh of relief. "She would never have been able to bear it, if I had died under the other treatment. Women feel so strongly about these things. I am glad to know that — for her sake, — poor mother!" He turned again, and slept.

It was late evening when he roused and spoke again. He found himself in great suffering. He called petulantly, and demanded to be told where that doctor was. Some one answered that the doctor had been in while he slept. The room was darkened. He dimly perceived figures, — Mr. Butterwell in the doorway, and women; two of them. He beckoned to his hostess, and tried to tell her that he was glad she had obtained assistance, and to beg her to hire all necessary nursing freely; but he was unable to express himself, and sank away again.

The next time he became conscious, a clock somewhere was striking midnight. He felt the night air, and gratefully turned his mutilated, feverish face over towards it. A sick-lamp was burning low, in the entry, casting a little circle of light upon the old-fashioned, large-patterned oilcloth. Only one person was in the room, a woman. He asked her for water. She brought it. She had a soft step. When he had satisfied his thirst, which he was allowed to do without protest, the woman gave him medicine. He recognized the familiar tumbler and teaspoon of his homœopathically educated infancy. He obeyed passively. The woman fed him with the medicine ; she did not spill it, nor choke him ; when she returned the teaspoon to the glass, he dimly saw the shape of her hand. He said, —

" You are not Mrs. Butterwell."

" No."

" You are my nurse ? "

" I take care of you to-night, sir."

" I — thank you," said Yorke, with a faint touch of his Beacon-Street courtliness ; and so fell away again.

He moved once more at dawn. He was alarmingly feverish. He heard the birds singing, and saw gray light through the slats of the closed green blinds. His agony had increased. He still moaned for water, and his mind reverted obstinately to its chief anxiety. He said, —

" Where *is* that doctor ? I am too sick a man to be neglected. I must see the doctor."

" The doctor has been here," said the woman who was serving as nurse, " nearly all night."

"Ah! I have been unconscious, I know."

"Yes. But you have been cared for. I hope that you will be able to compose yourself. I trust that you will feel no undue anxiety about your medical attendance. Everything shall be done, Mr. Yorke."

"I like your voice," said the patient, with delirious frankness. "I have n't heard one like it since I left home. I wish I were at home! It is natural that I should feel some anxiety about this country physician. I want to know the worst. I shall feel better after I have seen him."

"Perhaps you may," replied the nurse, after a slight hesitation. "I will go and see about it. Sleep if you can. I shall be back directly."

This quieted him, and he slept once more. When he waked it was broadening, brightening, beautiful day. The nurse was standing behind him at the head of the bed, which was pushed out from the wall into the free air. She said : —

"The doctor is here, Mr. Yorke, and will speak with you in a moment. The bandage on your head is to be changed first."

"Oh, very well. That is right. I am glad you have come, sir." The patient sighed contentedly. He submitted to the painful operation without further comment or complaint. He felt

how much he was hurt, and how utterly he was at
the mercy of this unseen, unknown being, who
stood in the mysterious dawn there, fighting for
his fainting life.

. . . He handled one gently enough ; firmly,
too, — not a tremor; it did seem a practiced touch.

The color slowly struck and traversed the young
man's ghastly face.

" Is *this* the doctor ? "

" Be calm, sir, — yes."

" Is *that* the doctor's hand I feel upon my head
at this moment ? "

" Be quiet, Mr. Yorke, — it is."

" But this is a woman's hand ! "

" I cannot help it, sir. I would if I could, just
this minute, rather than to disappoint you so."

The startled color ebbed from the patient's
face, dashing it white, leaving it gray. He looked
very ill. He repeated faintly, —

" *A woman's hand !* "

" It is a good-sized hand, sir."

" I — Excuse me, madam."

" It is a strong hand, Mr. Yorke. It does not
tremble. Do you see ? "

" I see."

" It is not a rough hand, I hope. It will not
inflict more pain than it must."

" I know."

" It will inflict all that it ought. It is not afraid. It has handled serious injuries before. Yours is not the first."

" *What shall I do?*" cried the sick man, with piteous bluntness.

" I wish we could have avoided this shock and worry," replied the physician. She still stood, unseen and unsummoned, at the head of his bed. " I beg that you will not disturb yourself. There is another doctor in the village. I can put you in his hands at once, if you desire. Your uneasiness is very natural. I will fasten this bandage first, if you please."

She finished her work in silence, with deft and gentle fingers.

" Come round here," said the patient feebly. " I want to look at you."

III.

SHE came at once. She stepped before him at the bedside, and stood there without moving. She let him look at her as long as he would. It was not long. He felt very ill. He regarded her confusedly. He perceived a woman of medium height, with a well-shaped head. He felt the dress and carriage of a lady. His eye fell upon her hands, which were crossed lightly on the edge of the little table where his medicines stood. Sick as he was, he noticed unusual signs of strength in her fingers, which were yet not deficient in delicacy. Yorke had always judged people a good deal by their hands. He repeated his nervous phrase : —

" I am in a woman's hands ! "

She spread them out before him with a swift, fine gesture; then made as if she put something unseen at one side from them.

" Let me send for the man I spoke of. You are irresolute. You are losing strength and time. This is a mistake as well as a misfortune. I can't help being a woman, but I can help your suffering from the fact."

" No, — not yet. No. Wait a moment. I wish to speak with you. Will you pardon me if I ask — a few questions ? "

" I will pardon anything. But they must be very few. I shall not stand by and see you spend your breath unnecessarily."

" Are you an educated physician, madam ? "

" Yes, sir."

" A beginner ? "

" I have practiced several years."

" Do you think you understand my case ? "

" I think I do."

" This old man you speak of, — this other doctor, — what is he ? "

" His patients trust him."

" Do you think I should trust him ? "

" No, sir."

" Are you the only homœopathist in this region ? "

" There is one at Cherryfield ; others at Bangor ; none within thirty miles."

" Can you get consultation ? "

" I have already telegraphed to Bangor for advice : there is an eminent surgeon there ; he will come if needed. I know him well."

" How much am I hurt ? "

" A good deal, sir."

" Where are the injuries ? "

" In the head, the foot, and the right arm."

" What are they ? "

" I do not wish you to talk of them. I do not wish you to talk any more of anything."

" Just this, — am I in danger ? "

" I hope not, Mr. Yorke."

" I see you can tell the truth.'

" I *am* telling the truth."

" I begin to trust you."

She put her finger on her lip. He stirred heavily, with an ineffectual attempt to writhe himself into another position.

" I cannot move. I did not know my arm was hurt before — Ah, there ! "

As he spoke, blood sprang. The doctor made towards him a motion remarkable for its union of swiftness with great composure. Her face had a stern but perfectly steady light. She said calmly :

" Lie still, Mr. Yorke," and with one hand held him down upon the pillow. He perceived then that a bandage had slipped from a deep wound just below the shoulder, and that a severed artery was oozing red and hot. He grew giddy and faint, but managed to keep his wits together to watch and see what the young woman would do. She quickly bared his arm, from which the sleeve was already cut away.

"Mrs. Butterwell," she called quietly, "will you please bring me some hot water?"

During the little delay which ensued on this order — a momentary one, for Mrs. Isaiah Butterwell was one of those housekeepers who would prefer a lukewarm conscience to a lukewarm boiler — the doctor gently unrolled the bandage from the wound, which she then thoroughly sponged and cleansed. The patient thought he heard her say something about "secondary hæmorrhage;" but the words, if indeed she used them at all, were not addressed to him. The hot water did not stop the blood, which seemed to him to be sucking his soul out.

"Hold this arm, Mrs. Butterwell," said the young lady — "just so. Keep it in this position till I tell you to let go. Do you understand? There. No, stay. Call Mr. Butterwell. I want two."

She drew her surgical case from her pocket, and selected an artery forceps. She opened the wound, and instructed Mr. Butterwell how to hold the forceps in position while she ligated the artery. She bandaged the arm, and adjusted it to suit her upon a pillow. She had a firm and fearless touch. Her face betrayed no uneasiness; only the contraction of the brows inseparable from studious attention.

The patient looked at the physician with glazing eyes.

"Write to my mother," he said weakly. "Don't say you are not a man. Only say you are not an allopath — and that I have given my case unreservedly to you. Tell her not to worry. Give her my love. Tell her "—

And with this he fainted quite away.

This faint was the prelude to a hard pull Days of alternate syncope and delirium followed. Short intervals of consciousness found him quiet, but alarmingly weak. His early anxiety had ceased to manifest itself. He yielded to the treatment he received without criticism or demur. In fact, he was too ill to do anything else. This condition lasted for more than a week.

One day he awoke, conscious and calm. It was a sunny day. There seemed to be a faint woody perfume in the room, from some source unknown. A long, narrow block of light lay yellow on the stiff-patterned brown carpet; it was by no means, however, a cheap carpet. There was an expensive red and gold paper on the walls, and marble-topped furniture. There were two pictures. One was a framed certificate setting forth the fact of Mr. Butterwell's honored and honorable career as a Freemason. The other was an engraving of the Sistine Madonna. Yorke had hardly noticed the contents of his room before. He observed these details with the vivid interest of a newly-made invalid, wondering how long he was likely to lie and look at them. As his eye wandered weakly about the room it rested upon the bureau, which stood somewhat behind him. A vase of yellow Austrian glass was on the bureau ; it held a spray of apple-blossoms.

While he lay breathing in their delicate outlines like a perfume, and feeling their perfume like a color, the half-opened door pushed gently in, and a woman — a lady — entered with a quick step. She was a young lady ; or at least she was under thirty. She stopped on seeing that he was awake, and the two regarded each other. She saw a very haggard-looking young fellow, with a sane eye and a wan smile. He saw a blooming creature. She had her hat on and driving-gloves in her hand Her face was sensitive with pleasure at the change in the patient. She advanced towards him heartily, holding out her hand. He said, —

" Are you the doctor ? "

"Yes, sir."

" What is — excuse me — but, madam, I don't know your name."

" My name is Lloyd. You are better to-day ! "

" Infinitely ! Wait, please . . . . I have seen you before. Where have I seen you ? "

" Three times a day for a week, without counting the nights," said the young lady, with mischief in her voice. She had a pleasant voice. She spoke a little too quickly, perhaps. She stood beside his bed. She stood erect and strong. Her hair was dark, and she had rather large, dark blue eyes. He thought it was a fine, strong face ; he did not know but it might be safe to call it beautiful. She wore a blue flannel dress.

" I know ! " he said suddenly. " You are the caryatid."

" *What*, sir ? "

" You are the blue caryatid — Never mind. I am not deranged again. Have I been very crazy ? "

" Sometimes," said the lady gravely. Her expression and manner had changed. She sat down beside him and opened her medicine-case, which she laid upon the table. He smiled when he saw the tiny vials. She either did not observe or did not return the smile. Her face had settled into an intent and studious form, like a hardening cast. He thought, She is not beautiful.

She took out her note-book, and began to ask him a series of professional questions. She spoke with the distinct but rapid enunciation which he had noticed before. She wrote down his answers carefully. Many of her questions were more personal than he had expected; he was not used to what Mrs. Butterwell called "doctoring." This young lady required his age, his habits, family history, and other items not immediately connected in the patient's mind with a dislocated ankle.

"Now your pulse, please," she said, when she had reached the end of her catechism. She took his wrist in a business-like way. The young man experienced a certain embarrassment. The physician gave evidence of none. She laid his hand down again, as if it had been a bottle or a bandage, told him that she was greatly gratified with his marked improvement, prepared his powders, and, drawing the little rubber clasp over her medicine-case, gave him to understand by her motion and manner that she considered the consultation at an end.

"One powder in six tablespoonfuls of water; one tablespoonful every four hours," she said, rising. "Are you quite able to remember? Or I will speak to Mrs. Butterwell myself as I go out. She will be with you soon, and I have directed that some one shall be within call whenever you are left alone. You do not object to being alone somewhat?"

"I like it."

"I was sure of it. I prefer you to *be* alone as much as you can bear now. But you will not be neglected. I will see you again at night."

"I should like to talk with you a little," stammered Yorke, hardly knowing what was the etiquette of this anomalous position. "Cannot you stay longer?"

She looked at her watch, hesitated, and sat down again.

"I can give you a few minutes. I have a busy day before me."

"Did you write to my mother," began the patient, "and what has she answered?"

"If you go on improving at this rate, you may read your letters to-morrow, Mr. Yorke."

"Not to-day?"

"No."

"You are arbitrary, Miss — Dr. Lloyd."

She gave him a cool, keen look.

"That is my business," she said.

"What has been the matter with me?" persisted the young man. "What are my injuries? I wish to know."

"A dislocation of the ankle; a severed artery

in the arm; and concussion of the brain, — besides the minor cuts attendant on such an accident as yours. Each of these is doing finely. You have now no cause for alarm. It was a beautiful dislocation!" added the physician, with enthusiasm.

"Have I been dangerously ill?"

"Yes."

"Have you had consultation?"

"By telegraph every day, your worst days; by letter when I have thought you would feel easier to know that I had it."

"How soon shall I be about again?"

"I cannot promise you anything at present. You are doing remarkably well. But you will have occasion for patience, sir."

"I must have seemed very rude — or — distrustful of you, at the first."

"On the contrary, Mr. Yorke, you have shown me every reasonable confidence, — far more than I could have expected under the circumstances. I have appreciated it."

That sensitiveness had come into her face again; she gave him a direct, full look; and he thought once more that she was a beautiful woman.

"Believe," he said earnestly, "that I am grateful to you, madam."

She smiled indulgently, bowed, and left him. He heard her quick step in the hall, and her voice speaking to Mrs. Butterwell; then he heard her chirrup to her pony, and the sound of wheels. She drove rapidly, and was soon gone.

The day passed in the faint, sweet, hazy way that only the convalescent knows. No other creature ever gets behind that glamour. Returning life paces towards one so solemnly that the soul would keep upon its knees, were it not so weak; one dares not pray; one ventures only to see the frolic in the eyes of the advancing power, and dashes into joy as bees into rhythm, or as flowers into color. Waldo Yorke was very happy. He thought of his mother; his heart was full. He looked at the block of yellow light upon the carpet; at the apple-blossoms in the vase; at the patch of June sky that burned beyond that one open window. Life and light, he thought, are here.

Mrs. Isaiah Butterwell, however, was there too. She was extremely kind. She entertained the young man with a graphic account of his accident and its consequences. Mr. Butterwell himself came in, for a moment, and briefly considered it (although the Bangor horse was killed) a lucky thing.

"When he brought you home," observed the

lady, " I said, ' He 's dead.' I must say I hoped
you were, for I said to my husband, ' He 'll be an
idiot if he lives.' It always seems to me as if the
Creator was thinking he had n't made enough of
'em, after all, and was watching opportunities to
increase the stock. But our doctor 's been a match
for him this time ! " added Mrs. Isaiah, with a
snap of her soft eyes.

" Why, — Sar-ah ! " rebuked her husband,
gently.

" Well, she has ! " insisted Sarah ; " and I don't
see the harm. He made *her*, too, I suppose, did n't
he ? I think he ought to be proud of her. I 've
no doubt he is, — not the least in the world."

" Why, *Sar*ah ! " repeated Mr. Butterwell. He
had the air of being just as much surprised by
these little conversational peculiarities in his con-
sort as if he had not wintered and summered them
for better and worse for forty years. This amused
the invalid. He liked to hear them talk. He was
so happy that day that Mrs. Isaiah seemed to him
really very witty. He drew her out. She dwelt a
good deal upon the doctor. She explained to him
her difficulty in concealing the fact of the physician's sex from him those first few days.

" I would *not* tell a fib for you, Mr. Yorke, even
if you did die. And when you ran on so about

seeing the doctor, I was hard up. I could n't say 'she,' and I would n't say 'he,' for she was n't a 'he,' now was she? Once I got stuck in the middle of a sentence; and Mr. Butterwell was here, and I said, 'Sh — Isaiah! — he;' so I cut the word in two, don't you see? Only I spelled it with an extra *h*. But I'd rather sacrifice my spellin' than my conscience. And Isaiah asked me afterwards what I sh-shd him up for, when he had n't opened his mouth. He did n't open it very often while you were sick, Mr. Yorke. But he spoke about your uncle, and was blue enough. I had to make up my mind to do the talking for two when I married Mr. Butterwell. What time did Doctor Zay say she should look in again, Mr. Yorke?"

"Doctor Zay?" repeated the young gentleman blankly.

"Oh, we call her Doctor Zay. You see there were two of them, she and the old man; and, as luck would, they must have the same name. I suppose he was ashamed of his, — Adoniram; I don't blame him. At any rate, there's the sign, 'Dr. A. Lloyd.' And she has some kind of a heathen name herself; I never can pronounce it; so she takes to 'Dr. Z. A. Lloyd,' and that's how we come by it. Everybody calls her Doctor Za.

But she spells it with a y herself. We love the sound of it," added Mrs. Butterwell gently. "So would you, if you 'd been a woman Down East, and she the first one, of all you 'd read about and needed, you 'd ever seen."

"But I 'm not a woman," interrupted the patient, laughing. "I can't call her Doctor Zay. The young lady has done admirably by me ; I 'll admit that. How much I must have troubled her, to come here so often ! "

"I would n't waste your feelings, sir," observed Mrs. Butterwell, dryly. "Feelings are too rich cream to be skimmed for nothing. Doctor would have done her duty by you, anyhow ; but it 's been less of a sacrifice, considering she lives here."

The subsiding expression of weariness on the sick man's face rose to one of interest. He repeated, "Lives here ? " not without something like energy.

"Yes, I 've had her a year. She was starving at the Sherman Hotel, and I took her in. I used to go to school with some connections of hers, so I felt a kind of responsibility for her. And then I 'm always glad of society, as I told you when I took you. I 'm social in my nature. I suppose that 's why Providence went out of his way to marry me to Mr. Butterwell. If my lot had been cast in Portland, or Bangor, I'm afraid I should have been frivolous, as I said to Doctor Zay, the first time I saw her, — it was chilblains; I thought I could trust her; I didn't know her then, you see. Do you mean to say you didn't notice her sign? Then, if she'd got sick at the hotel they'd have said she was A WOMAN. I had the cause to consider," added Mrs. Butterwell, solemnly.

The physician came again at night, as she had promised. She was later than usual. Yorke listened for her wheels, and got restless. It made him nervous when the country wagons rolled up and rumbled by. He had flushed with the end of the day, and was feverish and miserable. He attended to his sensations anxiously. He wished she would come. It was quite dark when the low wheels of the phaeton came smoothly and suddenly to a stop in the great back yard; he heard the doctor's voice speaking cheerily to her boy. "Handy," she called him. Handy took the horse; a light step passed the corner of the house, and vanished. "She must have gone on to the office door," thought Yorke. He found himself absorbed in a little uneasiness; he wondered if she would take her tea first.

She did not. She came to him directly. Her things were off; her hair smoothly brushed; she stood beside him, her pleasant figure, in its house-dress, cut against the light that fell through the open door. She began at once: "There are patients in the office, — I am late; I was detained by a troublesome case. I can give you five minutes now, or come back when they are gone. Let me see!" She went out and brought the lamp, scrutinized his face closely, sat down, and felt his pulse; she did not count it, but quickly laid his hand aside.

"Please come by and by," urged the young man. Already he felt unaccountably better. "I can wait." She hesitated a moment, then said, "Very well," and left him. She was gone half an hour.

"Have you had your supper?" asked Yorke, when she came back.

"Oh, my supper is used to waiting," said Doctor Zay, cheerfully. "You have waited quite long enough, sir. Now, if you please, to business."

The note-book, the pencil, the medicine-case, and the somewhat stolid, studious look presented themselves at once. Yorke felt half amused, half annoyed. He wanted to be talked to, as if she had been like other women. He thought it would do him more good than the aconite pellets which she prepared so confidingly. He was just enough better to begin to be homesick. He asked her if he might try to walk to-morrow. She promptly replied in the negative.

"I *must* walk next week," urged the patient, setting a touch of his natural imperiousness against her own. She gave him one of her composed looks.

"You will walk, Mr. Yorke, when I allow you," she said, courteously enough. She looked so graceful and gentle and womanly, sitting there beside him, that all the man in him rebelled at her authority. Their eyes met, and clashed.

"When will that be?" he insisted, with a creditable effort at submission.

"A dislocated ankle is not to be used in ten days," replied the doctor quietly. "It is going to take time."

"How much time?"

"That depends partly on yourself, partly on me, a little on" —

"Providence?" interrupted Yorke.

"Not at all. God made the ankle, you dislocated it, I set it; nature must heal it."

"Mrs. Butterwell might have said that."

"Is it possible," said the young lady, with a change of manner, "that I am growing to talk like Mrs. Butterwell?"

This was the first personal accent which Yorke had caught in the doctor's voice. Thinking, perhaps, to pursue a faint advantage, which he vaguely felt would be of interest to him when he grew stronger and had nothing else to do but study this young woman, he proceeded irrelevantly : —

" I did not know that you stayed here, till to-day. It has been fortunate for me. It will be more fortunate still, if you are going to keep me on this bed all summer. Our hostess has been talking of you. She gave you such a pretty name ! I 've forgotten exactly what it was."

" We will move you to the lounge to-morrow," replied the doctor, rising. Yorke made no answer. He felt as if he were too sick a man to be snubbed. He found it more natural to think that his overthrown strength ought to have appealed to her chivalry, than to question if he had presumed upon the advantage which it gave him. In the subdued light of the sick-room all the values of his face were deepened ; he looked whiter for its setting of black hair, and his eyes darker for the pallor through which they burned. But the doctor was not an artist. She observed, and said to herself, " That is a *cinchona* look."

She moved the night-lamp, gave a few orders,

herself adjusted his window and blinds, and, step-
ping lightly, left him. She did not go out-of-doors,
but crossed the hall, and disappeared in her own
part of the house. He heard, soon after, what he
now knew to be the office-bell. It rang four or
five times ; and he heard the distant feet of patients on the graveled walk that led to her door.
After this there was silence, and he thought,
"They have let her alone to rest now." It had
not occurred to him before that she could be tired.
He was restless, and did not sleep easily, and
waked often. Once, far on in the night he
thought it must have been, a noise in the back
yard roused him. It was Handy rolling out the
basket phaeton. Yorke heard whispers and
hushed footfalls, and then the brisk trot of the
gray pony. There was a lantern on the phaeton,
which went flashing by his window, and crossed
his wall with bright bars like those of a golden
prison. He wished the blinds were open. He
thought, "Now they have called that poor girl
out again!" He pictured the desolate Maine
roads. A vision of the forest presented itself to
him : the great throat of blackness ; the outline of
near things, wet leaves, twigs, fern-clumps, and
fallen logs ; patches of moss and lichens, green
and gray ; and the light from the lonely carriage

streaming out; above it the solitary figure of the
caryatid, courageous and erect. He hoped the
boy went with her. He listened some time to
hear her return, but she did not come.

When he awoke again it was about seven
o'clock. He was faint, and while he was ringing
for his beef-tea, the phaeton came into the yard.

"Put up the pony, Handy," he heard her say;
"she is tired out. Give me Old Oak, to-day."

Yorke listened, feeling the strength of a new
sensation. Was it possible that this young woman
had practice enough to keep two horses? He
knew nothing of the natural history of doctresses.
He had thought of them chiefly as a species of
higher nurse, — poor women, who wore unbecom-
ing clothes, took the horse-cars, and probably
dropped their " *g*'s," or said, " Is that so? "

It was later than usual, that morning, when
Doctor Zay came round to him. It was another
of those sentient, vivid June days, and the block
of light on the brown carpet seemed to throb as
she crossed it. The apple-blossoms on the bureau
had begun to droop. She herself looked pale.

"You are tired!" began the patient impulsively.

"I have been up all night," said the doctor
shortly. She sat down with the indefinable air

which holds all personalities at arms-length, and went at once to work. She examined the wounded arm, she bathed and bandaged the injured foot; she had him moved to the lounge, with Mr. Butterwell's assistance. She was incommunicative as a beautiful and obedient machine. Yorke longed to ask what was the matter with her, but he did not dare. He felt sorry to see her look so worn; but he perceived that she did not require his sympathy. She looked more delicate for her weariness, which seemed to be subtly at odds with her professional manner. He would have liked to ask her a great many things, but her abstraction forbade him. He contented himself with the pathological ground upon which alone it was practicable to meet this exceptional young woman, and renewed his entreaties to be allowed to use his foot.

"You do not trust me," she said suddenly, laying down the sponge with which she had been bathing his arm.

"You wrong me, Doctor Lloyd. I think I have proved that I *do*."

"That is true. You have," she said, softening. "Trust me a while longer, then. No. Stay. Put your foot down, if you want to. Gently — slowly — but put it down."

He did so. A low outcry escaped him; he grew very pale.

"Now put it back," said the doctor grimly. But with that she melted like frost, and shone; she hovered over him; all the tenderness of the healer suffused her reticent face.

"I am sorry to let you hurt yourself, but you will feel better; you will obey me now. Is the pain still so sharp? Give me the foot." As if it had been her property, she took the aching ankle in her warm, strong, and delicate hands, and for a few moments rubbed it gently and gravely; the pain subsided under her touch.

"What am I going to do?" cried Yorke, despairingly.

"You are going to do admirably, Mr. Yorke, on invention for a while, on courage by and by. Your crutches will be here to-morrow night."

Waldo Yorke looked at the young lady with a kind of loyal helplessness. He felt so subdued by his anomalous position that, had she said, "I have sent to Bangor for your work-basket," or, "to Omaha for your wife," he would scarcely have experienced surprise. He repeated, "My crutches?" in a vague, submissive tone.

"I sent to Bangor for a pair of Whittemore crutches three days ago," replied the doctor quietly

" I should not want you to use them before to-morrow. The stage will bring them at five o'clock. If I should be out, do not meddle with them. No, on the whole, I had them addressed to myself. I wish to be present when you try them. One powder dry on the tongue, if you please, every four hours. Good-morning."

" Don't go, please," pleaded the young man; " it is so lonely to be sick."

An amused expression settled between her fine, level brows. She made no reply. He realized that he had said an absurd thing. He remembered into how many sick-rooms she must bring her bloom and bounteousness, and for the first time in his fortunate life he understood how corrosive is the need of the sick for the well. He remembered that he was but one of — how many? dependent and complaining creatures, draining upon the life of a strong and busy woman. He let her go in silence. He turned his face over towards the back of the lounge ; it was a black hair-cloth lounge. " I must look as if I were stretched on a bier, here," thought the young man irritably. All his youth and vigor revolted from the tedious convalescence, which it was clear this fatally wise young woman foresaw, but was too shrewd to discuss with him. He remembered, with a kind of awe, some invalid friends of his mother's. One lay on a bed in Chestnut Street for fifteen years. He recalled a man he met in the Tyrol once, who broke his knee-pan in a gymnasium, — was crippled for life. Yorke had always found him a trifle tiresome. He wished he had been kinder to the fellow, who, he remembered, had rather a lonely look. Yorke was receiving that enlargement and enlightenment of the imagination which it is the privilege of endurance alone, of all forms of human assimilation, to bestow upon us. Experience may almost be called a faculty of the soul.

He was interesting himself to the best of his brave ability in this commendable train of thought, when something white fluttered softly between his heroically dismal face and the pall of smooth haircloth to which he had limited his horizon. It was a letter, and was followed by another, and another, — his mother's letters. The big, weak, tender fellow caught them, like a lover, to his lips — they had taken him so suddenly — before he became aware that they fell from a delicately-gloved hand suspended between him and Mrs. Butterwell's striped wall. He turned, as the doctor was hurrying away, quickly enough — for he was growing stronger every hour — to snatch from her face a

kind of maternal gentleness, a beautiful look. She
was brooding over him with this little pleasure;
he felt how glad she was to give it. But instantly
an equally beautiful merriment darted over the
upper part of the doctor's face, deepening ray
within ray through the blue circles of her eyes,
like the spark in the aureola of ripples where a
shell has struck the sea.

"Another fit of the sulks to-day, if you dare!"
she said, and, evanescent as an uncaptured fancy,
she was gone.

IV.

WALDO YORKE was right in foreseeing for himself a tedious recovery. Had he at that time known the full extent of the shock he had undergone, that beautiful submission to the inevitable which he flattered himself he was cultivating to an extent that might almost be called feminine, and assuredly was super-masculine, would have received an important check. To his perplexed inquiries about certain annoying symptoms in the head and spine, his medical adviser returned that finely-constituted reply which is the historic solace and resource of the profession, — that he had received a nervous strain. This is a phrase which stands with a few others (notably among them "the tissues," "the mucous membrane," and "debility"), that science keeps on hand as a drop-curtain between herself and a confiding if expectant laity.

The young man got upon his crutches in the course of the week, but kept his room. He discovered the measure of his feebleness by the measure of his effort. He wrote cheerfully to Boston about both. In fact, he found himself more cheerful than one would have expected to be, under his really unusual circumstances. He wrote that Mrs. Butterwell read to him, and asked for more books. He deprecated distinctly a modest maternal plan for proposing to the eminent Dr. Fullkoffer to travel from Boston to Sherman to consult with the local physician. He assured his mother that he had every reason to be satisfied with his treatment. He still, from motives of consideration, neglected to reply to her minute inquiries as' to the nature of the practitioner.

" My mother wants to know whether he is ' high ' or ' low.' What does she mean ? " he asked. " And are you a gentleman or a quack ? And does he ' alternate,' — what 's *that ?* And does he use ' attenuations,' — do you ? — and something — I forget what — about what she calls ' triturations.' It seems to be a very important point. I was not to omit to answer it. Then there was a treatise on — I think she called them ' aggravations.' Don't go just yet, Doctor Zay — I beg your pardon ! I get so used to it with Mrs. Butterwell."

" Oh, never mind," she said, with her gentler manner ; it was one of her easy days, and she had leisure to be kind.

" I wish you would tell me," pleaded Yorke

" if you *don't* mind, how you came to have such an uncommon supply of initials. I've never even heard your name."

" Atalanta," said the doctor, looking up pleasantly from the powder-paper she was folding with mathematical precision. He always liked to see her fold powders ; it brought all the little delicate motions of her firm hands into play.

" Ah, the apple-blossom ! " said Yorke impulsively. The powder-paper remained for an instant motionless in Doctor's Zay's hand ; she turned her head slightly in the attitude of attention towards the hair-cloth sofa. He thought, " She meant to do it." Her eyes were bent. He thought for a moment he could see the mischief beneath the lids, and that she would ripple into frolic over his daring speech, like any other young lady. Nothing of the sort happened. The doctor's countenance presented a strictly scientific basis. " She dropped it by accident," said Yorke.

He contented himself with observing that it was an unusual name.

" I had a mother who liked the name," proceeded the doctor, leaning back in her chair, and looking over his head out of the window into the young June day. " When I was a baby she had this fancy for romantic names. She called me

Zaidee, to begin with. Then she happened on this. She always said it was cruelty to infants to impose names on them about which they were never consulted, and I should have my choice of either. I dropped the first, till I came here to practice. Then I had to make some compromise with fate as regarded Dr. Adoniram. There was something absurd in seeing 'Atalanta' on a Down East doctor's shingle, — I have known women do such things in that way ! I had a classmate who took out her diploma in the name of *Cubbie* Smith, M. D. ; and there was one who was let loose upon a defenseless public as Dr. *Teasie* Trial. So I had recourse to the discarded initial. My patients have made a pretty use of it. I rather like it, myself."

She gave that ominous snap to the elastic on the well-worn green morocco medicine-case which had become philosophically associated in the invalid's mind with the cessation of a pleasure. She was going. He hurried to say, —

" Do you object to telling me how you came to settle in this village ? There are so many things I should like to ask. I never knew a lady physician before. The whole thing interests me. So it will my mother ; she is familiar with such subjects. I believe she once consulted a doctress herself. I shall tell her about you when I get a little better; when it is too late to worry."

" I will give you any facts about professional women that may interest you, certainly," replied the doctor, rising, " when I have time."

" You *never* have time ! " cried the patient.

": Have I neglected you, Mr. Yorke? " she asked, coloring slightly ; her color became her. She wore a black dress that day, of almost extravagantly fine cashmere ; she was always well dressed. There was a carmine ribbon around her high, close collar of immaculate linen. The fastidious sick man wondered where this Down East doctress had her origin.

" You have asked me all sorts of personal questions," he went on, with his masculine insistence. " You know all about *me*."

" It is my business," said the doctor, coldly, " to know all about you."

" In other words, it is none of mine to feel the faintest human curiosity in a scientific fact like yourself. You are candid, Doctor Lloyd."

" And you are nervous, Mr. Yorke. Good-morning. I will send Mrs. Butterwell to read to you."

He held her to her promise, however ; and the next time she came he returned to the subject. It was her mood to be tolerant of him that afternoon ; indeed, she was tolerant of everything. She had just brought a patient triumphantly through a mortal attack of erysipelas : she had been a good deal worn by the case for some time ; now her cruel care had slipped radiantly from her young shoulders. He had never heard her talk so naturally, so much like other women. It seemed to him at the moment as if she were really communicative. Afterwards, he remembered how little she had said; and began to analyze the fine reserve upon which all her ease had been poised, like the pendulum of a golden clock upon its axis. She told him that she had been in active practice for four years ; that she was originally a Bangor girl ; that she came to Sherman for a complexity of reasons which might not interest him. She paused there, as if there were nothing more to be said.

"But where did you get your medical education ? " asked Yorke. " I don't even know where such things are to be had."

" At New York, Zürich, and Vienna."

" But why did you select this wilderness to bury yourself in ? " he repeated, his surprise overcoming his civility. " You who had seen — Is it possible you have been abroad ? "

She laughed outright at this, but did not otherwise comment upon it. A fine, good-natured scorn hovered over and seemed to be about to light upon her. He perceived at what a disadvantage he was showing himself; he might as well have said point-blank, "I thought you a crude, rural agitator." He felt his cheeks burn with the quick fever of illness, while she went on indulgently to say, —

"I used to come here summers, once. I knew Mrs. Butterwell and some people here. I must make my blunders somewhere. And then I had learned how terrible is the need of a woman by women, in country towns. One does not forget such things, who ever understands them. There is refinement and suffering and waste of delicate life enough in these desolate places to fill a circle in the Inferno. You do not know!" she said, with rare impetuousness. "No one knows, Mr. Yorke, but the woman healer."

"What led you to see it? How came you to *want* to see it?" he asked, reverently. "How came you to make such a sacrifice of yourself? — such a young, bright life as yours! I cannot understand it."

She did not answer him at once; and when he raised his eyes he perceived that her own swam with sudden tears. She held them back royally, commanded herself, and answered in a very low voice: —

"It was owing to — my mother. She had a painful illness. There were only we two. I took care of her through it all. She spent that last summer here in Sherman, — it was cool here. She suffered so from the hot weather! My mother was greatly comforted, during a part of her illness, by the services of a woman doctor in Boston. There was one when we were in Paris, too, who helped her. I said, When she is gone, I will do as much for some one else's mother."

Waldo Yorke was lying with his hands clasped behind his head, his thin face upturned towards her while she spoke. He did not say anything; but his sense of sympathy with this lonely woman vibrated through him to the last sick nerve. He had, for a moment, that vague consciousness of gaining an unexpected hold upon an unknown privilege, which is one of the keenest allurements and bitterest delusions of life. He dared not speak, lest he should startle her, — lest he should touch the rainbow in a bubble. She saw his hand tremble; her manner changed at once.

"And so I became a doctor," she said, with superficial cheerfulness. "Is there anything more you wanted to know?"

"I want to know everything," said Yorke, in an undertone. She ignored this little slip, as she would a rise in his pulse after dinner, or a faint turn on a hot day.

"If I knew what kind of information would interest you,"— she continued good-naturedly, "but I have had a very simple history. It is like that of many others in my profession. I really have nothing to tell. It came to me the more easily because I always had a taste for science; I found that out in my Sophomore year. And I inherited it besides."

"Sophomore?" repeated Yorke vaguely.

"I was a Vassar girl," said the doctor quietly.

"I have seen educated women before, though you might n't think it," returned Yorke, with humility. "My mother has them at the house, sometimes. I never saw one like you. I never noticed them very much."

"You must have been too preoccupied, — a young man in your arduous profession, Mr. Yorke. I can readily understand that you would have little leisure to study feminine types."

"It is unfair to be sarcastic with a patient, Doctor Lloyd! I was going to say it was unmanly. I have never been busy in my life. You know it as well as I do."

She scintillated for an instant with that charming merriment she had, but made no reply.

" Instead of being successful, I have been rich." he said bitterly. " If I had had to work for a living, I might have been worth something. There is nothing in life so fatal as to be fortunate."

" Ah," she said indifferently, " do you think so ? "

" Indeed I do."

" Have you had that stinging pain in the right side of the head, Mr. Yorke ? "

" Yes."

" And the dizziness you complained of ? "

" A good deal. How many years did you study, Doctor Lloyd ? Did you never shrink, — never want to give it up ? "

" It was hard sometimes in the foreign lecture-rooms, among the men. They were very courteous to me. I never had anything to complain of. But they could not make it easy. I never saw a woman rudely treated but once ; that was her own fault. Then the dissecting-room was a trial to me, at first. It would have been easier if my mother had been living ; if I could have gone home and talked to her. I was only twenty-one. But courage, like muscle, grows by exercise. No ; I never wanted to turn back."

"How many years did you study?"

"Three years are necessary to a diploma from any reputable school. The fourth I spent abroad. But of course one always studies. That is one of the advantages of the Maine wilderness. If I had settled down among people I knew in a town, there would have been too many minor demands. It is never even a professional necessity, down here, to get into one's best clothes; and there's been but one wedding reception since I've been here. I went to that on my way to a scarlet-fever patient. I couldn't come afterwards, with the risk. I did waste a pair of gloves, but I went in my woolen dress, the one I meant to sacrifice to that case. I *do* miss the concerts," she added; but hastily collected herself, with the air of a woman who had been drawn to the verge of a grave moral imprudence.

"Were you ever in Boston,— to stay, I mean?" asked Yorke.

"Oh, yes."

"I wish I had known it! I suppose it is unpardonable to ask where you were?"

"Oh," she said pleasantly, "I used to stay with different people. at the Shirleys' sometimes, and the Waynes'. I saw more of New York in my gay days; we had more relatives there, and I liked it better than Boston. I used to be at the Garratts', when I was a child. They were very kind to me, I remember, when I cried because I was homesick ; they never noticed me at the time, but always gave me orange marmalade for lunch-eor after it. When I got home I used to feel un-appreciated, because tears and marmalade did not retain the relation of cause and effect."

" Is it possible," cried Yorke, " that you are the little girl from somewhere who used to come over to our house with Susy Garratt, once in a while, to blow soap-bubbles ? You had two long braids of black hair, and blew bigger bubbles than I did. I hated you."

" Very likely," said the doctor, laughing as she rose. " I don't remember it. I have n't been to the Garratts' for years. Or anywhere else, for that matter."

" You have had better things to do than to blow our soap-bubbles."

She nodded gravely.

" How many times have you walked across the room to-day, Mr. Yorke ? "

" Oh, wait a minute. Don't go yet."

" *How many times, I ask*, have you walked about the room ? "

" Oh, ten, I believe, — yes, ten."

"I hope to get you out-of-doors next week. Are you suffering from restlessness? Do you feel that rebellion you spoke of at the tediousness of the case? I wish I could hasten your convalescence."

"I don't," said Yorke bluntly, "though I am rebellious enough."

She swept upon him the full fine rebuke of her professional look. He returned it with a certain defiance. She was a woman. She should not thrust him aside like this.

"I believe I shall give you Nux," observed the physician, after a silence which the patient had felt was fraught with a significance he could hardly believe she failed to perceive or share. He flushed painfully.

"Doctor Lloyd," he demanded, "did you ever have a man for a patient before?"

"Oh, yes," quietly. "I am treating a Mr Bailey now, — the erysipelas case I spoke of. His wife is a patient of mine; and Bob, the boy, and all the babies. They live about four miles out, beside the Black Forest."

"Do you often have us?" persisted Yorke.

"I do not desire it, — no. It will sometimes happen. Most of my patients are women and children. That is as I prefer it."

She was sweeping away. She had almost a society manner, like any other young lady. She spoke haughtily. She was evidently displeased. He had never seen her look so handsome. But he dashed on : —

"Did you ever treat a young man, — a fellow like me ? "

" Certainly not."

" I never should have known but you had them every day, — never."

" And why should you ? " she answered coolly. She left him without another word. He listened for her to call Handy ; for the nervous steps of the pony ; for the decreasing sound of the phaeton wheels, which had become so familiar and vital an event in the invalid's dull day. He knew that he had made himself successfully wretched until he should see her once more. He knew that he had followed to the verge of folly a pathological, and therefore delusive, track in that region which lay marked upon the map of his nature as " unexplored." He knew that he should lie and think of it, regret it, curse it, set his teeth against it, and do it again.

" I must get well," said the young man aloud ; as if that result awaited only the expressed intention on his part, and fate, like woman, needed nothing but the proper masculine handling. He got over on his crutches to the tall bureau, and looked into the old-fashioned gilt-framed glass. He saw a fierce-looking fellow, all black and white, — a thundercloud in the eyes, symptoms of earthquake about the jaw, the fragility of mortal illness in the sunken cheeks. What kind of a man was that to command a woman's respect? He must be on a level in her mind with, say, a case of measles. What a pity he could not have had the whooping-cough, and done with it!

It occurred to him that he would go out-of-doors. It struck him just then that he should go into a decline if he housed himself here like an old tabby any longer. He hunted up his hat, and rolled Mrs. Butterwell's somewhat accentuated red and black striped afghan anyhow about him, and hobbled to the front door. The day was damp and cheerless. It did not rain, but would have done so if it had dared. Yorke looked at the clouds grimly. "They are probably ordered by their physician not to go out," he thought. He got down upon the graveled walk, and stumped along towards the gate. He had never felt more guilty since, at the conscientious age of eleven, he kissed Susy Garratt without asking. As he stood there he caught sight suddenly of the doctor's phaeton.

She was turning a distant corner, over by the post-office. He maintained his ground sullenly; at least he would not run from her. She did not see him, he was sure; she was driving very fast. He watched her till she was out of sight, and then returned at once to the house. Mrs. Butterwell, at the rear kitchen window, was making lemon pies, — a conscientious, not to say religious, process. No one observed him. As he came up the walk he caught a glimpse of the doctor's sign, and wondered, with the idle curiosity of illness, what her part of the house might be like. He felt himself extremely faint, after his exertion, and sank exhausted on the hair-cloth sofa, beneath the blazing but generous afghan. He looked at the marble-topped bureau, the Madonna and the framed certificate, the red and gold striped walls, the brown carpet, where the block of sunshine was conspicuously absent. The clock was striking ten. He tried to read. Sparks of fire darted before his eyes, and his ears rang. There was no mail-stage till four o'clock. Doctor Zay might not make her evening call before eight or nine.

"How *dare* men ridicule or neglect sick women?" thought Waldo Yorke.

The day dragged piteously enough. He felt unusually ill. He asked Mrs. Butterwell to stay till she dilated before his eyes, and her head swelled and flashed fire like a jack-o'-lantern. He let her go, to call her back because her vacant chair undertook to rise and hop after her as she went. She read till he entreated her as an act of charity to stop, and talked till he begged her in self-defense to read.

" I 'm worried to death about Doctor," observed Mrs. Butterwell, by way of saying something cheerful. It was the sick man's habit to discourage his hostess in gossiping about the young lady ; perversely, to-day, he let her run on ; he had already that prevailing sense of having broken the ten commandments, which made the absence of an eleventh seem a philosophical lapse on the part of the Giver.

" She will be worked half out of her wits," proceeded Mrs. Butterwell, with that exasperating serenity which ignorance of one another's mental processes gives to the most perceptive of us at times. " East Sherman has the scarlet fever. It 's something about drains. There 's no society in East Sherman ; they 're a miserable lot. Doctor will be up and down day and night, now, you 'll see. She has no more consideration for herself than a seraphim. She 'll *be* one, if she don't mind. The poorer they are, the more no-

body else goes near 'em, the more they get of *her*.
I 've seen her go on like a lover to creatures you
or I would n't touch with our winter gloves on —
hold 'em in her arms — dirty babies ; and once
there was a woman at the poor-house — but there !
I won't go into that. You would n't sleep a wink
to-night. She has such a spirit ! You 'd expect
it if she was n't smart. When a woman ain't
good for anything else she falls back on her
spirit ! You don't look for it when she 's got
bigger fish to fry. But there ! There 's more
woman to our doctor than to the rest of us, just as
there 's more brains. Seems to me as if there was
love enough invested in her for half the world to
live on the interest, and never know they had n't
touched the principal. If she did n't give so
much, she 'd be rich on her own account before
now."

"Give so much what, — love ? " asked Yorke,
turning with the look and motion of momentarily
arrested suffering.

"Practice," said Mrs. Isaiah severely. "She
will do it, for all anybody, when folks ain't able
to pay. Why, Mr. Yorke, if Doctor got all that 's
owin' her she 'd do a five-thousand-dollar practice
every year of her life ; as it is, she don't fall short
of three. She 's sent for all over the county."

" Five thousand dollars!" echoed the sick man faintly. "That girl!" He had never earned five hundred in his life.

" And that, I 'd have you understand," pursued " that girl's " adorer, " is only because she shuts herself up down here with us, bless her! If she lived in New York, I 've no doubt it would be TWENTY-FIVE, — not the least in the world. What are you laughing at, Mr. Yorke? There is a woman out West that makes twenty."

"I don't dispute that it might be seventy," groaned Yorke.

" Not that there 's the remotest need of it," proceeded Mrs. Butterwell loftily. "Doctor is quite independent of her practice."

" I never had heard of that!" exclaimed Yorke savagely.

" Well, she is, all the same. Her father was one of the rich men in Bangor, — a doctor himself; she used to be round his laboratories, and so on, with him, when she was little. He died when she was fifteen. This girl is the only one left, and has it all. You don't suppose Providence did n't know what he was about when he planned out *her* life! He sets too much by her. He never 'd let *her* go skinning round in medical schools, do your own washing and gesticulate skeletons or go out nursing, to make a few dollars."

"It is a remarkable case," murmured Yorke. "And I must have been a remarkable donkey."

"Oh, I would n't dispute that, sir," replied Mrs. Isaiah gently.

"Why, *Sara*h!" objected Mr. Butterwell, whose prudent gray head appeared at the half-open door in season to receive the full force of this characteristic reply.

"Well, I would n't. I never argue with sick folks. You want to know what she does it for, Mr. Yorke? I see you do. Well, I 'll tell you. Don't you know there are women that can't get through this valley without men folks, in some shape or 'nother? If there ain't one round, they 're as miserable as a peacock deprived of society that appreciates spread-feathers. You know the kind I mean: if it ain't a husband, it 's a flirtation; if she can't flirt, she adores her minister. I always said I did n't blame 'em, ministers and doctors and all those privileges, for walkin' right on over women's necks. It is n't in human nature to take the trouble to step off the thing that 's under foot. Now, then! There are women that love *women*, Mr. Yorke, care for 'em, grieve over 'em, worry about 'em, feel a fellow feeling and a kind of duty to 'em, and never forget they 're one of 'em, misery and all, — and nonsense too, may be, if they had n't better bread to set; and they lift up their strong arms far above our heads, sir, like statues I 've read of that lift up temples, and carry our burdens for love of us, God bless 'em! — and I would n't think much of him if he did n't!' "

" Why, Sarah, Sarah !" said Mr. Butterwell. The sick man answered nothing. He tossed upon the hair-cloth sofa, and looked so uncommonly black that Mrs. Butterwell, acting upon an exceptionally vivid movement of the imagination, went to make him a blanc-mange. It was the whitest, not to say the most amiable, thing she could think of. She feared the patient was not improving, and experienced far more concern for Doctor Zay's professional venture in the matter than if it had been her own.

It was half past nine that evening before the doctor got, upon her rounds, to Mrs. Butterwell's spare chamber. The patient watched her dreamily, as she crossed the room through that mysterious half-light, in which he was so used to seeing her that he always thought of her in beautiful hazy outlines, standing between himself and the lamp upon the entry floor.

" How are the fever patients ? " he began, with a stupid idea of deferring personal consultation.

"I have changed my dress," said Doctor Zay, — "every article. There is nothing to fear."

"I never *thought* of *that!*" cried Yorke. She paid no attention to his thoughts, but sat down, and abruptly took his hand to count the pulse. He was in high fever.

"It is just as I expected," she said shortly. "You will discontinue the other remedy, and take these powders dry on the tongue, every two hours."

She brought the light to prepare the medicine. Her face, bent over the green morocco medicine-case, was stern. She did not talk to him. She rose, took up the light, and left the remedy and the room in silence.

"Come back, please, Doctor!" called the culprit, faintly. She stood, the lamp in her hand, looking over her shoulder. It was a warm night, and she had on a cambric dress, of one of the "brunette colors;" he did not know what to call it.

"I am afraid I did a wrong thing to-day," he began meekly. "I went" —

"It is unnecessary to talk about it, Mr. Yorke. I saw you."

"What don't you see!"

"Very little, I hope, which it is my business to see."

He had thought she would say more, but perceived that she had no intention of discussing the matter with him ; he keenly felt this dignified rebuke.

" I don't suppose I did quite right," he admitted hastily, " but I am not versed in medical ethics. I did not realize, till I felt so much worse, how wrong it was by you."

" It was not honorable. But the real wrong is to yourself. We will not talk of it, if you please. I must go. I have had nothing to eat since twelve o'clock."

He saw how tired she looked, and his heart smote him. He smothered an ineffectual groan. He felt that she was very angry with him, and that he deserved it. He would have pleaded with her. Unreasonably, he felt as if his suffering ought to appeal to her pity. Where was the woman in her that Mrs. Isaiah prated of ? Was there no weak point where his personality could struggle through and meet her own, man against woman, on level ground ? What an overthrow was his ! He called impetuously : —

" Doctor Zay ! "

" Sir ? "

" One moment " —

" I have no moments for you, at present, Mr.

Yorke." Her peremptoriness was the more incisive for being punctiliously polite. " It would be
perfectly just if I were to refuse to keep your case
another day. You have disobeyed and distrusted
me. You would have no right, after what I have
done for you, sir, to complain, if I turned you
over to old Doctor Adoniram to-morrow morning.
Good-night." And the woman of science left him,
without a relenting word. It struck him forcibly,
perhaps for the first time, that these exceptional
women had an unfortunate power of looking beyond that gentle pressure of the individual, which,
like the *masque* veils that their sex wore, heightened the complexion, if it did not brighten the
eyesight. Obviously, her interest in her professional reputation overpowered her interest in her
patient. He accepted his fate and his fever.
This was easier to do, as he was quite ill for several days.

V.

SHE took care of him conscientiously and skill-
fully. On his worst day, she even melted and
brooded in that gracious, womanly way of hers
that he watched for; but as soon as he began to
get better again he felt that she distanced him.

"You are harder than Heaven, Doctor," he
said. "You cannot forgive."

"Forgive what?" She looked up; she was
bandaging his ankle. "Oh, that disobedience of
yours? Honestly, I have been so hard-worked, I
had almost forgotten it."

"Then what is the matter, Doctor Zay?"

She glittered upon him for an instant with her
professional look. It was as if she held out a
golden sceptre to measure the width at which she
would keep him. There was no invitation in her
eye. He did not press his question. When the
consultation was over she told him that she should
not be in again till the next morning.

"You no longer need two calls a day, Mr.
Yorke. I will be here as usual, after office hours,
before I start off, and will see you safely out upon

the piazza. I wish you to keep out, now, from one to three hours a day. I will superintend the experiment, to begin with. But you are perfectly able to dispense with this frequent attendance."

Was she thinking of her — bill, perhaps? The young man had really forgotten, till that moment, that any embarrassing basis of this sort awaited himself and this lady.

"Oh, indeed, I don't think I am well enough, at all," he hastily said. "I — really — I have such troublesome sensations towards evening. I beg you will continue to come as you have, Doctor Lloyd."

That amused look flitted for a moment over her bowed forehead; he could see it in the little movements about the temples. She said, —

"It is impossible for me to call where I am not positively needed, just now. You do not realize how driven I am. You will find one daily call quite sufficient for your case. We will hope to dispense with that, before long."

She was as bad as her word, and he did not see her for twenty-four hours.

When she came again, she looked at him and frowned. He was clearly worse.

"I have found out now what my mother meant by 'aggravations,'" said the patient. "This must be one."

She did not smile, as he had expected. Neither did she express the sympathy which he felt that the physician's heart ought to keep on tap, like cider, and gush to order, at least upon a reasonably interesting invalid like himself. She leaned back in her chair with a look of annoyance, drumming lightly upon the table, with that nervous protest of the fingertips, which is a more natural expression of irritation among men than women. As she sat there, looking steadily at him, it occurred to him that she was about to say something of novelty and importance. A certain swift illumination of her thoughtful eyes struck him, and fell, like a ray of intercepted light. It was somehow made apparent to him, also, perhaps from the fact that she refrained from saying what she purposed, that it would not have been a matter of pleasurable interest to himself.

" I will get you out-of-doors, now," she observed, rising. She had never made him so short a call. He protested that he was too ill to go to-day; and, in fact, he had no heart or health for it. He was full of aches and ails; those, especially in the spine, were not of light importance; he was thoroughly dejected.

She paid no attention whatever to his opinions, but helped him out upon the piazza, overlooking the process carefully; when she had him located to her mind, in the proper hygienic relations to wind, wet, sun, and shade, she gathered her driving-gloves, as if to go. "You have not changed the medicine, Doctor," he said, with difficult carelessness.

"I do not propose to."

"Excuse me. I thought perhaps you had forgotten it."

"A physician cannot always give a patient the remedy he wants, you will understand; only the one he needs. I expect to find you better, when I come to-morrow."

It was hardly possible, he thought, to be mistaken in attributing a significance to these words. Yet so ineffably fine are the intonations by which souls become articulate for each other, and so exceptional was the acoustic position of these two, that the young man experienced a modest and taunting doubt whether he might rate himself even of value enough to his physician to receive a clearly personal rebuff.

There exists, and there must exist, between woman and man, an exquisite chromatic scale of relations, variable from the sublimest passions which glorify earth to the most futile movements of the fancy; from the profound and eternal sacrifices to the momentary deification of self ; from divine oneness, past conscious separation, all the way down to little intellectual curiosities, and the contented reverences of slight and beautiful approach. Somewhere in this wide resource of harmony, thought Waldo Yorke, we *must* belong. Then where ?

It was apt, he remembered, to be the woman whom nature or fate, God or at least man (the same thing, doubtless, to her), had relegated to the minor note. It occurred to him that in this case he seemed to have struck it himself.

He did not seek to detain her. They parted in silence, and she went to her day's work. Handy was at the gate with the gray pony. Handy always wore hats that were too big for him, and coats that never by any mistake were large enough. The doctor went down the long front walk, drawing on her gauntleted gloves. She had the decisive step which only women of business acquire to whom each moment represents dollars, responsibilities, or projects. Yet he liked to see that she had not lost the grace of movement due to her eminently womanly form. She had preserved the curves of femineity. He had never even seen her put her hand upon her hip, with that masculine angle of the elbow, the first evidence of a mysterious process of natural selection, which goes on in women thrust by fate or choice to the front and the brunt of life; and the last little peculiarity to leave them if, by choice or fate, they suffer a military recall to the civil status. She saluted him lightly with her free hand, as she gathered the long blue reins into her left, and, turning once, shot over her shoulder a sudden smile. She had, when she felt like it, a lovely smile. He found himself ridiculously better for it. He leaned back in the easy-chair where she had imprisoned him, and watched her drive away. The gray pony exhibited professional responsibility in every clean step that morning, and the consciousness of having made a timely diagnosis in each satisfied movement of her delicate ears. The doctor had on her linen dress and sack, and her figure absorbed the July morning light. Her color was fine. She was the eidolon of glorious health. Every free motion of her happy head and body was superb. She seemed to radiate health, as if she had too much for her own use, and to spare for half the pining world. She had the mysterious odic force of the healer, which is above science, and beyond experience, and behind theory, and which we call magnetism or vitality, tact or inspiration, according to our assimilating power in its presence, and our reverence for its mission.

It seemed to the nervously-strained patient on the piazza that he received a slowly-lessening strength from the doctor's departing figure, as he received warmth from the sun, at that moment threatened by a cloud. It seemed to him a cruel thing that she should not permit him to see her for twenty-four hours more.

It cannot be said that the young man did not chafe under his unprecedented consciousness of dependence. He did. It had struck him yesterday that he was in danger of making a fool of himself. He had devoted the day to this inspiring discovery, and to those select resolves and broad aspirations by which the Columbus in the soul is moved. His present relapse, not to say collapse, was the humiliating result. As he sat there, patient and weak in the strong summer morning, thinking these things sadly over, he recognized the fact that he was still too sick a man to be wise. The grave urgencies of illness intercepted him. He was caught between the fires of a higher and lower species of self-defense. All that a man hath, particularly his good sense, will he give for his life.

"Let me get well, first; I will be prudent afterwards," thought Yorke.

He waited to see her return at noon. He found himself strengthened — such is the hygienic influence of possessing an object in life — and calmed, as the morning wore away. It was a warm morning; would have been hot, outside of Maine. The soft, sudorific glow upon the small leaves of the acacia-trees in the front yard; the opaque color of the dust in the dry, still street; the contented cluck of a brood of yellow chickens, that made futile attempts at acquaintance with him, around the shaded corner of the house; the faint purr of unknown domestic mysteries in Mrs. Isaiah's distant kitchen; and then the sky, of whose intense blueness he was conscious, as if he had been a star gone out in it and become a part of the burning day, — these things emphasized the dreamy struggle after strength, in which he seemed to be alternately the victor and the vanquished, and to fight for high costs, and cover large arenas, and to live a long time in the hours of a short July morning. Well people will not understand.

Mr. Butterwell came out and sat with him a while; he tipped his chair back, and rocked on its hind legs, not having felt at liberty to be individual before since his guest was hurt. He talked of his horse, of Uncle Jed and the estate, of the doctor, of her horses, of Handy, of the lumber trade, and Sherman politics.

"I hope you find it comfortable to be sick, Mr. Yorke," he added hospitably. "I hope you don't mind it, bein' on Sarah's hands. Why, she *likes* it. The worse you were, the more she 'd enjoy it. Sarah is a very uncommon woman. She and I used to argey one spell about profession. Sarah is a professor. Seems at first she could n't sit down to it that I should n't profess alongside of her. But she gave it up after a while. Women are curious creeturs about what they *call* religion. It looks as if nature gave 'em their meetin's and hymntunes much as she give men a store or a counting-room. They want places to go to, — that 's what they want. They ain't like us, Mr. Yorke. There 's a monstrous difference. Why, there 's the doctor! She 's a good girl, Doctor Zay is, if she is cute. There is n't a horse in town, without it 's mine, can make the miles that pony can. Look there! The creetur wants her dinner. See how she holds her? No blinders nor check-rein on *her* horses. She drives 'em by lovin' 'em. There 's *woman clear through that girl's brains.* You should see her in January. There ain't three men in Sherman I 'd trust to drive that mare in January without a good life insurance before they set out. Now, Mr. Yorke, may be you don't feel as I do, but to my mind there's no prettier sight under heaven than a brave girl and a fine horse that understand each other. I guess I'll speak to the little doctor."

This was a long speech for Mr. Butterwell, who clearly took advantage of what he thought the first well-bred opportunity to relieve himself of his unwonted conversational responsibility. He was fond of Mr. Yorke, but he adored the doctor, who never wasted good English herself, and had cured the big sorrel of rheumatism. Yorke watched the two standing in the bright, unshaded yard. Mr. Butterwell patted the pony, and it seemed, although she did not touch him, as if the doctor patted the old man. There was a beautiful affectionateness about her, — Yorke had either never noticed or never seen it before, — a certain free, feminine impulse, which it is hard to describe, unless we say that it showed itself chiefly in the motions of her delicate chin. She nodded pleasantly to her patient as she came by, but did not stop.

Presently the dinner-bell rang, and she came through the long hall behind him, and out upon the piazza. He saw then that she had changed her " scarlet-fever dress " for a fresh cambric, before coming near him. She had a vine whose name

he did not know, in her hand. She dropped it
lightly over his shoulder ; it floated down, and fell
slowly ; it was a delicate thing. She said, —

" Do you know too much about the spontaneous
movements of plants ? I have some books that
you may like, when you are strong enough, — one
of Darwin's especially. It is a subject that interests me greatly. I found this sensitive thing step-
ping straight over the shrubs and logs for a certain
birch-tree it fancied, to climb there ; it went as if
it were frightened, or starved, — like a creature. It
made me feel as if it had a nervous system, and
that the lack is in us, not in it ; we have not the
eyes fine enough to find its ganglia, that is all."

" It seems to shrink from my touch, like a
woman," said Yorke.

" It was so delicate, I thought you would like it,"
observed the doctor. " But come ! I must send you
back to bed. I will have your dinner brought in.
You have been here twenty minutes too long."

He went, peaceably enough. He felt ridiculously, vaguely, pitifully happy.

VI.

EAST SHERMAN, as Mrs. Butterwell had not
untruthfully observed, was a place lacking in " society." The people were miserably poor, and proportionally ignorant, — foreigners, largely : French
and Irish lumbermen, and householders of the
lesser sort, who raised cabbages, aspired to potatoes, and supported a theory, if not their families,
— the theory being that they were farmers.

There are advantages in remoteness, solitude,
and unlimited opportunity to appreciate nature,
but advanced sanitary conditions are not, even in
the State of Maine, necessarily among them. East
Sherman raged with scarlet fever and diphtheria
through that long July, and Doctor Zay had her
expressive hands full. She was busy day and
night. The exhausting rides of the country physician extended themselves through the neighbor-
ing towns, to disheartening lengths. Old Oak relieved the gray pony now regularly every day
The office bell rang to the verge of confusion.
Handy, plunged in gloom, rolled out the phaeton
at midnight, or waited vainly, deep through the

late summer twilights, for the "blessedest, best sound" of low wheels returning down the lonely road. Handy had one spot in the back yard, by the wood-pile, where he stood to exercise what might be called his mind upon the medical and moral subjects connected with his calling. He dug his foot — the right one always, and he took off his shoe for the purpose — spirally into the sawdust, a process not widely understood for its tendency to develop thought, and retired deeper than usual into his hats. He had two. The felt one was the bigger; he wore it altogether during the prevalence of the epidemic. Handy regarded the scarlet fever as a serious infliction, chiefly on horses, not to mention indirectly persons by occupation devoted to equine interests. He made unsuccessful attempts to explain this scientific theory to the doctor; but found her the slave of established medical prejudices, not predisposing one to accept popular discoveries. When Handy was especially aggrieved, he alluded to his injury as "an Ananias 'n' Sapphiry shame." No one had ever traced the etymological derivation of this figure.

One evening, as the clock was striking eight, Handy, having reached that depth of spiral action on the sawdust heap which expressed resignation, not as yet hope, expectation, or disappointment,

and still as far from the pessimistic as it was from
the optimistic view of life, found himself, like
many a better and wiser soul that in facing duty
wrests content from the teeth of despair, suddenly
plunged into undreamed-of (but plainly deserved)
delight.

The doctor was coming home.

" Some of 'em 's better," observed Handy,
wriggling out of the sawdust, and into his shoe, an
artistic attitude which joggled his hat an inch or
so lower than usual over his nose. " Or some of
'em 's dead. Somebody 's cured. Or somebody's
killed. *I* don't care which. Well, Doctor ? "

" Don't water her for thirty-five minutes," said
the doctor, throwing the reins over the dasher.
" She 's too warm."

" Gointerwanteragin ? " asked Handy, in one
agonized breath.

" Not to-night. Put her up. Have you fed
Old Oak? Very well. That 's all."

" Bobailey was after you 'safternoon. The Bai-
leybabyswuss. 'Relse it 's better. I forget. It 's
one or t'other. It always *is* one or t'other," added
Handy in an aggrieved tone. " Haintgoterseeit-
aginaveyer ? "

The doctor did not answer Handy. If she had
been a man, one would have said she strode by

him into the house. As it was, she had a long nervous, absorbed step, that Handy knew very well. He and the gray pony looked at each other with a confidential air through the twilight of the deserted back yard.

" It 's dead," said Handy, " ain't it?" He stroked the pony's chin. The horse returned the boy's gaze with soft, tired eyes, and seemed to nod.

" I thought so," said Handy. " You need n't tell *me* you ain't glad of it. Got your supper an hour sooner. Accommodatinbabywarntit ? "

He leaned his face against the pony's, and whistled, as he led her to her stall, a polka made popular in Maine by the Sherman Brass Band. The horse and the boy went gayly into the barn together, cheek to cheek, as if they both belonged there. Suddenly Handy appeared in the barn door, and made a dive (chiefly over the flower beds) after the doctor's retreating figure.

" Oh, I say, Doctor ! I forgot ! Hewantsyer, mostpartiklertoo. I 've got too much to do to keep rememberin' *him*," said Handy, with a look of disgust.

" What *is* the matter, Handy ? " The doctor stopped, not without a touch of annoyance.

" Why, the fellar in the house. He 's wuss,

too. They 're all wuss to-day," cried Handy, with professional glee. "It 's one of our days. It 's pretty much all wussness. We 've got our hands full, I tell yer, younmenthehosses."

"But I went to see Mr. Yorke this morning," said Doctor Zay, rather to herself than to Handy. She pushed off her hat, and passed her hand over her forehead wearily. There was an irritable, almost a womanish accent in her voice; as if she would have said, "What *shall* I do?" or, possibly, would have cried a little, if she had not been ashamed to. But only Handy heard her, and the gray pony, neighing through the barn door for her supper. Both of them discriminated finely, up to a certain point, in the doctor's tones; but she had passed that point.

"Can't help that," said Handy; "yervegoter-go. He said so."

She bathed, and changed her dress, and took her supper, before she obeyed Mr. Yorke's order; but she obeyed it. He was on the lounge in his room, in the familiar position, and the lamp was in the entry; she came through the half-light, towards him, against the Rembrandt-like background. He watched her in silence.

"Well?" she said, stopping before him. She made no movement to sit down.

"Why, Doctor, you're cross!" said the young man, with an indefinably masculine touch in his tone; half frolic, half tenderness, as if he sported with her retreat, and put it aside as something not important to the case, or even as a thing which it might be in his power to overcome, if he chose.

"Handy said you were worse, and needed me," replied the doctor, gravely. Plainly, she was not a woman to be meshed by these little nets.

"I did not tell Handy I was worse. But I do need you."

"So do many other people. If there are no new symptoms, Mr. Yorke" —

"*Symptoms!*" breathed the patient, all but inaudibly. "There are new symptoms every day."

She made a nonchalant little gesture with one hand.

"If that is all," — there was a very fine emphasis, too light to bear italics, too clear to pass unnoticed, upon the "that," — "you will excuse me, to-night. I am — tired."

"Bring the light, please," said Yorke, with a change of manner. "No, sit down. I can do it myself. Take the easy-chair. No, take the lounge. I can sit up a few minutes perfectly well. I won't keep you more than a few minutes. Please! Why not? Where's the harm? How tired — how tired you are!"

He had hobbled over, and brought the lamp: it was a little lantern, that he had made to swing upon his arm, — one of the contrivances of convalescence, the offspring of necessity, like all the great inventions of history; it had a Japanese paper shade. He stood leaning upon his crutches, looking down. She had silently taken the empty chair.

Doctor Zay had borne her epidemic superbly. Her bloom had subsided a little, it is true, but only enough to increase the delicacy rather than detract from the vigor of her strong face. He had all along perceived in her a person practically supported by what we are accustomed to call, with the most imperfect apprehension of the phrase, a scientific passion.

Against the strain of exhausted sympathy she had set the muscle of intellectual conquest. It could not be denied that in a certain sense the doctor enjoyed her terrible work. She gave out of herself, as if she possessed the life everlasting before her time. She had bread to eat that he knew not of. He could not think of her as sinking, dejected, in need, ahungered. Her splendid health was like a god to her. She leaned against her own physical strength, as another woman might lean upon a man's. She had the repose of

her full mental activity. She had her dangerous
and sacred feminine nerve under magnificent training. It was her servant, not her tyrant; her
wealth, not her poverty; the source of her power,
not the exponent of her weakness. She moved on
her straight and narrow way between life and
death, where one hysteric moment would be fatal,
with a glorious poise. The young man acknowledged from the bottom of his heart that she was a
balanced and beautiful creature. He had read of
such women. He had never seen one.

It was not without a thrill of reverence, amounting almost to awe, that he perceived, when he
swung his fantastic little lantern full in her face,
that she was undergoing some intense emotion,
which, in almost any woman that he knew, would
have weakened itself in vehement vocal expression.

"I had a letter from my mother," he began,
"and I thought — it was about you — I had told
her at last — and it was such a pleasant letter.
I meant to read it to you. She sends a long
message to you. I really am not such a brute as
I seem. I thought perhaps it would amuse you.
Doctor Zay, I had no more idea you were so over-
worked than I had that you were " — He broke
off.

"I never *saw* you look so!" he murmured, with rebellious, almost affectionate anxiety. "It's not easy when you've done so much for him, for a man to look on, like a woman, this way. Isn't there anything I can do? If you would stay a while, I could read to you. We will send for Mrs. Butterwell, if you would rather. I could do something, I know I could! Just let me try."

"You cannot help me," she said, gently enough. "Nobody can. I have lost a patient."

Yorke was on the point of crying, "Is that all?" but saved himself in time, and only said, —

"Who is it?"

"The little Bailey baby. It was doing so well, — out of danger. The mother took it over to a neighbor's. You cannot conceive the ignorance and recklessness that we have to manage. She took the child out, like an express bundle, rolled in her shawl. Coming home, it got wet in that shower. I had ceased to visit there every day; they did not send at once, — I suppose every doctor makes these excuses for himself; what would become of us, if we couldn't? — but when I got there, I could not do anything. The little thing died at half past seven."

She sat looking straight before her at the Japanese lantern. Yorke felt that the personality of the red and purple paper men on it came as near her at that moment as his. He could not think of anything to say which would not present the edge of an intrusion upon an experience so far without the pale of his own. The young man's imagination was well stocked with comfortable material for the lesser sympathies. If she had lost a steamer to Liverpool, or a ticket for a Christmas oratorio, or a picture bidden for in the last great art craze, he could have comforted her. She had lost only a miserable child out of a beggarly home. What could he say?

"I don't believe every baby in Sherman is worth your looking like that!" he cried, with an impulse whose only virtue lay in its honesty. He really perceived that something more than scientific pride was hurt in Doctor Zay. He felt, with a kind of senseless triumph, which he put aside to analyze by and by, that he had found the woman in the doctor.

"It was a dear little thing," she said, softly, "and fond of me. I had always taken care of it, ever since it was born. It was just beginning to talk. It wasn't a big, noisy baby, like the rest of the family. It is terrible that a child should die, — terrible! It ought never to happen. There is no excuse for it. I can never be reconciled to it!"

She rose impetuously, and left him without another word. The patient looked after her. She
had forgotten him. He and the paper men regarded each other. It was not for them to help
her in her trouble. She went across the entry,
and on into her own rooms, and he heard the door
shut. Only one patient rang the office bell that
night. He was glad she was left to herself. Mr.
and Mrs. Butterwell came in. They too, were
much moved by the doctor's grief. They all sat
together in the sick-room, and mourned about that
baby as if it had been one of the family.

"It's always just so," said Mrs. Butterwell, wiping her eyes. "She has n't lost but two patients
since she came to Sherman, — except old Father
Foxy, that nobody counts; for the Lord himself
could n't have saved *him*, — eighty-seven, and
drunk since he was seventeen. The Sherman Tem-
perance Lodge used him for a warning in good and
regular standing, till he got to be about fifty, he
kept such excellent health; and sixty, then they
fought shy of him; and seventy, but did n't die;
and when he came to be eighty they gave him up
as a bad argument. But there! It *kills* Doctor
Zay to lose a patient. I never saw anybody mind
anything so. She acts as if she 'd murdered 'em.
You 'll see! She 'll be all but down sick over

this. She 'd better take it as a blessin'. I would. Those Baileys have got seven now, and poor as Job's Monday dinners. I tell you, Providence knows what he 's about, if folks don't. He will drown the extra kittens, when he can. *I* say he ought to be thanked to mercy for it. But we never do. We up and blame him, the more fools we ! "

" Why, *Sar*-ah ! " said Mr. Butterwell, placidly.

Upon the sill of the open window, during the unwonted domestic excitement of that summer evening, a felt hat with a boy under it had sympathetically and prudently reposed. Nobody minded Handy. He looked in and out unnoticed, with wide-apart, dumb eyes, like the pony. Sometimes Yorke wondered dimly if anybody had fed and watered him ; but even that was an intellectual effort disproportionate to the proposition. It was a long time since the doctor had lost a patient. Handy regarded it as an epoch in human history. He felt that the event reflected importance upon himself, who might be said to have had a share in the glory of the circumstance. He felt above the company of the pony and Old Oak that night ; and though the bosom of the family, as expressed by the window-sill, was a little hard, there is a compensatory pleasure in finding one's social level.

Handy remained there, after Mr. and Mrs. Butterwell had gone. It seemed to him that this lame gentleman encroached somewhat upon his (Handy's) rights in exhibiting so much interest in that dead baby. That was a professional matter mainly between himself and the doctor.

Mr. Yorke, left alone, after a few moments' thought, bent his head upon the top of his crutch, sitting quite still. The red and purple light of the Japanese gentlemen on the little lantern, flashed and defined his profile. Handy vaguely resented its expression. The old felt hat slipped softly from the window-sill, and betook itself confidently to the doctor's side of the house. The office door was open to the warm night. Handy peeked. He peeked without a qualm. He regarded it as one of his privileges to follow the doctor's private career. Who had as good a right ?

Doctor Zay was sitting by her office table. A half-open drawer showed surgical instruments. Rows of vials exhibited mysteries of white pellets and powders. Medical books lay open underneath her hat and gloves, which she had tossed down on coming in. But Handy regarded these points with the apathy of familiarity. The environment did not interest this scientific child. Doctor Zay, who drove the fastest horse in Sherman, who always knew by an awful omniscience whether you missed a pailful or shook the oat-measure; Doctor Zay, who had got old Doctor Adoniram's practice half away from him; *Handy's* Doctor Zay, was bent and bowed over her office table, her face crushed into her resolute hands, as if she had been stricken down by a power that no man could see.

If Handy's education had progressed a little farther he would have called this a phenomenon. As it was, he could only say, —

" It's a thunderin' Ananias 'n' Sapphiry shame. Nothin' but a Bailey baby ! "

It occurred to Handy, as he walked sadly away, over the heavy wet heads of the clover-tops, back to the sawdust heap by the wood-pile, that perhaps he had peeped as far for that one night as the perquisites of his calling allowed.

" Two of 'em," reflected Handy. " Heads down, like unlucky coppers. One on his crutch. T'other on her learnin.' Bobailey 'n' all his tribe ain't wuth it."

Handy was confusedly jealous of something. He imagined it was Bob Bailey.

The doctor was called out that night to see a poor girl, three miles away. Handy accompanied **her.** As they drove through the chilly dawn alone together, Handy's emotions waxed mighty within him.

"Doctor?" he said, in a pleasant confidential way.

"Well, Handy?"

"Is Mr. Yorke wuss?"

"Why, no, Handy."

"Ain't wrong in his head or nothin,' is he?"

"Oh, no, Handy."

"Well. I did n't know. While you was takin' on so about the Baileybaby, he flopped over on them Bangor crutches, and says he, 'Poor girl!' He says it out loud. I heern him. Now, you know, you *ain't* a girl; you 're a *doctor*. I thought may be he was a mite loony, and we 'd ought to look after him. Do you keep any medicine for loons, Doctor?"

She made her call, as usual, the next morning; a very short one. Yorke had hoped he knew not what, he knew not why, from it; she left him only his powders and his disappointment. It was impossible to draw her within telescopic sweep of a personality. She had seemed near to him in that outburst of grief, last night, as if some kindly or friendly impulse in her reached out its hands to him; precisely by the width of that impulse was she now removed. He had his day's orders from his doctor; nothing more. She looked, as Mrs. Butterwell had prophesied, really ill. He thought of her; he thought of her till he was ashamed to think how long it was since he had thought of anything else. The terrible leisure of invalidism gaped, a gulf, and filled itself with her. If he could have arisen like a man, and bridged it, or like a hero, and leaped into it, she would never, he said to himself doggedly, have this exquisite advantage over him. He lay there like a woman, reduced from activity to endurance, from resolve to patience, while she amassed her importance to him,— how idly!— like gold that she gave herself no trouble to count.

He was surprised that night at receiving a second visit; but his momentary gratification quickly spent itself. Her errand was to inform him that she should not come again.

"I do not understand you, Doctor Lloyd," said the young man, with an effort at composure; his breath shortened, and he felt dizzy and faint.

"Oh, I mean, if you are able, won't you come to the office?" she answered wearily. "I am preoccupied, and begin wrong end foremost. I do not mean to neglect you. But I really think you able to get around to my door. The air and exercise will be beneficial to you. There is no reason for my coming to you so often. You can take the morning hour, from eight to nine, or the one at noon, as you prefer."

She gave that slight and fine emphasis of hers to the word " reason."

" This means that I am not to see you — here — any longer? "

" Not unless it is necessary."

" Suppose I find it necessary, Doctor Lloyd ? "

" I must be the judge of that, Mr. Yorke."

" Very well," said Yorke, after a moment's thought, " I will come to your office to-morrow."

He went. He stumped around on the Bangor crutches over the piazza to the office door, which set forth the legend " Z. A. Lloyd, M. D.," in modest little letters of gray and gold. The reception-room was partly full. Five or six women sat there, and a child or two ; one man, a lumberman, who said Puella said she wanted more powders for that crookedness in her mind. Another man came, while Yorke waited, with what he called an " order " for an immediate call on his wife. Doctor Zay nodded to Yorke pleasantly when she came out, but did not speak. He perceived that he was to bide his turn, like any other patient. The doctor said, " Next ? " as if they had been children at school. She was abstracted and pale. She had that look of application which failed of being beautiful. The reception-room was rather pleasant. It was clear that the young lady furnished her own part of the house. Yorke took in an idle, luxurious sense of familiar photographs and even a high-art carpet. There were flowers all over the room, and a table covered with books and periodicals for the patients. Some of the women were reading. He took up yesterday's Boston Advertiser, and hid his amusement, if not his embarrassment behind it.

Presently he realized that they had all gone. Doctor Zay stood waiting for him, gravely. He followed her into the office; a tiny room, hardly more than a generous closet. She shut the door, and motioned him to a chair. She took her own at the desk where the vials were. Her ledgers and note-book, and one or two volumes of Materia Medica, were lying about. The office, he saw at once, was lined from floor to ceiling with book-cases, all full. The doctor waited a moment, as if for him to begin his daily report. He did not. She raised her eyes quickly to his face, and that sensitive change he liked so much crossed her own. Then, for the first time, he saw signs of embarrassment in her. She colored a little, and he smiled.

"Really, Doctor," he said, "do you think this is an improvement?"

She hesitated before she answered: "Really, I — don't know."

"Keeping me here among all those ladies, — the only fellow, except Puella's. *He* did n't stay by me long. I think, for my own part, it was much better in my room."

"Perhaps it was," she admitted, "but" —

"But you don't want to come any longer?"

"Frankly, Mr. Yorke, no."

"Then you sha'n't. I won't be more disagreeable than I must. I will come to the office, as you wish. But why cannot I have a separate hour, after the women are gone? It seems to me it would be quite as pleasant, and much less" — he, too, hesitated before adding, "noticeable."

"I hardly know," said Doctor Zay, knitting her brows. "There are no precedents, exactly." He had never seen her irresolute before. She looked fatigued and annoyed. "There are new questions constantly arising," she went on, "for a woman in my position. One ceases to be an individual. One acts for the whole, — for the sex, for a cause, for a future. We are not quite free, like other people, in little perplexities. It is what Paul said about no man's living to himself. We pay a price for our privilege. I suppose everything in this world renders its cost, but nothing so heavily, nothing so relentlessly, as an unusual purpose in a woman. Nothing is more expensive than sustained usefulness, — or what one tries to make such. I hate to think of petty things!" she added, with some fire.

"Then don't!" urged the young man. "I cannot see the need of it, in a case like yours. You are an antidote to pettiness. You eat it out, like a swift and beautiful vitriol. You would make us all ashamed of it. It cannot exist where you are. I felt that in you the first time I saw you. And pretense, — I had got so tired of pretense. You went on your way so simply. You were so *thorough*. I said, There is a trained woman. She is honest all through. She has the modesty of knowledge. I thought all this while you were tying that artery, before I fainted. What a faint that was!"

"You overestimate me, Mr. Yorke," said the doctor, rather distantly. And yet he was sure that he had not displeased her.

"I have sometimes wondered," he went on, with an awkward courage, "what you thought of *me*, the first time you saw me. I dare say you could n't remember. I don't presume, believe me, that it was of so much importance."

"Oh, yes, I remember perfectly," said Doctor Zay, laughing. "I thought, Concussion and dislocation! Possibly a fine compound fracture. I have never had a compound fracture. I've always wanted one."

"And I have always thought, always maintained, that the scientific temperament is the hardest among civilized types. 'He broke himself against that flint,' I heard said once of a sensitive man, in a miserable instance, — it happened to be a marriage, but that does n't affect the point. One comes upon such a nature as against the glacial period: it solidifies against you; it never bends nor shatters " —

"Nor melts?" she asked, smiling (he could see) out of pure mischief.

"In the course of ages, I suppose. Too late to be of practical service. One freezes in the process."

"The best thing that could happen!" she said quickly.

A white light darted over the young man's face, and passed. He was a remarkably fine-looking fellow in these swift pallors. He shook himself, as if to shake his weakness off.

"Come, Doctor," he said, lightly enough. "Tell me! Was that all you thought when I fell into your remorseless hands?"

"No," she said gravely and gently. "I thought — His mother would not know him."

"Was I so hideous?"

"Yes, you were badly mangled."

"Well, I am even with you. That first time you touched me, I thought I was in hell."

"Yes, sir; you made the fact quite evident, particularly when I set the ankle."

"And now," he said, leaning his head back in the office chair, and dreamily regarding her across the little distance that separated them, — " now I am in " —

The doctor looked at her watch, and moved back her chair.

"I have spent fifteen minutes on you!" she said, in a tone of vexation too genuine to be mistaken by the blindest feeling for a freak of feminine coyness. "So long out of this short morning! And I have thirty-two calls to make before supper. Continue the remedy that you have, till to-morrow. Then call on me again, — here. Come at noon; the office will not be so full, then. You may be a little late, if you like. You may come to me twice a week, now, for an office call. If you need extra attention, — but I do not think you will, — I will call on you, as formerly. You must excuse me now."

" Twice a *week !* " cried the patient. She made
him no answer, rang her bell for Handy, and putting on her feathered hat, walked rapidly away.

Yorke sat in the office a few minutes where she
had left him ; he looked confusedly about. It
seemed to him that he was taking her up in new
and unknown conditions, like the second volume
of a novel. He turned the leaves with a dull uneasiness. Something in him urged, " Throw the
book down ! " He searched his soul for power to
arise and do so. He found there only a great com-
pulsion, as silent and as terrible as the thread in
the hand of Lachesis, which he knew would bind
him down to read on to the end.

VII.

He did not go at noon. It occurred to him in the morning that he was well enough to wait till the evening office. He dreamed away his day on the piazza, watching her as she went and came; lost in admiration of his own self-restraint, and in a nebulous impression that it was time to take matters into a more strictly masculine control.

She did not come home till eight o'clock. The July twilight was already deepening down. Handy came up from the depths of the sawdust-heap and retired from public life with Old Oak; the doctor went to her supper; and Yorke got around into the reception-room, and waited for her in the dusk. No other patients were there. Roses were in the room somewhere, — he could not see them. The folds of the long muslin curtains drifted in the warm wind. The rows of books in the office, seen through the open door, looked fuller for the darkness. Beyond them, another door led into the doctor's private parlor. He had heard Mrs. Butterwell say that her lodger had three rooms below ("two and a half," Mrs. Butterwell called them), and one up-stairs. This other door was half open, swinging idly on its hinges in the perfumed air. He sat and watched it till she came in. It did not open; it would not shut.

She did not see him at first, and he admired the fine unconsciousness of her movements as she crossed the rooms. She lighted her German student lamp on the office table, and, pulling a formidable professional book towards her, without a moment's irresolution, plunged into its contents with the headlong dash which only an absorbing intellectual passion gives. She leaned her head upon her hand, with her controlled profile towards him, while she read. He contrasted this little act cruelly with his invalid reveries.

A woman who *says*, "My life is too full to have need of you," will be met by the historic masculine privilege of reply, "You take the trouble to mention it. I reserve the benefit of the doubt." Doctor Zay took the trouble to mention nothing.

The young man had seen for himself what all the little feminine protest in the world could never have made patent to his imagination: a woman absorbed in her business, to whom a man must be the accident, not the substance, of thought.

He rose at once, and made her aware of his

presence. She expressed the slight, superficial surprise of a preoccupied person, whose life brings her in constant contact with the unexpected. She met him very cordially. He vaguely felt that she approved of him for staying away half a day longer than was necessary. He limped over to the office chair. She shut the door, and he surrendered himself to the brief medical consultation. She found it necessary to examine the injured foot, upon which she laid for a moment her vital, healing touch.

"You would get on much faster if this foot could be properly treated every day, Mr. Yorke. There is not a *massage* rubber short of Bangor. You need one now. You have reached the stage where I should recommend it decidedly. I am sorry."

Yorke made no reply; he dared not, he was so sure that he should say something unexpected to himself and annoying to her; and she brought the consultation to an end. As he went away she told him that she desired him to ride the next day. His ankle, she thought, would bear the motion, — one of the last experiments before walking, — and he would have a driver, of course. She gave the order lightly, the means by which it was to be obeyed not being the physician's concern.

"I should like it, of all things," said Yorke, impulsively, "if I may. But it is so dull with a driver, and Mr. Butterwell is going to Bangor, you know, for several days. I don't doubt he would offer to take me, if he were here. I wish " —

" Why, I suppose I might take you," said Doctor Zay, after a scarcely perceptible pause. " I never thought of it ! "

" I did n't suppose you did," said Yorke, laughing ; " but I don't see why I should n't go, — if you won't let me bore you, that is, — do you ? "

" Certainly not. I will take you with pleasure. I often take patients in the summer. It is stupid waiting. You won't find it an exciting process, I warn you. But it will be better for you than moping on the piazza. You have done enough of that."

" Quite enough, I think," said Yorke, looking fully into her upraised eyes.

" Persistent pallor ! " said the doctor, in a meditative tone. " Tendency to fixed ideas. This accords with other symptoms I have noted. I must look it up carefully ; but I feel pretty sure I shall give you " — her face lighted with the fervor of the symptomatologist — " I shall give you *carbo vegetabilis !* "

They rode. They rode three hours through the warmth and scent of roadside things, while the summer morning waxed indolently towards the splendid noon. Yorke bore the experiment with remarkable success. The doctor attributed this to the carbo vegetabilis.

She chatted cordially with him, as they drove over the long, solitary intervals that separated one call from another; or she came from a grave case to sit in the phaeton silent and distrait, and mind him no more than if he had been Handy; or a patient was responding to a difficult diagnosis or a pet theory, and she radiated her happiness upon him. He did not try to talk much. He absorbed her idly, as he did returning life and the throbbing day. He had never been beside her for so long before. He thought of that first ride through the Maine forest, and said dreamily, —

" It seems like a modern magazine serial that I should be driving with the caryatid. But I have not overtaken Atalanta. There is the Greek tragedy. No, don't turn to your note-book. I am not delirious — yet. You need not " —

" Need not what, sir ? "

" Need not change the remedy. It works well."

" You speak in figures," said the woman of science, curtly. " I am a person of facts. I fail to follow you."

They called at those Baileys' who had become

historic during the scarlet fever, and Yorke looked about him with vague reminiscences. The woman came to the door to welcome the doctor, extending her lean arm.

"There! It's the sign-post woman!" cried Yorke. "We owe it all to her."

"You are strangling in allegory, again. It is a case of asphyxia," said the doctor, handing him the blue reins.

"I mean, we owe it to her that I ever got to Sherman, — a precious sort of debt you think it! Your eyes laugh loud enough to be heard in Bangor. You might spare a shattered man so innocent a delusion. Science would be none the less exact for it. Hang — no, bless Mrs. Bailey! It was she who put me up to — By the way, Doctor, *did* you drop it by accident, or did you mean " —

"How's that leg of Bob's?" asked the doctor, in her happy soprano. She was half-way up the dreary front yard. The children ran to meet her, — a forlorn little batch, — and the woman clung to her with an uncouth, pathetic gesture, half reverence, half fearless love. Mrs. Bailey never thought of paying a doctor's bill, but she wore new mourning for her baby. Her affection was none the less genuine for that. Doctor Zay did not grudge her the sleazy alpaca.

There was a sacredness to the physician beyond the pale of enlightened social science, in the clasp of those scraggy black arms. Mrs. Bailey might outrage political economy, and retard the millennium by becoming a pauper; but she trusted her doctor, and had lost her baby.

Yorke knew little about people of this sort; he had left the lower orders of society to his mother, with a dim sense of their usefulness in providing an outlet for her superfluous sympathies. Boston women must always have an outlet. His mother kept herself supplied with several. He thought, as he sat in the phaeton waiting for this unusual young lady to exchange the society of the Baileys for his own, that she possessed a power which was far more masculine than feminine, of absorption in the immediate task. He thought it would go hard with a man to haunt her. She would shake him off for what she called objects in life, as a fine spaniel shakes off the drops after a plunge into the sea; earth is his element, after all.

Bob Bailey had cut one of the femoral muscles on a mowing-machine. The doctor etherized him, and sewed the leg up, enthusiastically. The odor of the ether permeated the fresh morning, and Yorke sickened over it in the phaeton. She came out presently, with that cool, scientific eye which stimulated more than it defied him.

"I had forgotten you were here!" she said, as she took the reins. "Are you tired waiting?"

"I am not patient by nature, but may become so by grace. I am cherishing a host of feminine virtues," replied Yorke, stretching his big dimensions in the little carriage. "I shall make rather a superior woman by the time I get well. Like the man who had a damp cellar: it was good for nothing else, so he grew mushrooms in it. These beautiful characteristics which suffering or you, — it's all the same thing " —

" Why, *thank* you ! "

— " Are cultivating in me, are " —

" Mushrooms ? "

"I'm afraid so. They won't live long. I am *not* a woman, unfortunately. I am only an arrested development. It is something, though, in this world, to be even a lost opportunity."

" Call it a rudiment," was the scientific suggestion. " And I am glad you reach the subject of mushrooms, Mr. Yorke, of your own accord. It is precisely the point to which I wish to conduct your botanical education. When one knows enough not to expect a mushroom to be, say, an aloe, one is prepared for life. You will recover. I like the symptom."

" Symptom ! " cried the young man irritably.

"Everything, with you, is a symptom. I am growing nervous over the sound of the word."

"Morbid sensitiveness to trifles. I must consider that in your next remedy. Well, and why not, Mr. Yorke? Most things are symptoms. Life is only a pathological experiment."

"That is a narrow professional view."

"All views are narrow. Let me advise you to have as few as possible."

"I am tired of being advised," said Yorke wearily.

Her eyes brimmed with frolic. "Do you want to go home? Or change your doctor?"

"Sometimes I think I will do both, to-morrow."

"You could not do a better thing," said Doctor Zay, carelessly.

"Do you think me able to travel so far?"

"I did not say that. Much depends on the patient. There are collateral dangers in all cases. Many cures consist in a fine choice of risks. Therapeutics, as Hamilton said of conversation, is always a selection."

Yorke regarded her steadily. "I shall not go," he said with decision, after a moment's pause.

They rode. He drank in the divine healing of the day. They talked of safe subjects, — anæsthetics and Materia Medica. Yorke had always be-

fore, regarded homœopathy as a private hobby of
his mother's. He was interested in this young
woman's clear-headed exposition of a theory to
which he was compelled to acknowledge himself a
grateful, if not a convincing testimony. With the
irresponsibility of the laity, he amused himself
with her fervor, while revering her skill. When
she alluded to the Divine Truth in connection with
her sugar-plums, he laughed. But when they
drove over that bridge whence the Bangor pony
had plunged to his last account, the young man
grew respectfully grave. He experienced at moments a species of awe of this studious and instructed lady; not so much because of her learning, which was unquestionable, nor of her beautiful inborn fitness for the art of healing, which was
as clear as the flash of her eye, as for the fact that,
in spite of these circumstances, she could be a
charming creature.

The swift morning grew into the high, hot noon.
The dew dried on the white clover by the road-
side. The dust flew a little. Yorke was tired, de-
spite himself, and glad when the doctor took a
cross-cut through a wood-path to make her last call.
It was a poor girl, she said, who had few friends.
They passed a saw-mill, as they drove to this place.
The wheel was silent. The water dripped from it

with a cool sound. The men were separating to their dinner; one remained at work above the dam. Yorke observed with admiration his practiced step upon the slippery logs which floated, chained, over the deep, black pool.

Doctor Zay drove to the foot of the hill, and stopped. She would leave him in the shade, she said, and walk up to her patient's; it was but a step. Yorke made no protest. He had long since learned that it was hopeless to argue with his physician. He sat and rested in the green coolness, till she returned.

She was gone about twenty minutes, and came out abstracted and stern. She did not speak at first, or take the reins, but sat still, with a twitching of all the delicate facial muscles which in other women would have meant a shower of tears or a tornado of anger.

" Well?" asked Yorke, conscious how imbecile the monosyllable sounded, but not daring to add another.

" She has just told me who it is that is to blame!" said the physician in a low, surcharged voice.

Yorke uttered a sympathetic ejaculation, as her meaning flashed upon him. He felt touched both at the simplicity and the solemnity of her words.

Nothing of the sort had occurred to him, when she spoke about her " poor girl." Nothing could have revealed to him, as did this little shock, the gravity and sacredness of her work. Alas! what could have so betrayed to him the gulf between her dedicated life and his own ?

" I have tried for some time to learn," said the doctor, with unwonted agitation. " The poor thing opened her heart to me just now. You cannot think how such things affect me. He was perfectly free to marry her. There is nothing too bad for him! I have no mercy for such men, — none ! I wish — Excuse me, Mr. Yorke," she interrupted herself. " There is a professional thoughtlessness; I hope I do not often fall into it. I was overborne by the poor thing's trouble. She is such a pretty creature. It would break your heart to see her. And the women all depend on me so; they think there is nothing beyond my power. Why, she clings to me as if she thought I could undo it all, — could make her what she used to be again! I believe she does. It is more than I can ear."

His own eyes filled, as he saw the slow, strong tears, beaten back and dreaded, gather on her lids. All the littleness and pretense and shallow barrier of the world slipped away from them, as they sat there together in the forest. They did not seem any more to be young and unfamiliar, or even man and woman, but only two human beings, who could arise and go hand in hand to meet the solemn need of all the world. To Yorke it was a moment that he wished might never end.

She was the first to speak, and she said gently, —

" I have tired, or perhaps shocked you. We will go home now. It is not my habit to speak of my cares to my patients. You must " —

" Help, *Help !* Oh, for God's sake, HELP ! "

A terrible cry interrupted the doctor. It came from the mill-pond, whose dam frowned over their heads. The thin cascade of the falls drooped like lace against the wall of stone. The trees gathered close about the water, and Yorke looked up to the sky, as out of a well. He could see nothing else. The cry died in a gurgling sound. Yorke sprang, putting the woman by ; he forgot her.

" Mr. Yorke, stay *just where you are !* "

An imperious voice, a firm hand, barred his way.

" Let me go ! " demanded the man.

" Not an inch ! To lame yourself for life, and help nobody ! You never can get up there. Sit back ! Take the reins ! Drive on for help ! There must be men at dinner behind that barn. Do as I bid you ! Do as I ask you, — please."

He obeyed her; he cursed his helplessness, but he obeyed. She was already out of his sight, behind the saw-mill. The next instant, as he drove, lashing the pony, he saw her run swiftly out upon the chained logs above the dam. He closed his eyes. She poised herself like a chamois. He saw her sink upon her knees, — had she slipped? His breath came fast and feeble. The road darkened before him, and the forest whirled.

" Am I going to do such a lady-like thing as to faint ? " thought the sick man. He fixed his eyes fiercely upon the blue reins, — they seemed to remain knotted in his fingers; he had a vision of the flying road, of the sudden sun, of dashing down upon a group of men, of seeing figures dart, of cry answering to cry; and his next precise impression was that he had been sitting in the bottom of that phaeton, with his head on the cushions, longer than he supposed. He was alone, by the barn she spoke of. All the men were gone. He gathered his soul together, and drove back as he had come.

A cluster of men hung on the bank above the dam. A motionless figure lay on the ground in the centre of the group. For an instant Yorke could see nothing distinctly.

" Turn him over ! " rang out a clear, sweet, imperious voice. " No, not so. *So*. This **way** There ! Now, here, Jenley ! You help me."

" All right, Doctor ! " said an unseen man. Silence followed. Yorke bowed his face upon his crutch, with a confused idea of saying his prayers. All he could think of was the Apostles' Creed and Fairy Lilian. The trickle of the fall fell cheerfully over the dam.

" Tompkins, *you* here ! " came the word of command, in that calm, refined voice. " Work at his feet, as I bade you. Keep the arms, Jenley. Tear the shirt, — don't wait. Harder, Smith ! Get more blankets from the house, — bed-quilts, anything. And flannel cloths, — all you can muster. Be quiet. Work more steadily. Don't get excited. I want even motions, — so."

Fifteen minutes passed. One of the men spoke in a lone tone : —

" He don't budge, Doctor."

She made no answer. They worked on silently. Yorke looked at his watch. Twenty-two minutes.

" Make that chest movement just as I told you, Jenley ! — patiently. Have courage. Give me the flannel, Smith. No. Rub *upwards*, not down ; I told you twice. Harder. Here, I 'll show you."

Twenty-six minutes. Half an hour. The lumbermen began to mutter. Yorke could hear their faint gutteral protest.

" You can't resusentite a dead man, Doctor."

" He's dead, that's gospel sure, — deader 'n Judas."

" A critter's legs don't hang that way if he's livin'."

" You hain't seen so many drownded lumbermen as we have, young lady."

" My *arms* ache," said one big fellow earnestly. " I've rubbed a long spell.   Give him up, Doctor?"

" Give him up ?   *No!*" came down the ringing cry.

Yorke quivered with the pride he felt in her. He leaned over his watch, as if it held the arrested heart-beats of the human life for which the brave girl fought.

Thirty-five minutes.   Forty.   Forty-one — two — three.   Forty-four minutes.

A low, awed whisper began to rustle through the group.   Some of the men dropped on their knees.   One ran towards the house.   She seemed to call him back, to utter some rapid order; he started off again.   As he ran past the phaeton he called to Yorke, —

" *Gor a' mighty she's fetched him!*"

This man did not return.

Yorke was sitting in a picturesque heap, with

his crutches, wondering where was the precise point at which a newly-acquired tendency to faint ceased to be physiology and became psychology, and how long he should maintain himself at that credi able juncture in philosophical experience, when he felt her hand upon his own.

" Drink this," she said laconically. He looked up, and saw that she had coffee in her hand ; he swallowed it obediently.

" We have got him into the house," she said, speaking rapidly. "Everything goes well. I know this has hurt you. But I don't want to take you home yet. I have a reason. Can you eat, — if I desire it very much ? "

"I can try," said Yorke, smiling at her tone ; she really pleaded.

" Then I will sit here with you, and we will have luncheon together. You need your dinner. You will be good for nothing with an empty stomach. There ! It will gratify me if you will eat half this bread."

She got into the phaeton and sat beside him, leaning back, and watching him with a gentle eagerness which he would have dared to call tender if he had not remembered that it was professional. " I will eat it all," said Yorke.

She made a pretense of sharing the slice with

him, but he could see that she was keenly excited.
"Now," she said, when the bread and coffee were
gone, "are you better? Are you strong enough
to hear what I want of you?"

"Try me, and see."

"They are together there," — she pointed to
the poor girl's house, — "those two, who ought to
be together for all their lives. *He* is the man."

"The drowned man?" cried Yorke. She
nodded fiercely.

"I want you to come up there with me. I want
you for a witness. I may fail in the thing, but
it's got to be tried. I can't have any of those fellows there, and there's nobody at home but a
young step-mother, who won't come near us. Are
you able to do this?"

Yorke replied by silently taking the reins. He,
too, felt excited and strong. They drove up the
steep, short hill, and close to the poor place. At
the gate stood a wagon, containing an elderly and
gentlemanly but very impatient person. A few
men were hanging about the door-steps. The doctor helped her patient out, and he followed her
into the house, asking no questions.

They went into a low, clean room on the ground
floor. A man was there upon a lounge, swathed
in blankets; he was ghastly white. A girl hung

over him : she uttered low, inarticulate cries ; she
rained her tears upon his face, his hands, — nay,
her kisses on his great, coarse feet, as if he were
her saviour. The doctor shut the door softly, and
Yorke stood uncovered beside her. The girl noticed them no more than if they had been spirits.

" Why, Molly ! " said the fellow weakly.
" Why, *Molly !* I hain't done so well by you that
you should — kiss me — now. I don't deserve it,"
he added, after a moment's thought.

" Molly," said the doctor, coming forward with
her nervous step, " leave Jim to me a minute. I
want to talk to him."

Molly gathered herself together, — a miserable
little effort, — shame and love and tears, — and
obeyed. She was a pretty girl, with blonde hair.

" Deserve it ? " said Doctor Zay, in a changed
manner, as soon as the girl was gone. " *Deserve*
it ? You have behaved to her like a coward and
a sneak. She is behaving like — a woman. She
loves him, I suppose," added the doctor, in an undertone. " That is the way with these women.
Now, then, Jim Paisley ! I have just this to say
to you. You are able to sit up. Let me see you
do it."

The resuscitated man struggled to an obtuse angle against the pillows.

" Very good. I wish you could stand up, but that will do. I want you to marry Molly. I will call her back."

" But, Doctor " — began Jim.

" No shilly - shallying," returned the doctor sharply. " Not a word. Let me see it done before I leave the house. I sent Henry for the minister the first breath you drew, — out there on the shore, — before I sent for the brandy, before you gasped twice. He is sitting at the gate this minute, with a borrowed horse, too, that he's in a hurry to get back to a man who is mowing. Don't waste any more of our time. It's too precious for you. Come ! "

" But Doctor, how can I be married, done up in blankets like a mummy. It's — so — ridiculous ! " pleaded Jim. " I 'd have liked my best close on."

" Paisley ! " said the doctor, towering and superb, " did I work over you fourteen minutes after every man in Sherman would have given you up for dead ? Fourteen minutes longer than is laid down by Hering, too, if I remember," she added, turning to Yorke.

" Well, Doctor, I s'pose you did."

" Did I bring back the soul to your senseless, sinful body, after it had gone God knows where, but where you 'll never go again till you go to stay ? "

"That's a fact, Doctor. Yes, marm."

"I've got some rights in your life, have I, Jim?"

"Yes, marm. I don't deny you brought me to."

"Do you suppose you were worth *touching*, except that you had it in your miserable power to right a poor wronged girl? Come! Do you?"

"No, marm."

"If you don't marry Molly before I leave this house, every lumberman in Sherman may throw you into the mill-pond, — and some of them will. I'll stand by and see them do it. I won't lift a finger for you."

"You're hard on a fellow," complained Jim. "I hain't said I wouldn't. I only said I'd rather wait and get my best close. I vum, when I come to, and — Good Lord! did you see her, Doctor? I hain't done right by her, that's a fact. I told her so."

"Well, well!" said Doctor Zay, softening. She went at once to call the girl, who lay crouched like a spaniel outside the door, upon the bare entry floor. "Come here, Molly," she said, with ineffable gentleness. "Jim wants to be married."

Molly stood still. The color slowly crept over her delicate neck.

"He hain't asked me himself," she said. Jim held out his hand to her.

"The doctor thought I was n't fit to ask you, Molly. She ain't far out, either."

The girl advanced slowly, looking at him searchingly. Then, with a certain dignity, she gave the man one hand, and said, —

"Very well, Doctor."

The minister came, talking about his borrowed horse. He was worried and hurried.

"Where is your certificate of intention to marry?" he asked shortly; "we require five days' notice of intention in our State."

"The marriage will be legal," replied Dr. Zay, promptly. "I 've had occasion to look into that. Whatever formalities are necessary, I will attend to myself. I will pay your fine, if you are called to account for this."

"It is a large fine," said the minister, slowly.

"I will be responsible for it," persisted the Doctor. "I must see the thing done now. Something might go wrong with the case yet. The man is very weak."

The old minister yielded his point after a little feeble protest; he wanted to get back to his mowing.

Yorke and the physician witnessed the marriage.

And the young stepmother, out in the front yard, gossiped with the lumbermen through it all.

Doctor Zay took her patient home immediately when the painful scene was over. He was greatly exhausted. She sent him at once to bed, left minute orders for his care, and went off on her afternoon rounds.

In the.evening she came to him again. She sat some time. She was anxious, gentle, half deprecating. She gave her professional tenderness a beautiful freedom. He felt her sympathy like a sparkling tonic. She atoned for what she had cost him by a divine hour.

She did not mention the poor girl. But Yorke thought of the caryatid lifting marble arms to hold the Temple "high above our heads."

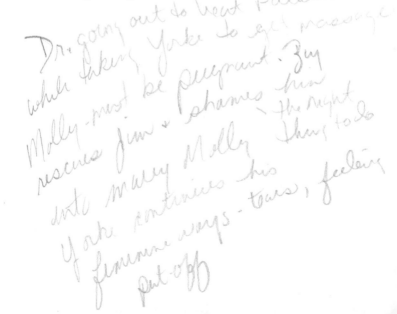

VIII.

THE patient continued for several days clearly worse for the episode of Molly and Jim. The physician was penitently assiduous in her attentions. As soon as he was better they cooled off quietly, but so obviously that Mrs. Butterwell turned her soft eyes, not without sympathy, upon her invalid lodger.

"She's like a candle, — knows her mould, and gets into it, and no fuss. Some folks are like ice-cream; can't freeze without churning. Doctor's always just so with patients. I wouldn't notice her, — she has to be; they'd lean her life out."

It fact, Yorke found himself reduced to his office-calls again, and to a limited allowance of those. He now took occasional meals with the family, and thus sometimes met her at the table. She was very irregular. The office-bell pealed, or Handy summoned her authoritatively; or she was hours behind time. She nodded to him kindly when she came, or they chatted a few moments. She glanced at him with her direct, brilliant, healthy look. He watched her with his sad, refined, in valid eyes. She poured her abundant personality into half a hundred empty lives a day. He received into his vacant hours the influences of the moment. She went; he stayed. He suffered; she acted. He remembered; she forgot.

One day he called her, as he sat on the piazza. She was coming from the dining-room, after a late and hurried dinner. She had her hat and gloves in her hand. " Doctor," he said, " do you know that this is August?"

" It is the 3d, — yes."

" I thought you would n't know. How did you happen to?"

" I always date my prescriptions."

" I might have known there was a scientific reason. For, as nearly as an ignorant layman can observe, the seasons slip away from your attention like cured patients. One is like another, to you. Doctor Zay, do you know that you have never asked me yet to call on you?"

" To *call* on— Oh, you mean "— She stopped.

" As a person, I mean, not a patient. Is there any reason why I should n't?"

" Why, no! " she said cordially, — " none in the world."

" Only you never thought of it."

" That is all," quietly.

" *All!* " cried Yorke.

She swept upon him a fine look; half rebuke,
like a monarch's, half perplexity, like a little girl's.
He hastened to placate this expression.

" Would you like to have me come? I had
rather be denied than endured."

" That is manly. So should I. Certainly, I
should like to see you. Only I never am at home.
I suppose it was rude not to ask you before. I am
so out of the way of — all these little things."

She spoke the last three words with an accent
before which his heart shrank. But he only
said, —

" May I come — to-night? "

" Oh, yes," she answered lightly; " any time
you like, after office-hours and before your bed-
time."

" I 'm coming," he said, in a low, significant
tone.

" What did you say? "

He rose and confronted her. He leaned upon
his crutch, but she felt that the man was waxing
strong.

" I 'm *coming*," he repeated firmly.

She had turned to go, but regarded him for an
instant over her shoulder. A beautiful mocking
light darted from her lip to her eye. She did not

say a word. But he heard every nerve in the woman defy him. It was like the challenge before a battle. The convalescing man welcomed the signal of contest.

He went that evening, "after office-hours and before bed - time," dutifully, as she had bidden. It was a superb evening, and he lingered a moment outside the door to watch the western colors behind the forest. He had already acquired that half-plaintive sympathy with the setting sun which is so noticeable a feature in the lives of invalids. Is it because the hour marks another finished period of suffering, or that it promises renewal of life, which is always resurrection of hope ?

It was a quiet sunset of pale chromes and violets, sinking gently into gray below, melting to the deep blue of advancing night above. The long forest, with its procession of pine outlines, cut the horizon. The heavy mists of the Maine evening rose from the little river and the mill-ponds. This fog caught fire, and the village seemed to stagger in it. Mr. and Mrs. Isaiah Butterwell were picking currants together in the garden, stooping to their task in the level light ; they did not watch the sunset. Handy was watering Old Oak at the spring in the pasture behind the barn. The stage was late, and the two worn horses struggled, with hanging heads, up the lonely street. Two or three lumbermen followed the stage, singing. They sang a chorus which ran, —

> " Thus with the man, thus with the tree,
> Sharp at the root the axe shall be."

Mr. Butterwell called out to the driver to toss him over a paper. The stage crawled on, and turned the corner to the post-office. The fire fell from the mists, the deserted road grew gray, and Yorke felt damp as soon as the color dropped.

The solitude of the scene oppressed him at that moment, as if he had known that he should never have power to separate himself from it. The limit of life in this poor place, its denial, its desolateness, came to his consciousness with the vividness and remorselessness of personal fate. He thought of that wealthy nature, that glorious vigor, that delicate youth, impoverished here. He thought of going back to Boston, and leaving her. He rang the office-bell sharply, and entered without waiting for it to be answered.

No one was in the reception-room, and he passed through. The office was empty. All the doors were open. As he stood hesitating, she came from the parlor beyond. She stood in the door-way, and held out her hand.

" Ah, it is you ? " she said graciously. He was

confused by a consciousness of change in her, but could not have told what it was. As he followed her into the room, he perceived that this impression came from her dress. She wore a muslin gown of a violet color; it was finished at the throat and wrists by fluttering satin ribbons and lace; it was a cool, sheer thing, as befitted the warm night, — a parlor dress, sweeping the floor. He had always seen her in her business clothes.

He was not sure at first that he liked to see her in any other way. He felt a vague jealousy of her individuality, on which this dainty feminine gear seemed to encroach. But in a moment, when he had accustomed his eye to the transformation, he acknowledged that he would not have missed it for the world.

" What is the matter ? " she asked, in her outright fashion ; her profession had cultivated in her, to perhaps an extreme limit, what was probably great native directness of manner.

" Excuse me. Was I staring ? I have never seen you in a — don't you call them trails ? "

She blushed a little, looking over her shoulder down at the wave of purple color, out of which she seemed to rise, as if she floated on it.

" I do not wear such things. I do not respect them," she said, with a latent vexation in her

voice. "I feel as if I ought to apologize to ideal
womanhood every time I encumber my feet and
other people's in this way. But it was so warm,
and this is the coolest thing ·I have. I had been
dusty and uncomfortable all day. And it *is* pretty,
in itself, I think; don't you?"

"I shall not — that is to say I cannot — tell
you what I think," he answered. The undisguised
admiration in his eyes roamed over her with daring leisure.

It was characteristic of these two people — and
to which the more creditable, one can hardly say
— that it no more occurred to the young man that
there was a remote touch of pardonable feminine
coquetry in the coincidence of his call and the violet muslin, than it did to the lady that he might
think so. Doctor Zay knew how often she wore
that gown on warm evenings, shut in alone in her
dark little parlor, after the last patient was gone,
after the care and fever of the long day were
spent, — when the doctor melted into the woman.
And Yorke was beginning to know Doctor Zay.

He took the easy-chair which she offered him,
quietly observing the scene upon which he had
fallen, and in which the violet muslin was only
what artists would call the "high light." After
his hair-cloth sofa and framed certificate, this

young lady's parlor affected him like a restored
and precious painting. He felt the powerful influence of the cultivated interior, to which he
yielded with that composite emotion, half home-
sickness, half instinct, which we all know, and
which, like a magnet, draws back the exile from
what we are pleased to call "the world."

Yorke, as he sat and talked of little things, as-
similated his surroundings gently : the books, the
engravings, few but fine, the bronze Psyche, the
little landscape of Gifford's, magazines, newspa-
pers, reviews, and colors that he had not seen since
he left home.

While she busied herself in drawing the long
curtains and lighting the lamps, he noticed the
Chickering upright across the corner, and a curious
afghan, knit of dull harmonious tints, like a Per-
sian rug. There were flowers, too. The lamps
had green and yellow globes. There were many
pillows in the room, of odd shapes, and all sorts of
hospitable things to sit on ; an open fire-place,
filled now with ferns : yet nothing seemed to be a
reproduction of a fashionable craze. There was no
incoherent attempt at affecting cracked bricabrac,
deteriorated Japanese art, or doubtful colonial fash-
ions. One did not even think of Queen Anne or
Louis Quinze, but only of Doctor Zay, who had a
pleasant room and lived there.

It affected Yorke strongly to meet his doctor
here, — a lady, like other ladies, in a shelter,
among little lovely things, quiet and set apart,
protected from encroachments, forgetful of care.
He was glad that the patients were never allowed
to come into that room. He felt dizzy with his
own privilege.

He leaned his head back against his boldly modern but proportionally easy-chair, and watched
her, while they chatted pleasantly. They talked of
Boston, of books, of people, of well things. Left
to herself, he noticed that she avoided all pathological subjects with a rigor which in itself was all
that reminded him of their existence. She made
no inquiries about the state of his prevailing sensations, nor alluded in any way to his relation as a
patient to herself. She had a fine tact in this,
which made him feel as if he were a well man
again. He rested in her dainty vicinity, the quiet
things she said, the sound of her voice, the delicacy of her dress, in herself. He forgot for one delicious hour the real and rugged world in which
she lived. Or rather, perhaps, if he analyzed his
feeling, he had a vague sense of mastery, as stimulating as it was unprecedented, as if he himself
were the agent, not the subject, of a new experience, in which he drew her from a consecration to
a dream.

He asked her to play to him.

" No," she said, " you are a Bostonian."

" But not a critic."

" Impossible ! You approve the Handel and Haydn, and patronize the Symphony. You do your duty by the prevailing artists ; hold them at arm's length as I do my last new babies, with about the same complacency in their existence, as if the Creator had an obligation to you for the fact. You are like the man who declined to be a vegetarian on the ground that *pâté de foie gras* was good enough for him. I had a patient once who abandoned smoking because his taste had developed so fastidious a quality that he could find no tobacco fine enough for him."

" I am still a crude smoker. Play to me; please ! "

" I know two tunes: one is China, and the other is n't. Which will you have ? "

" The other one. Play to me ! "

" It is a Scotch song. Do you like Scotch song ? "

" Do you sing ? "

" Not in the least. I can play you the accompaniment."

He made a little movement of impatience. He was by nature of a restless, not to say an imperious temper which his illness (or perhaps it would be more precise to say, his physician) had subdued rather than excited.

Her ready merriment came to her eyes.

"You cannot make me believe," he insisted, "that you are not musical. Physicians are."

"That is true enough," she answered, quickly warming to the subject. "Science is harmony. Music and science are twins. Music is the feminine, though, I think."

"It is a fine marriage. Oh, you call them twins, though."

"You are not so far out of the way. There is an element of twinship in all absolute marriage." This was said with her scientific expression, as if she were dissecting a radial artery.

"How many 'absolute' marriages have you known?" asked Yorke, as nearly as possible in the same tone.

"Just three," said Dr. Doctor Zay.

"In all your experience? Only three that would — that *you* would have been satisfied with?"

"It is not a question of what would satisfy one's self," she said, freezing swiftly and slightly, like thin November ice. "It is a matter of psychological investigation."

" What a horrible advantage over mankind your profession gives ! " said Yorke, between his teeth. She nodded gravely.

" It is unmatched, I believe. Even the clergy have a poor one beside us. We stand at an eternal confessional, in which the chance of moral escape or evasion is reduced to a minimum. It is holding human hearts to count their beats. When you add the control of life and death, you have a position unique in human relations. When I began, it seemed to me like God's. My mother used to " — She stopped.

" What did your mother do ? " asked Yorke, gently.

" She encouraged that feeling," said Doctor Zay. " She said no one was fit to enter the profession who did not have it."

" I wish I had known your mother," he ventured.

" You would have loved her," said the doctor, simply.

" And I wish you knew mine ! " continued the young man, fatuously.

" She would not be interested in me," returned Doctor Zay, coldly. It was good, honest December ice now. He could have skated on the barrier she had thrust between them, he neither knew how nor why.

"Oh, you don't know her" — he began. At this moment the office-bell rang. Handy answered it, and knocked at the parlor door to announce (with evident pleasure) the presence of a patient who "was in an Ananias 'n' Sapphiry hurry. Guessed it was somebody dyin' or smushed."

The doctor rose leisurely, too used to these interruptions to expend nerve force on little haste or premature excitement, and went into the reception-room. She did not excuse herself to her visitor. She left the doors ajar, and he could hear her hearty voice : —

"Ah, Mr. Beckwith ! What now ? "

"Wall," replied the man's voice that Yorke had heard on his first office-call, "Puella, you see, she 's bad. She 's took screechin' bad ag'in, and don't give none of us no peace. She wants you right away. She made me tackle up so 's to bring you myself. I *told* her, says I, 't was a kind of shame ! — you 'd be all beat out, this time o' night. But, Doctor," plaintively, "it ain't no use *to* tell Puella things."

"Anything new, Mr. Beckwith ? Any serious change in the case ? What are the symptoms ? "

"Wall," said Mr. Beckwith slowly, "I can't

say 's it 's so very *noo*. It 's that same crookedness in her mind. She suffers a sight," solemnly, "from crookedness in the mind, Doctor."

"I 'll send her something," said the doctor kindly. "I do not think it necessary for me to go to-night. There! One powder dry on the tongue, if you please, every two hours. I will look in to-morrow."

"I *told* her you would n't come," said Mr. Beckwith, triumphantly. "And what 's more, I said, says I, Puella, I would n't if I was her, says I. But says she, You don't none of you know what it is to have crookedness into your mind."

Silence succeeded. The doctor returned, closing the doors as she came. She made no comments on the interruption. She drifted into the quiet room, past the green and golden lamps, in her violet dress, and resumed her chair in silence. Yorke looked at her without speaking.

"What are you thinking?" she asked abruptly. There was a dash of something which he could almost have dared to call friendly freedom in the tone of the question.

"I was thinking that you harmonize with your environment."

"That would be the acquisition, as it is the aspiration, of one's life-time. The compliment is too large for the occasion."

For answer, he glanced about the room and back at herself. She smiled, not without a touch of scorn, or it might have been of bitterness.

" But then," he continued dreamily, "you are of course an exception, not a representative, among women who adopt your vocation."

" You only exhibit your ignorance by such a remark," said the young lady quietly. " Among the thousand of us now practicing medicine in this country, there are many more successful than I, and abroad there is some superb work done. I should like to give you the figures some time. They are very interesting. But I won't bore you now. It would be like putting sermons in a novel."

" What is the proportion of ladies in the profession ? " asked Yorke, with a slight shrug.

" What is the proportion of gentlemen in the profession ? "

" Except that I really know nothing about it, I should suppose it is larger."

" It probably is a little. Until recently it needed force rather than fineness to bring a woman to the surface of a great progressive movement. We are coming to a point where both are to be absolutely necessary to success in the art of healing. A union of these qualities will be demanded of women, be-

cause they are women, such as has never been expected of men, or perhaps been possible to them.
We have a complex task before us."

" It seems a dreary one to me," said Yorke,
rather sadly. "And yet you find it" —

" Bright ! " she said quickly ; " bright, bright ! "
Her earnest face fired.

" You really seem happy," he urged.

" I *am* happy ! " she cried, in her resonant, joy-
ous tone.

" I wonder if I could say as much, if I had done
as much ? " queried the sick man.

Her whole expression changed instantly. Both
felt what neither said, that they had approached
difficult and delicate ground.

" I do not take as dark a view of your case as
you do," she said.

" In other words, I am not lost to your respect,
because I have not become an eminent jurist at the
age of — I am only twenty-eight, after all," he
added.

" I am a year older than that," she smiled. " I
ought to have done more. What is the trouble,
Mr. Yorke ? Don't you get any clients ? " She
took unconsciously the professional tone she had
so long assumed to him, as if she had asked,
" Does n't your dinner agree with you ? "

" I had one divorce case last winter; I lost it."

" You resent my asking questions. You ought not to."

" I feel it. I do not resent it."

" That is kind in you, and discriminating. You silence me."

" No, go on. Say what you think of me. Tell me, — I can stand it. What a consummate donkey a man of my sort must seem to a woman of yours! And yet I'm not a donkey; I am really a very good sort of fellow."

" You are rudimentary," said the doctor, with an inscrutable look.

" Hum — um — um."

" Honestly, Mr. Yorke, my diagnosis of you is different from — It is my own, at any rate, be it worth little or much."

" You have had some chance to form one, I'll admit," said Yorke. " Let me make a guess at it: Inherited inertia. Succumbed to his environment. Corrosion of Beacon Street upon what might, in a machine-shop, for instance, or a factory, have been called his brain. Native indolence, developed by acquired habit. Hopeless correlation of predestined forces. Atrophied ambition. Paralyzed aspiration. No struggle for existence. Destitute of scientific basis. Reductio ad absurdum, — Laborare est orare, — Facilis descensus. No correspondent in the Materia Medica. Hahnemann knew not of him. (*He* was mobbed for a great cause.) The Organon foresaw him not. There is no divine remedy for him. Give him *sac. lac.* powders, and send him back to Beacon Street. By the way, Doctor, did you ever give me a sugar powder?"

" Once."

" When was that? I 'll know, or I 'll never forgive you."

" The day you disobeyed me about going outdoors, and caused me an unnecessary call."

" On your honor, is that the only time?"

" By my diploma! — the only time."

" You did not say whether I had hit the diagnosis, Doctor Zay."

She did not answer him at once, and when she spoke he felt, rather than saw, that it was with her guarded look.

" I do not make it a case of paralysis, exactly. I should rather call it one of hyperæsthesia."

" Hyperæs — that was what was the matter with me when I could n't let Mrs. Butterwell shut a door, or drop a thimble; when the horses kept me awake, stamping in the barn. You mean that you do me the honor to infer that I have ideals, despite my failure to give an inquiring world evidence of the fact, and that (if I do not strain your goodness) the idealizing fibre is not without superfluous sensitiveness ? "

" Superfluous, and therefore injurious, sensitiveness. You experience a certain scorn of the best into which you know yourself capable of resulting. You cherished this scorn, at one time, as a silent proof of superiority of nature, patent only to yourself, and the more precious, like family lace or jewels worn out of sight. You were met at the outset of life by the conviction that you were without extraordinary gifts, and it struck you as original to snub the ordinary ones, as if it were their fault. I am not sure that it was even original ; it certainly was not admirable. But you have outgrown that. I recognize now a genuine modesty at root of your inertia. Your self-estimate is calculably less than that of almost any other Boston man I ever met. I prognosticate that the next phase of experience will be a healthier and haughtier one. I think you capable of service." The young lady uttered these sentences slowly, with palliative pauses between them ; she had an absorbed and studious look.

" I always thought I might have made a good head-waiter," said the young man grimly.

" Take me as you please," persisted the doctor

"I have paid you a compliment; my first — and last. Cut yourself with it, if you want to. It would be malpractice, but I am not the surgeon."

Yorke made no reply. He sat and watched her, thinking that he would not have borne from any other woman in the world what came like a fine intoxication from her; he drank her noble severity like gleaming wine.

"You are not a great man," she urged gently, as if she had to say, "You have a spinal injury," "but you have uncommon qualities, — perhaps I should say quality; you have hardly taken the trouble, as yet, to indicate what your qualities are. You could be successful if you chose. The difficulty has been that you have not respected what we are in the habit of calling success."

"Frankly, no; it has never seemed worth while."

"The Christians have a phrase," said Doctor Zay, "which expresses the deficiency in most of our standards. They talk of consecration. It means something, I find."

"Are you a Christian?" asked Yorke.

"I do not know — yet," she answered, gravely.

"Now, I have always thought I was," he said, smiling sadly.

"Are you?" She looked at him wistfully.

"At least I was confirmed once, to please my mother. It may belong to that pervasive weakness of nature, which you classify so indulgently as sensitiveness, that I never have grown away as far from all that as many fellows I know. There, now, is an ideal! Where in history or philosophy can it be mated? Faith *is* beauty. I should like to hold on to my faith, if I can, — if I had no other reason, just as I should wish to keep my paintings or bronzes. But I know it is harder for a camel to go through the knee of an idol, as the little boy said, than for a student of science to enter the kingdom of heaven. Are you one of the two atheists, in the historic three doctors?"

"God forbid!" she cried. "I am a seeker, still. That is all I mean to say. And I know I must seem" — She paused, stricken by an unprecedented and beautiful blushing embarrassment.

"What must you seem?"

"It was nothing, — a foolish speech. It is time for you to go home, Mr. Yorke, and go to bed."

"What must it make you seem? I will go when I know. Tell me, — you shall! Indulge me, please." He limped over towards her; his words fell over each other; his figure towered above her.

She gave one glance at his agitated face, and

collected herself by a movement swift and secretive as the opening of a water-lily.

"I only meant to say that a woman usually — naturally, perhaps — is the guide in matters of belief. Spiritual superiority belongs to her historically, and prophetically too, I do not dispute. It occurred to me, at that moment, how it must strike a man, if she were below him on that basis; if she had no power to heighten or deepen his ideal, — that was all. Good-night, Mr. Yorke. If you don't sleep, take that powder marked 'Cham. 5 m.' Now go!"

"You heighten and deepen every other ideal I have," said the young man, solemnly. "You cannot fail me there. It will not be possible to you."

His agitation had urged itself upon her now, against her will; he was half shocked, half transported, to see that a slow pallor advanced like a spirit towards him, over her resolute face. He watched it with a kind of awe, and made a gesture with one of his thin hands, as if to check an invisible presence which he was not strong enough to meet. It was the movement of a sick man whose physical strength was spent by emotion. The physician perceived this instantly.

"There is the office-bell," she said, in her business tone. "I will answer it as I help you out."

He made no reply, and they left the parlor in uneasy silence. He had tried to come on one crutch that night; now, weakened with excitement, he made bad work of the experiment.

"Put your hand on my shoulder," ordered Doctor Zay.

"You are not tall enough," he objected.

"I am strong enough," she insisted.

He obeyed her, and thus came limping to the front door between the lady and the crutch. The patient who had rung the office-bell stood in the doorway. It was a man. It was a gentleman. It was a stranger. At sight of him Doctor Zay colored with impulsive pleasure. She said: —

"Why, Doctor!"

The stranger answered: —

"Good-evening, Doctor."

Yorke found this dialogue monotonous, and removed his hand from the violet muslin shoulder.

"Walk in," said the lady, turning heartily to her guest. "Go right through into the parlor. I will be with you in a moment."

The stranger, bowing slightly to Yorke, stepped in and passed them. By the sharp light of the kerosene entry lamp Yorke perceived a man of years and dignity; in fact, a person of distinguished appearance.

"I will not trouble you to go any farther with me," said Doctor Zay's patient, stiffly.

" Nonsense ! "

The soft, warm shoulder presented itself with a beautiful — it seemed to Yorke a terrible — unconsciousness, leaning towards him like a violet indeed.

" No, no," he said, roughly ; "I don't want it. It won't help me. Don't you understand a man better than that ?"

As soon as the words were uttered, he would have given, let us say, his sound ankle to recall them. She shrank all over, as if, indeed, he had stepped on a flower, and, gathering herself with a grave majesty, swept away from him.

IX.

YORKE limped back to his room, and sank into the first chair that presented itself. It happened to be the high rocker, and he put his head back, and thrust his hands into his pockets, and got his ankle across another chair, and for a few moments occupied himself in a savage longing for a smoke. His physician had forbidden him his cigars, pending the presence of certain spinal symptoms which she was pleased to consider of importance to her therapeutic whims. A good square disobedience would have relieved him. He would have liked nothing better than that the odor of the tobacco should steal around through her parlor windows, while she sat there in that trailed gown making herself lovely to that fellow. Was it possible she knew *he* was coming when she put the thing on? . . .

Yorke found himself engulfed in a chasm of feeling, across which, like a bridge whereon he had missed his footing, ran one slender thought : —

" I ought to have gone home three weeks ago."

It was quarter past nine when she sent him to

his room. He sat in the big rocker, in the dark, without moving, till ten. No sound had come from the doctor's side of the house. Acting upon a sudden impulse, of which he was half ashamed, half defensive, and which he owned himself wholly disinclined to resist, he groped for his crutches and got out upon the piazza, where he could see the light from her windows making a great radiance upon the acacia-tree, and showing the outlines of the short, wet grass. A honeysuckle clambered over the nearest window. When the curtain drifted in the warm wind, the long-necked flowers seemed to look in. The subdued sound of voices came to his ear. He went back, and got upon the lounge. As he lay there, the lumbermen returned, sing-ing, —

> " Thus with the man, thus with the tree,
> Sharp at the root the axe must be."

Mrs. Butterwell came in to say good-night. She held a candle, which made fickle revelations of her black silk dress and sallow cheeks. She expressed surprise at finding her lodger in the dark, and lighted his Japanese lantern assiduously. She thought Mr. Yorke had been calling on the doctor.

"She sent me to bed," said Yorke. "She has another fellow there."

"They will come at all hours," replied Mrs. Butterwell, serenely. "More blame to 'em!"

" *Who* will come at all hours?" gasped Yorke.

"Why, patients, of course. Who else?"

"This is n't a patient. This is a gentleman."

"I want to know!" said Mrs. Butterwell, putting down the light.

"And so do I," said Yorke, grimly.

"A tall, dark-complected gentleman? Wears a crush felt hat and gray gloves, — a *beautiful* fit?"

"I did n't notice his gloves," savagely.

"A handsome man, was n't he?" pursued Mrs. Butterwell, cruelly. "Splendid figure and great blue eyes" —

"How should I know about his eyes?" groaned Yorke.

"Oh, it must be he," returned Mrs. Butterwell, placidly. "I wonder I did n't see him in the stage. I always mean to look in the stage. May be he drove, — he 's apt to."

Yorke made no answer. Every word of Mrs. Butterwell's caused an acute pain in his left temple, like the nail in the brain of Sisera; he put up his hand to his head.

"His name is Penhallow," hammered Mrs. Butterwell, — "Doctor Penhallow, of Bangor. He is a famous surgeon, — very famous. He sets the world by her."

"It can't be — it is n't the fellow she telegraphed to about my case, at the beginning?" cried Yorke.

"Oh, I dare say. Doctor did n't mention it to me. Doctor never talks about her cases. She admires Doctor Penhallow above all. He was her preceptor. He's old enough to be — well, it would be a young sort of father; but he's well along; he could n't be so famous if he was n't; nor she would n't feel that kind of feeling for him, — that looking up. He's the only man I ever saw Doctor look up to. She ain't like the rest of us; we wear our upper lids short with it. I declare! It seems to me in course of generations women would n't have had any eyelids; they'd be what you call nowadays selected away, by worshipin' men-folks, if Providence had n't thrown in such lots of little men, — mites and dots of souls, too short for the biggest fool alive to call the tallest. Then, half the time, she gets on her knees to him to make out the difference. Oh, I've seen 'em! Down on their knees, and stay there to make him think he's as big as he wants to be, and pacify him. Then another thing," added Mrs. Butterwell, gently, "is babies. You've got to look down to your babies, and that keeps the balance something like even. Providence knew what he was up to when he made women, though I must say it looks sometimes as if he'd made an awful botch of it."

"Is he married?" asked Yorke.

"Who? Oh, Doctor Penhallow? (I was thinking about Providence.) No. *He's* an old bach," said Mrs. Butterwell in a mysterious manner, " and only one sister, and she just married and gone to Surinam to live. It seems to make it such a useful place ; I never felt as if anybody lived there before. He used to have to have her home in Bangor till a gracious mercy removed her, for she was squint-eyed and had spells. He was a friend of her father's, too."

" Whose father's?" cried Yorke, desperately.

" Why, Doctor's father's, — Doctor Zay's father's. Old Doctor Lloyd and Doctor Penhallow were friends, the dearest kind ; he was his preceptor, too, and Doctor " —

" We are getting our pronouns, not to say our physicians, dreadfully mixed," interrupted the young man wearily. " And I suppose the lady has a right to her admirers, whether they meet our views or not. There really is nothing extraordinary about it, except the fact that it should never have occurred to me that she could have them, in this wilderness."

" Well, there! I should like to know why not!'

Mrs. Butterwell fired at once. "You don't suppose a woman ain't a woman because she's a doctor, do you? There was a fellow here last summer, — a family of summer folks at the Sherman Hotel, three brothers: one was a minister, and one was an editor of something, — I forget what, but he wasn't a widower, that I'm sure of, — and one had a patent on mouse-traps. I can't say much for the minister, for he preached on woman's sphere in the Baptist church, — may the Lord forgive him, if he ever heard the sermon, which I don't believe He did, — and the mouse-trap was engaged, besides having his front teeth out, and coming down here to wait till he shrank for a new set. But that poor little editor, Mr. Yorke, I wish you could have made his acquaintance. The table-girl at the Sherman House told my girl he'd lost his appetite to that pass he wouldn't eat a thing but shoo-fly potatoes. Think," added Mrs. Butterwell, with a gravity which deepened to solemnity, "of supporting an honorable and unrequited affection on shoo-fly potatoes!"

"I did not know," observed Yorke, acutely conscious of the indiscretion of his remark, "that physicians — men physicians — were apt to be appreciative of the lady members of the profession in any way, least of all in that. Many of these facts in social progress, you see, are novel to me. I am very dull about them."

"Well, I declare!" objected Mrs. Butterwell. "I must say I think you are. For my part, I can't conceive of anything more natural. When you consider the convenience of taking each other's overflow practice, and consulting together when folks die, and the sitting down of an evening to talk over operations; and then one boy would do for both sets of horses. And when you think of having a woman like Doctor to turn to, sharin' the biggest cares and joys a man has got, not leanin' like a water-soaked log against him when he feels slim as a pussy-willow himself, poor fellow, but claspin' hands as steady as a statue to help him on, — and that hair of hers, and her eyes, for all her learning! But there, Mr. Yorke! I've talked you dead as East Sherman. I'll fix your blinds for you and put in the pegs, and get your milk, and go. Don't you lie awake listening for him. He won't go till half past eleven. He never does. He ain't able to get over very often, for his business is tremendous, and he's sent for all over the State, consultin'. He's *famous* enough for her, if that is all," she added, by way of final consolation.

Mrs. Butterwell's prophecy proved so far cor-

rect that at quarter of eleven the hospitable light
still shone from Doctor Zay's parlor upon the aca-
cia leaves and clovers, and the slender-throated
honey-suckles, curious and dumb. It was with an
emotion of exultance, for which he blamed and
shamed himself with bitter helplessness, that
Yorke heard, at ten minutes before eleven, the office-bell struck by what he knew was the imperious
hand of a messenger in mortal need. He heard
Doctor Zay come out quickly to the wagon which
had brought the order. She did not wait for her
own horse to be harnessed, but was driven rapidly
and anxiously away. It seemed to him that he
heard Jim Paisley's voice, and that Jim said something about Molly. Yorke was sorry for Molly,
but he was not sorry for Doctor Penhallow, whose
distinguished footsteps echoed down the lonely
street, on their way back to the Sherman Hotel.

"I think, Doctor, if I was you, — which I ain't,
goodness knows, I don't mean to set myself up, —
I should go and look at Mr Yorke before you go
out," said Mrs. Butterwell, presenting herself at
the office the next morning. "He has a dreadfully
peakéd look, and he's got past Sally Lunn for
breakfast. As long as he took hi; Sally Lunns, I
knew you'd found THE REMEDY." (Mrs. But-

terwell pronounced these two words with that accent of confiding reverence by which the truly
devout homœopathist may be instantly classified.)
" But now I 'm afraid you have n't. He never
looked at a thing only his coffee, and he swore at
that, too. He thought I 'd gone, but I had n't."

" I never heard Mr. Yorke swear," observed
Doctor Zay dryly.

" Well, he did ; he said he supposed the sooner
he drank the infernal thing and done with it, the
better. I was clear across the entry, but I heard
him."

The doctor went as she was bidden, fortified by
her hat and gloves and full professional demeanor.
Yorke was on the lounge, glaring at his breakfast
tray. He pushed it aside when he saw her, and
held out his hand. She did not take it, but drew
out her note-book and medicine-case, and coldly
asked for the symptoms.

" I owe you an apology," said the patient at
once, drawing back his hand.

" You do indeed," she answered sternly.

" I can do no more than offer it," returned the
young man with spirit. " If you had ever been a
man, you would be less implacable."

" I am not implacable," she softened. " No one
ever called me that."

" It is possible that no one ever called you several things that I shall have occasion to," observed the patient, running his white hand through his hair, and sturdily meeting her eyes, which seemed to overlook him with a fathomless, fatal calm, as if he were a being of another solar system, speaking in an unknown tongue.

" Mrs. Butterwell said you were worse."

" I have had no sleep and no breakfast : it does not signify."

" It does signify," returned Doctor Zay ; " it is — ridiculous."

" You use sympathetic language, Doctor Lloyd."

" I do not feel sympathetic." She looked deeply annoyed ; she drew out her miniature vial with her tiny pincers in frowning hesitation. " I have no symptoms. Give me some symptoms before I prescribe."

" Where is your friend ? " asked Yorke abruptly. " Has he gone ? "

She evinced neither surprise nor displeasure at the question, but laconically answered, —

" Yes."

" Then you will not be engaged with him. Will you take me to ride to-night ? "

" What do you want to do that for ? "

" I am going home next week. I want a ride before I go."

Such a pretty person

"Very well," said Doctor Zay, after a severe pause. "Have it as you will. Only remember that I did not invite you."

"I promise you to remember as much as that."

"Did you take that powder, last night?"

"No."

"Why not?"

"I did not want your sugar!" with rising fierceness. He quickly repented this outburst, and as she was leaving the room, he asked, with what he thought a masterly effort to be civil, if not natural, "What does *Cham. 5 m.* stand for, Doctor?"

"Champs Elysées, five miles," she said, without turning around.

"That is a long tramp for a man on crutches."

"Altogether too long," retorted the doctor "He should n't try it."

The phaeton came to the door directly after an early tea, and Yorke went out, and got in without further invitation. Handy helped him. The doctor did not offer her shoulder. She came down the walk consulting her visiting list with an absorption which the vainest of men could not have interpreted as less than real. It bitterly occurred to Yorke that she had already forgotten even to seem to forget what had cost him more than he had nerve of soul or body to waste. She took the reins without speaking, and they drove for some time silently towards the large August sunset. She wore a white dress which, for some reason, did not become her. It was one of her plainest hours. He watched her studious and anxious face, on which lines of care were beginning — he had never noticed before — to notch themselves lightly, as if with the probational or preparatory motion which the heavy chisel - stroke must follow soon and surely. It came to his thought with a complex emotion, how dear she looked to him when she was not beautiful. It would have been hard to say why this discovery was so fraught with significance to him.

"You are anxious and tired, to-night," he ventured at length, when her silence had lasted so long that he felt it was veering over the margin between the oppressive and the dangerous.

"I have a diphtheria case that is going hard," she said, weariedly. "It is Johnny Sanscrit, the minister's little boy, — his only child. I never stand it well with only children. They sent Doctor Adoniram off, in their extremity, which makes it worse. That is too often the way: the patient comes into our hands just in time for us to sign the " —

"Death warrant ? " interrupted Yorke.

"The technical expression is death certificate; you can take your choice. This is the house. I must stop here first."

Yorke did not experience that acute anxiety in behalf of Johnny Sanscrit which perhaps should have been expected of a humane neighbor. He occupied himself with dwelling upon the modern disadvantages attending an interest in the Useful Woman, who has no time to be admired, and perhaps less heart. It occurred to him to picture one of Scott's or Richardson's stately heroes stranded meekly in a basket phaeton, with matters of feeling trembling on his lips, while the heroine made professional calls and forgot him. How was a man going to approach this new and confusing type of woman? The old codes were all astray. Were the old impulses ruled out of order, too?

But Johnny Sanscrit, as fate would, was better, and the doctor returned to the phaeton, transformed.

"It is a remarkable adaptation of *Lachesis*," she said, with a radiant smile.

"Is it?" said Yorke.

"And I hope you haven't got chilly?" She looked at him absently, with her hazy, happy eyes. She began to sparkle with conversation, and overflow with good humor. Yorke reminded himself that it was owing to Johnny Sanscrit.

She had regained herself, and looked superbly. The opacity of the white dress softened in the softening light. As the sun dropped, she drew over her shoulders a fine Stuart plaid shawl which he liked. He welcomed her moody beauty with exultance, as he had protected its absence with tenderness.

They drove to poor Molly's, who proved to be better. Everybody was better. The doctor was girlishly happy. They rode past the mill-pond and the silent wheel, and through the well of trees, and up the darkening hill ; and she said she had but one more call to make, and then they would go home. There was a wood-cutter's wife who expected her, if Mr. Yorke felt able to go. Mr. Yorke felt quite able, and they turned from the road into the narrow cart-path, that wound at that hour like a blazing green and golden serpent through the late light and long shadow, towards the forest's heart.

" Are you never tired of it ? " asked Yorke, suddenly, as they entered the cart-path.

" Of my work ? Never ! "

" I don't mean that. It would be like tiring of a great opal to be fickle with usefulness like yours."

" What a pretty thought ! " she interrupted,

with that delicate and gradual expression of surprise by which a poetic image always overtook her practically occupied imagination.

" I meant," explained Yorke, " don't you get tired of the surroundings you have chosen for it? Do you never feel the need of resetting it ? "

" What could be better ? " She pointed with her whip down the sinuous, shaded driveway. The trees met above it. The horse's feet sounded softly on the grass. The great shadows from the forest advanced. The great glory of the receding sun struggled through the shield of fine leaf-outlines. The entrance to the road, like its termination, was blotted out in splendid curves and colors, which seemed to bar the intruders in, as if they had trespassed upon some sweet or awful secret of the woods, with which they could not be trusted, if set free. It was one of those scenes, it was one of those moments, when the power of the forest overshadows the soul like the power of the Highest, and when Nature seems to approach us on her knees in the service of a Greater than herself, bearing a message too mystic for any but our unworldly, unspotted selves to receive.

Yorke looked from the face of the wilderness to the face of the woman.

" It is very beautiful," he said, " but it is very lonely."

She did not answer him, but, turning a sudden soft grassy corner, came to a halt at her wood-cutter's and forsook him for her patient with that easy adaptability to which he never became accustomed. She was not gone long, but it was darkening rapidly in the woods when she came out, and she drove slowly through the looming shadow, over the rude road.

" There is a short cut home through the woods," she said. " We will take it, unless it seems damp to you."

" No, let us take it," he said absently. They rode through the sweet, dry dusk among the pines. It was too dark to see each other's faces. The consciousness of her presence, their solitude, their approaching separation, arose and took hold of Yorke like a hand at his throat, from whose grip he was strangling. It was to him as if he struck out for his life when he said, —

" Miss Lloyd, I told you I was going home next week. I wish to tell you why."

" Don't ! " she said quickly. " *Don't !* "

He thrust her words aside, as if they had been women, with a fierce gesture of his invalid hands. " It is not for you to tell me what I shall do or not. I am not talking about my ankle or my spine. This is not a case of pellets and bandages and faints and fol-de-rol. I will not have your precautions and advice. I will say what I have to say. I will take no interference. I will speak, and you shall hear."

"If you speak, I must hear, but I warn you. I *beg* you not ! "

" And why, I demand, do you beg me not ? What right have you ? What " —

" The right of my responsibility," she answered, in a tone too low to be calm, and yet too controlled to be agitated.

" I relieve you of the slightest responsibility ! "

" You cannot."

" But I do assume that deadly burden. My shoulders are broad enough yet, — though I am a poor fool of a sick man, dependent on your wisdom, in debt to you for his unfortunate life " —

" Oh, please, Mr. Yorke " —

" I insist. You will oblige me by explaining why I should not say what I like to you, as well as to any other woman."

" Because you are not strong enough."

" I am strong enough to love you, at all events." He drew one great breath, and looked at her through the dark with straining eyeballs, like a blind man. She gave no sign of surprise or frail feminine protest. Although it was so dark, he could see (her long gloves were white) the steady pull of her hand on the reins, at which the pony was twiching and shying over the uneven road. After a moment of oppressive silence, she said, with cruelly gentle sadness, —

"That is exactly what you are *not* strong enough to do."

"Do you presume to tell a man he does n't know when he loves a woman?" cried Yorke, quivering, stung beyond endurance.

"You are not in love," she said calmly, "you are only nervous."

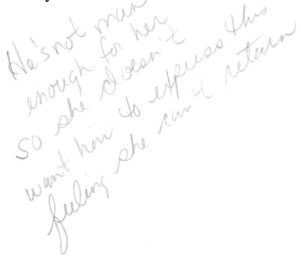

X.

THEY had come out now upon the open road. Faint colors remained in the west, — ashes-of-roses and alloyed gold. There was a young moon sinking behind the forest. The untrodden street stretched on, dimly defined in the immature light. The windows of the near village glimmered ruddily beyond.

"Drive faster," said Yorke. "I must get home." He had the heavy, painful pant of an exhausted man. She gave one glance at him, and one fleck of the whip to the pony, who put down her head, and took to her slender feet the wings of the wind. The night air came in warm gusts against their faces as they flew over the solitary road. She drove directly to her own side of the house, tied the horse, and resolutely presented her shoulder.

"I have hurt you," she said gently. "You must let me help you — this once."

He did not repulse her; he felt too sick. It seemed to make little difference what happened, and so he got into the house. She helped him

through into the parlor, and shut the outer doors.
Only one low lamp burned somewhere; in the office, he thought.   She groped for matches; he
lay and listened to the fine rustle of her linen
dress.   As more light flashed into the room, he
saw her standing in her white clothes. She looked
very tall and pale. She brought him a tablespoonful of brandy, which he swallowed obediently, and
for which he felt better.   Then, without perceptible hesitation, this remarkable young woman took
out her medicine-case.

"Are you a woman?" he panted.

"I am a doctor."

"Take away your sugar-plums!"

She drew the rubber strap over the case.

"As you please. Your condition calls for a
remedy. I can't have you subject to these nervous sinking-turns."

"I need no remedy — but one. It is the only
one, — the Divine Remedy in deed and truth. You
refuse it to me."

"I have refused you nothing."

"True; I have asked for nothing. But you
would deny me, if I did."

"Yes," she replied solemnly, "I should."

"Sit down by me," pleaded Yorke. "I want
to finish this."

You had much better wait," she urged with decision, but not without tenderness, — that ready, cruel, professional tenderness ; he would rather she had poisoned him.

" I will not wait. I am stronger. See ! — I am all right now, although, as you said, not strong enough to — What a merciless thing that was to say ! "

" I know it must have seemed so, Mr. Yorke. Believe, if you can, that I mean to be kind."

" It seems to me," said Yorke, struggling up against the bright *bizarre* sofa pillows, and turning his haggard face towards her, " that the only thing I *am* strong enough to do, yet, is to love you. I believe it is the only thing I have ever done strongly in my life. It will not be the last. I can see already how it is going to alter everything. Good God ! What is a man going to do, with life before him, and such a feeling in it ! It will take the work of ten to hold him. There is n't a woman of the whole of you that knows what it is. There 's more of you than any other woman I ever knew, but you don't know ; you *can't* know."

She sat on the edge of the chair, a little sidewise, leaning back, just as she had dropped there when he asked her to sit by him, her hands clasped over the medicine-case, with whose rubber strap she had bound her fingers down. She watched him with a look which no plummet in his soul could fathom.

" You are wrong ! " he cried. " You are cold, unnatural ! It was unwomanly in you to tell me I was only nervous ! "

" It is not the first time that a woman has been called unwomanly for saying the truth," said Doctor Zay, without flinching. " I do not doubt I have seemed unwomanlike to you in many other respects. Your ideal and my fact are a world's width apart."

" You have never seemed unwomanly to me, in all that we have been through, — never once ! " said Yorke. " I have thought you, from the very first — you have been to me the loveliest woman I ever knew ! " His voice shook. She sat, without a change either in her attitude or expression, regarding him with narrow, inscrutable eyes.

" I have not thought," he went on, with gathering strength, " I have not dared to think, that I had won anything from *you*, — a sick man whining on your little bottles for the breath of life ! And I know that others, other men — I understand my cruel disadvantage ; it is that that galls me so ! "

" Other men have nothing to do with it," she

said gravely. "I have had different things to do from thinking what would be pleasing to men. My life is not like other women's. It is not often that I am troubled in this way. I do not mean to treat you harshly, believe me. But I do not say hard things easily; perhaps I am out of practice."

"Surely," said Yorke, smiling despite himself at this, "you have known what it is to be loved."

"Yes, I have been beloved," she answered simply. "I suppose no woman avoids that. If I had not, I should have no right to tell you that you are not in love. I should not have any standard."

"Nothing can give you any such right!" he repeated feverishly.

"I do not know how to continue this discussion," she said, after a painful pause. "I seem to have few ideas and fewer words for such a purpose. I can find nothing to tell you but what I said in the carriage. My professional responsibility gives me my right."

"And I reiterate what I said in the carriage, — that I relieve you of what you call your responsibility."

"Then I must renew my answer, — that this is a thing you cannot do. So we are repeating ourselves, like history, and proving how worse than vain it is to talk in this way."

" You speak as if I were a creature lent to you, intrusted to you, soul and body!" blazed the young man.

"So you were," said the physician quietly. "So you are."

" If anything could make me *un*love you," said Yorke, with calm desperation, " such a speech as that would do it. But it works just the other way. Listen to me, Miss Lloyd. I *will* love you. You cannot help it. I will tell you so. You cannot help that. You must accept it. You must endure it. You must remember it. I shall not allow you to forget it."

One swift, dangerous gleam darted from her guarded eyes. The whole woman seemed impelled by some elemental instinct, mightier than he, mightier than herself, to warn him off. She did not trust herself to speak, and this gave him the first advantage he had felt; he hastened to avail himself of it.

" It is insufferable that any woman should treat any man as you treat me. Because I am a patient, am I not a man ? Because I dislocated my ankle and concussed my brain (as is quite evident now, if it never was before), am I to be set aside like a hysteric girl, for the state of whose limp emotions her medical attendant feels in honor bound to look out ? "

"Can you tell me any reason," asked Doctor Zay serenely, "why I should *not* feel the same sense of honor that a man would in the case you describe? But I have never called you hysteric."

"You consider my love a symptom, I suppose, — another symptom; like a nervous sinking-turn, or my afternoon headaches."

"Since you press the question, Mr. Yorke, I do, indeed. That is just what I consider it."

"It's a pretty serious one," fiercely, "as you will find out before you have done with me. It is beyond the reach of any pellet in your little case; the remedy is not included in your Materia Medica."

"That may be true. But Nature has her own unerring prescriptions. A single dose of absence — even in the first attenuation — will work a recovery which will astonish yourself, sir. It will not surprise me."

She said the last five words with a vague sadness, elusive as the sigh of a ghost, which did not escape the lover's fine ear. She rose as she spoke, and pushed back her chair. She stood looking down at him. For a silent moment his suffering and weakness seemed to plead with her splendid nerve and strength, and to find them implacable; yet to urge her, perhaps, against her own determination, into the tone of something like self-defense, in which she said, —

"What should I be, if I could take the charge of a man like you, — a sensitive man, struck down in perfect health by such a serious nervous shock, knowing nothing of its subtler effects ; a man brought up from the grip of death inch by inch back to life, dependent on the creature who saves him, confusing his gratitude and his idleness and his suffering with other feelings so much greater, — what sort of a woman should I be, if I did not feel responsible for him ? I should despise myself, Mr. Yorke, if I let you drift into such breakers as those ; if I *allowed* you to believe that this is love you feel for me. I should think it was the most unwomanly thing I ever did in my life ! "

He had risen to reply to her, and they confronted each other, flashing and pale.

"Not a word more to-night," she said authoritatively. "It is unsafe and wrong ; I cannot permit you talk in this way another moment. Go back to your room, and go to bed. Sleep if you can. Go home next week ; as you intended. It will be the wisest thing you have done for a long while."

"I must see you again to-morrow," said Yorke, stretching out his hand blindly.

"Very well," she replied, without hesitation. "I do not advise it, but I will not refuse it. Only go now, and — I hope you will sleep," she added sorrowfully.

She stood watching him as he tottered to the door. Had he seen the expression of her face he would have got no comfort from it; he would not even have understood it; yet he would have felt it to be an indefinable gain that he had not missed it.

"Mr. Yorke!" He turned drearily around. "Put yourself in my place for a moment. Reverse our positions."

Her words died before his protesting, passionate man's eyes. Just then she pitied them more than any woman's she had ever seen.

"I can't," he said hoarsely. "It makes a madman of me!"

XI.

THE next morning it rained. Mr. and Mrs. Butterwell therefore experienced astonishment when their invalid lodger appeared at breakfast with the request that Mr. Butterwell would drive him out to conduct some business relative to his uncle's estate.

" You look fitter to be abed and tended up," said his hostess, halting at that stage of latent sympathy which we are moved to express to the sick by active severity. " I 'll read to you, if that will keep you home and teach you sense. I 'll read poetry, if you like. I can. Isaiah has a copy of Tennyson's In Memorial (I gave it to him Christmas), though I must say I never could find head nor tail on it more 'n on a roasted chicken. I 'll read you anything but the Bible. It 's against my principles to read Bible to sick folks. It ain't cheerful enough. Mr. Butterwell had the liver complaint once, and he got such a shine for readin' in the Minor Prophets and the Imprecatory Psalms I told the Doctor it was the most serious symptom about him ; and it was. He 'd have pined right

along if I had n't got him into the genealogies in
Matthew, and so eased off on to the secular page
of the Congregationalist, and slipped him up one
day into Mark Twain's 'Innocents Abroad.'"

" Why, *Sar*-ah ! " said Mr. Butterwell patiently.
But he went out to harness his big sorrel at once,
since, if Mr. Yorke wished to ride, that ended the
matter.   Mr. Butterwell failed to see what his
liver complaint had to do with poor Jed's estate,
and more than ever realized his own deficiencies
in general conversation.

" It is time I began to thank you for an infinite
series of obligations, Mrs. Butterwell," said Yorke,
pushing back his chair from the breakfast table.
" I am going home next week."

" Infinite fiddlesticks ! " retorted Mrs. Butterwell.   " Going to — Surinam ! "   Her soft eyes
peered at him gently as a bird's over these terrible words.   " Why, Doctor has n't got half through
with you ! "

" I am afraid she has, quite through," said the
young man.   " I am going by Monday's boat, if I
can get over to Jonesboro' in season to take it.   I
shall find the best man I can round here, and leave
Uncle Jed's affairs in the hands of a local lawyer.
I am not strong enough to be bothered with them.
I have written to my mother that I shall join her
at Nahant as soon as possible."

"Does Doctor think you 're fit to take the journey ?" asked Mrs. Butterwell, after some studious consideration.

"I did n't ask her. She approves of my going."

"Doctor knows best about things in her line," replied Mrs. Butterwell, closely regarding her lodger. "But between you and me, there 's one thing that ain't in it."

"What is that?" asked Yorke, with a pale smile.

"Men-folks," said Mrs. Butterwell succinctly. She considerered this a truly scholarly reply, which it was not precise to amend by foot-notes. Her shrewd, homely face lengthened as Mr. Yorke limped away. Mrs. Butterwell had received a shock.

Doctor Zay was called out early that day, and kept out late. Yorke attended to his business, and made no effort to see her till night. She was away at dinner, and he took tea in his own room. The storm continued. He passed an idle, almost an entirely solitary day. He had some scientific books of Wallace's which she had lent him : he tried to read; the thing was impossible. The rain came in gusts upon the windows, with lulls between ; he listened to it with a sense of personal

irritation at the nervous combat of sound and silence, which served as a shallow outlet to the
steady torrent of his feeling.

We find it in our way, as we get well past these
sharp alternations of shine and shade, to miss something of sympathy with what time has blurred into
dim backgrounds for ourselves ; to see less of the
dignity, less of the pathos, more of the frailty, and
more of the folly of the great passions before which
youth and vigor and hope and rectitude are beaten
down like breath before the oncoming of cyclones.
And yet I think it is not the best way of aging,
to grow so gray at the heart, and that it were what
might almost be called a coarse thing to smile at
our young fellow here, writhing in the grip of his
first clench with life. He loved, or thought he
did.   It is better to be off with our hats and down
on our knees to illusions that we have long since
overthrown, than to withhold from the most trans-
parent of them the reverence which is the eternal
due of human conflict.

He sought her in the evening, through the steady
downfall of the storm. She had never invited him
to make use of that other door, which connected
her parlor with the body of the house. It was so
wet that he ventured to go before the office hours
were over, thinking that no one would be there.

He found himself mistaken. A patient was in conference with her, and he waited awkwardly in the office till the woman had gone.

This little misstep seemed, when they were left alone together, to give him an unnecessary disadvantage before her. He stood, embarrassed and savage, midway between the office and the lighted parlor. " I thought there was nobody here," he said confusedly.

" And there is n't," she answered, smiling up at him as if nothing had happened. Her sweet womanly graciousness, which set him at ease again, seemed subtly to put her out of it, and to give him a vague sense of having gained a mastery of the moment, which he did not see his way to use.

He did not try to use it, and followed her into the parlor, cursing his inadequacy.

" Won't you take the lounge ? " she asked, wheeling it lightly towards him.

" No. I must learn to sit up, if I am going Monday."

" Monday ? " She could not, or did not control a slight movement of surprise. He tried in vain to interpret it as one of regret.

" If I can. The sooner the better. You agree with me, I am sure."

" As a person, yes. As a physician, no. It

would be safer for you to wait till the next boat.
You are hardly ready for the journey.   You are
living on nerve."

"And shall till I get away from you," said
Yorke bluntly.

"Perhaps so," returned the doctor, sighing; "I
am of course a little at sea in such a case as this.
I wish to facilitate your departure as much and as
fast as I can."   She stiffened into her professional
manner.   He felt as if he had struck a glacier in a
clover-field.

"I want to talk this out before I go," proceeded
Yorke doggedly.

"It only wastes nerve-fibre," said the doctor in
an undertone.

"The physiological basis is not the only one on
which life is to be taken, Doctor Zay.   I have
told you before, that I am a man as well as a patient.   Try to remember it, if you can."

"What is the *use* in remembering it?" she said
unexpectedly.   He held his breath for a moment,
scrutinizing her averted face.

"Do you mind," he asked suddenly, "my asking whether I am so far too late in the declaration
of my feeling for you, that some other man would
have a right, or think he had, to " —

"I am not going to marry Dr. Penhallow, if that
is what you mean," she interrupted calmly.

" Thank you," said Yorke, after what seemed to her a long silence. He could not keep the rebellious hope out of his pale face. It dashed at her like a sunlit shower.

She looked up, saw it, and shook her head at it, as if it had been a word or outcry.

"It is not impossible, then," persisted he, " that you might some time begin to love me " —

" It is like the miracles," replied the doctor. " It is not logic to assume their impossibility. Their improbability is so great that it amounts to about the same thing. Put aside the thought of my loving you, Mr. Yorke, in justice and in mercy to yourself. I cannot demonstrate to you the futility of your hope. I can only state it. The sooner you accept it, the better for us both. Let us consider this a case of aphonia and aphasia, and be done with it."

" Explain yourself to the ignorant, my learned physician."

" Aphonia is inability to speak " —

"Oh yes; my Greek might have stood me for that. And aphasia is " —

" Inability to say certain things. Or at least that will pass for a popular definition."

" That is a scientific reply," said Yorke, regarding her keenly. " I am not sure that it is " — He checked himself. She did not ask him to finish his sentence, but sat with downcast, troubled lids before him.

"Suppose you could love me," he urged, "in the course of time, after a good while; suppose you did not thwart or deny the feeling of kindliness which I hope I may say you have for me; suppose you reconsidered the reasonableness of the miracle."

"It would make no difference; none at all!" She lifted her head, and her eyes, like sleepless sentinels, forced him off. All his manhood roused itself to defy them. He felt himself swept along by a power as mysterious to him as if he only out of the world had ever come into helpless and beautiful contact with it. All his lot, like a Pagan fate, moved on in its destined way to its appointed end. He experienced the terrible acceleration of a passion, and found that neither nature nor observation had given him any more prevision of the force of the torrent than they had power wherewith to stay it.

"I love you," he repeated, — "I love you!" as if the fact itself must be an appeal inexorable to her as the laws of light, or gravitation, or any natural code which she could not infringe without penalty.

She made a slight gesture, which seemed one of entreaty rather than of impatience, rose, and walked over to the window, which she flung open. A dash of rain swept through. She stood in the gust for a moment. The light from the globed lamps struggled out against the darkness, and Yorke could see a wet honeysuckle staring in ; the yellow flower dripped and nodded at him.

He got up and followed her, half unconsciously.

" You would not want to give up your profession," he began. " You should not give it up ! I would not ask it " —

A slow, slight smile curled the delicate corners of her lips.

" You will take cold," she said. She shut the window, and, turning, faced him. Her hair was wet with the rain, and glittered.

" Have you *nothing* for me ? " he cried.

" Nothing that you would care for. Men do not value a woman's friendship. They do not understand it. They do not know what to do with it."

" No ! I will not have your friendship ! " He turned his back to her, and stood, trembling.

" It would be perfectly useless to you, if you would," said Doctor Zay, a little drearily. " You are not well enough to try difficult experiments.

Make up your mind to let them all alone, — and me, too."

"I will never let you alone!" said the lover, under his breath.

"Oh yes, you will," said the woman of science quietly. "In a few months you will find it easier to let me alone than to shatter your nervous system over me in this way. Nothing could be worse," she added, "for those spinal symptoms."

"I believe they are right," answered Yorke, with dull bitterness; his imagination at that moment was denuded of hope. "A woman cannot follow a career without ruin to all that is noblest and sweetest and truest in her nature. Your heart is as hard as your lancet. Your instinct has become as cruel. If I had a fair chance, it should not be so. I would compel you to feel my presence, to recognize my claim. You should be wounded by a bullet that you could not find, — that slipped, and defied your probe, and rankled till you respected it."

He had made his way back, weakly, as he spoke, to the sofa, upon which he sank, pale and panting.

"The sick are at such horrible odds!" he cried. "It must be bad enough for a woman, but for a man " —

He stopped, startled. She had floated to him
with an impetuous motion. He saw her out-
stretched hands ; she leaned above him ; her resolute features broke.

" Stop ! " she said. " Please stop ! "

" What should I stop for ? " He held up his
arms. She retreated like a dream, and stood towering above him, like a statue. The agitation of
her face contrasted singularly with the massive-
ness of her attitude. He was sure that he saw
tears before she dashed them away as if they had
been ignoble impulses.

" Mr. Yorke," she said, in a tone of infinite gentleness, " the time will come when you will bless
me for what I am doing now, — for my ' heart-
lessness,' my ' cruelty,' my ' unwomanliness.' They
are three words easy to remember. I shall not
forget them — at once. You will retract them
some time. You will tell me that perhaps I deserved a — milder phrase. But never mind that !
It is not a question of what I deserve. It is a
question of what you require. Beyond doubt, that
is absolute separation from all this pathological
sentiment, and the exciting cause of it. I insist
upon this separation. I will not receive any more
expressions of your supposed feeling for myself.
Go home to your mother and your own people, —

to the kind of women you are used to, and understand. As you grow physically stronger, you will rebound to your own environment as naturally as you will walk without crutches. I have been nothing but a crutch to you, Mr. Yorke!"

He raised himself upon the pillows, leaning his head upon his hand and shading his eyes, watching her intently; he did not interrupt her. She went on, in a low, controlled voice: —

"Take it away, and go alone, and you will learn what you would never learn as long as you depended on it. I think you will always remember me gratefully and affectionately. I hope you will. Nothing is more valuable in life to a physician than the fidelity of a patient; it is surprising how little there is of it, after all. They go their ways when they need us no longer, and drop us out of their thoughts. After all, it is a solemn tie to fight with death together, as you and I have done. We will not break it flippantly. Believe me, that I shall — remember you. And some time, when you have righted all this little delusion about me, — somewhere, perhaps, — we may meet on fairer ground, when our views of one another would not, could not, be subject to this law of refraction which acts upon them now. You do not love me. You have needed me. I have been useful to you

I have occupied your thoughts. You may miss me. But that is not love. Go home, and find it out. Get well, and find it out."

While Doctor Zay was speaking, an increasing calmness had settled upon Yorke's face. It seemed to her that she could see the tide, for whose ebb she had watched, turning in his soul. She felt that it was her duty to welcome it, as it had been her fate to foresee it. He still sat with his hand above his eyes, which he had not once removed from her. He roused himself, and confusedly said, —

"You may be right, for aught I know. I will go, as you bid me; and thank you, as you suggest, whenever I can. I am able even now to appreciate your position. You are the only woman I ever saw who was able to save a man from himself!"

He took her hand with more self-control than he had shown for many days; and they parted, heavily and silently.

He went by the Monday's boat. Mr. Butterwell drove him to Jonesboro' on Sunday. Doctor Zay had been out all night, and most of the day. She was lying on the parlor sofa when he went to say good-by. She had flung herself down, exhausted, craving five minutes' rest. She had on that white linen dress, and the vari-colored afghan over her feet. It was a sultry August day, but her hand was cold; he had often noticed that it was so after she had been up all night. She rose when she saw him, and asked if he found the package of medicine, with the directions, and if he understood them all. He thanked her, and said they were quite clear. Her face had its stolid look. He searched in vain for its beautiful sensitiveness.

"I shall write to you," he said, hesitating, "if I may."

"Oh yes. Do, by all means. I shall wish to hear all about the journey, and its effect on you. Tell your mother if I had had two weeks more I would have sent you back in better condition."

"Or worse," he said, impetuously. She put her finger on her lips, and smiled. They shook hands. He pulled his hat over his eyes, and got away.

He looked back through the little oval buggy window, as Mr. Butterwell drove him off. Mrs. Butterwell was wiping the tears off her black silk dress. Handy, by the wood-pile, very large as to his hat and bare as to his feet, eloquently confided his emotions to the sawdust heap.

The phaeton and the gray pony stood at the doctor's gate. She did not come out. The big sorrel turned the post-office corner, and Mr. Butterwell observed that there was a fine lobster factory on the road. They canned 'em. Which had the worst of it, the consumer or the lobster, Mr. Butterwell would not undertake to say.

Half a mile down the Jonesboro' road, Mr. Butterwell reined up.

" There ain't but one horse in these parts that can overtake the sorrel," he said, leisurely. " I hear the pony after us."

Yorke looked back through the little buggy window. The gray mare, with a stiff head and clean step, was close behind them. Before he could turn his head, the doctor's phaeton overtook the buggy.

"Mr. Yorke has forgotten his brandy-flask," she called, cheerily. " Mrs. Butterwell found it out in the nick of time. You might have missed it on the boat." She stretched her hand over the wheel with the wicker traveling-flask, which Yorke took stupidly. He forgot to thank her. Their eyes met for a moment. She flung him a bright, light smile, turned dexterously in the narrow road, and whirled away. He leaned out of the buggy to look after her. All he saw distinctly was the Scotch plaid shawl folded on the empty seat beside her.

XII.

It was an ill-tempered December day, — gray from Passamaquoddy to Point Judith ; grimmer in the State of Maine than in any other privileged portion of the proud New England coast.

"We allers do hev everything wuss than other folks," said a passenger in the Bangor mail-coach. "Freeze and Prohibition, mud and Fusion. We've got one of the constitooshuns that *take* things. Like my boy. He's had the measles 'n the chicken-porx and the mumps and the nettle-rash, and fell in love with his school-marm 'n got religion and lost the prize for elocootin' all in one darned year."

A passenger from Boston laughed at this. He had not laughed before since they left Bangor, at seven o'clock in the morning, with the thermometer eight below, and the storm-signals flying from Kittery to Kitty Hawk. Of all places where it might be supposed that a man with a free will and foreknowledge absolute of his especial fate would not be on a December day, the Bangor and Sherman mail-stage was the most notable. The mud of forgotten seasons and unmentioned regions, splashed, tormented, and congealed, adorned the rotund yellow body and black, loose-jointed top of the vehicle. The high windows were opaque with the thick brown spatter. The laborious wheels, encrusted with frozen clay, had given place to gaunt runners, that " brought up " on the abundant inequalities of the road with a kind of moral ferocity, like unpleasant second thoughts or good resolutions after moral lapses. The driver swore at his horses, and insulted the passengers by looking perfectly comfortable in a new buffalo coat. Inside the stage, lunatic gloom and the chill of the Glacial Period descended upon the unfortunate travelers. The straw was cold and thin. The blankets were icy and emaciated. The leather seats seemed to have absorbed and preserved the storms of winters, the rheumatism of the past, the sciatica of the future. The Boston passenger, though protected by his individual traveling blanket and highly-becoming seal-bound coat, expressed an opinion that he was freezing to the cushions, which the jocose passenger honored by a stare and the comforting observation, —

" Why, we *expect* to."

This pleasant person got out, about four o'clock, at what he called his " store," — a centre of trade at some uncertain remove from the metropolis of East Sherman, — and the traveler from Boston had the impressive experience of finding himself alone in the stage during its passage through that segment of the Black Forest which the Bangor and Sherman route embraced.

He looked through the muddy windows upon the ghastly scenery with a sense of repulsion so active that it fairly kept him warm. The forest, through which the Machias stage-route ran nine awful miles unmet by a human habitation, turned its December expression upon him like a Medusa, before which the bravest pulse must petrify. Twilight and the storm were coming on. The runners made a fine, grating sound, like a badly-tuned stringed instrument, in the solidly-packed snow. Darkness already had its lair in the woods. Ice encrusted the trunks of the trees and the fallen logs. The stripped and tossing boughs moaned in the rising wind with an incredibly human cry. The leathery leaves that clung to the low oaks rustled as the stage crept by, as if they had been watching for it. It was too late to hear in the distant gloom the thud of the wood-chopper's axe. One leisurely and lonely rabbit, white against the whiteness, crossed the way and disappeared in the thicket. All the shadows on the snowy road were blue. The light that struggled from the sky was gray. The drifts were freshly blown over and deep, and the horses plunged and struggled in them, and panted up the little hills. In the forest the snow lay on a level of five feet. The silence was profound; the desolation pathetic; the cold deadly. It was like the corpse of a world. The vivid face of the young man in the fur-trimmed coat disappeared, at the end of the first mile, from the mud-bespattered stage window. He rolled himself up to the throat in his traveling-rug, pulled his hat over his eyes, and let the Black Forest severely alone. His whole soul sank before it. He thought of the lives barred in behind it, bound to their frozen places like its icicles. He thought of the delicate nerve, the expectant possibility, the bourgeoning nature —

"Poor girl!" he said aloud. "Poor girl!"

It seemed that he felt the necessity of commanding himself, or of defending himself from his own thoughts; for after a few moments' surrender to them he fumbled in his pockets for letters, and, selecting one, perused it with a studiousness devoid of curiosity, which implied that this was not the first or second reading. This done, he put the letter out of sight, and, leaning forward with folded arms upon the slippery ledge of the stage window-sill, stared out once more at the icy forest, with the look of a man who stood readier to fight his Gorgons than to flee them.

This was the letter : —

SHERMAN, *December* 10*th.*

MY DEAR MR. YORKE, — I suppose you 've forgotten us, but it don't follow. We talk a good deal about you, and should feel honored if yon would visit us. *I* should be pleased to see you some time in holidays, for it 's as much as your soul 's worth to stand holidays in Sherman. If the Lord had had to be born in Maine at this time of year — But there! Isaiah says I 'm growing profane as I grow old, and I don't know as he 's far out. The Baptists are getting up a tree to head off ours. They are depending on a new recipe for a gingerbread donkey, and turkey-red candy-bags. Our committee have sent to Bangor for cheap *bon-bons,* to spite 'em. I 've bought some greens of a peddler, and Doctor asked me to find something suitable for her to give the cook. (I 've had three since you were here.) The peddler was drunk, and the cook is going to leave next week. This is the extent of our Christmas news. Doctor is very busy, and Isaiah isn't very well. He 's got sciatica. He talks a good deal about your uncle,

and the estate, and you. The big sorrel is dead.
This has been a great affliction to him. It would
be a great pleasure to him to tell you about it.
It is the only thing that has happened in Sherman
since you left. I hope you are in improved health,
and that I have not made too bold in writing you
this letter. I never wrote to a gentleman before,
unless he began the correspondence. I have n't
mentioned it to Isaiah, nor to any of the folks.
Wishing to be respectfully remembered to your
mother, I am truly yours,

SARAH J. BUTTERWELL.

P. S. Doctor has had the diphtheria. She
caught it of Molly Paisley. She was sick enough
for a week, and got out long before she was able.
I look to see her down with something any day.
It 's been an awfully sickly winter, and they 've
worked her enough to kill five men and ten ministers. Dr. Penhallow 's been here, and he talked
with me about it. He said she was carrying it
too far. He was very anxious about her. But
nobody can manage Doctor, any more than you
can a blocking snow-storm. If Providence himself undertook to manage her, he 'd have his hands
full.

S. J. B.

The stage had wrestled through its last important struggle, known to the passengers as the "long drift," more familiar to the profane driver as the "d——d long drift," and the Black Forest lay at length behind the traveler. He let down the window to take a look at it, as they turned the familiar corner at the cross-roads, made immortal by an apple-blossom. They were close upon the still unseen village, now, and the night came down fast. The forest rose, a tower of blackness, like a perplexity from which one had escaped. He could just see the narrow road, winding gray and snow-blown through; it pierced the gloom for a space, and vanished with mysterious suddenness. There was one low streak of coppery yellow in the sky, upon which the storm was massing heavily in stratified clouds. The protest of the wind in the woods was like the protest of the sea. A few steely flakes had already begun to fall; they cut the faint light with meagre outlines, as if the very snow were starved in this famishing place. They struck Yorke in the face; he shivered, and put up the window impatiently. As he did so, he heard the sudden sound of sleigh-bells, and perceived that some one was passing the stage, almost within his hand's reach. The sleigh was a low cutter, overflowing with yellow fox-skins and bright woolen robes. The horse was a gray pony, closely blanketed. The driver was a lady, solitary and young. She wore a cap and coat of seal, trimmed with leopard's fur. She had a fine, high color. Her strong profile was cut for an instant against that last dash of yellow in the sky, before she swept by and vanished in the now implacable twilight. She had nodded to the driver with a smile, as she passed him, — one of those warm, brilliant, fatally generous smiles that an abundant feminine creature bestows anywhere, and takes no thought where they may strike, or how. The driver touched his cap with his whip. His pet oath stuck half-way in his throat, and gurgled away into "Evenin', Doctor!" as he yielded the narrow road to the pony, and struggled on with unprecedented meekness into the silent, frozen village street.

It occurred to Waldo Yorke, leaning back there in the stage, with his hand over his eyes, after she had swept by, that it was impossible for him to chatter with those people before he should see her. It was unbearable now that there should be anybody in the world but herself and him. It was incredible. What man could have believed that one look would undo so much, would do so much? She seemed to have sprung on him, like a leopard·

ess indeed. He panted for breath, and thrust his hand out, alone there in the dark stage, with a motion as if he could have thrust her off for life's sake.

The driver reined up at the post-office, and the passenger got out. He walked over to the Sherman Hotel and called for supper, and tried to calm himself by a smoke in the dingy office. But his cigar disgusted him, and he threw it away. He got out into the freezing air again as soon as possible, and walked up and down, for a while, in the middle of the road. The sidewalks were not broken out; the drifts lay even with the fences; there were no street-lamps, and between the scattered houses long wastes of blackness crouched. There were no pedestrians. Occasionally a sleigh tinkled up to the post-office; the drivers clapped their ears with blue-mittened hands, and crouched under old buffaloes worn to the skin.

He passed the town hall, where a sickly handbill set forth that the celebrated Adonita Duella, the only female child drummer in the world, would perform that night, and could be seen and heard for the sum of twenty-five cents.

He passed the Baptist church, where the vestry was lighted for a prayer-meeting, and a trustful choir were pathetically rehearsing Hold the Fort, with what they were pleased to call a cabinet or gan and a soprano who cultivated a cold upon the lungs. The frost was as thick as plush upon the windows of the vestry.

It was too early for either of these sources of social diversion to be open to the public. Yorke met no one, and walked as slowly as he could without congealing, stumbling through the dark, over the drifted road, till he came in sight of Mr. Butterwell's familiar square house. He came first upon the doctor's wing. Lights were in the office, and in her parlor. The reception-room was dark. Encouraged by this to think that the office hour was either over — it used to be over by seven o'clock — or else that no one was there, he pushed on, and softly made his way up the walk and to the piazza, where he paused. It was now snowing fast, and he stood in the whirl and wet, overwhelmed by a hesitation that he dared neither disregard nor obey. His thoughts at that moment, with a whimsical irrelevance, reverted to the letter he wrote when he first got back to Nahant, in which he had asked for her bill. She sent it, after a scarcely perceptible delay. He thought it rather small, but dared not say so. She had not written since. Now, after a few moments' reflection, he softly turned the handle of the door, without ring

ing. There was no furnace in the house, and the entry was cold. The door of the reception-room was shut. He opened this, also, without knocking, and, closing it quietly behind him, stood for a minute with his back to the door. She was not there, or she did not hear him. There was a soapstone stove in the reception-room, in which a huge fire burned sturdily. Plants were blossoming somewhere, and he perceived that there must be carnations among them. The office door and the door into the parlor were both open; a delicious, even warmth, summer-like and scented, pervaded all the rooms. He stepped on into the office, and stood still. The snow was sprinkled on his fur collar and black hair and beard.

" Handy ? " she called from the parlor, in that rapid way he had noticed when he first knew her, and which he had come to associate with her anxious or wearied moods. " Handy, is that you ? Come here."

Yorke made no answer, but advanced a step or two, and so met her — for, startled by silence, she had risen immediately — on the threshold of the inner room.

His heart leaped to see that she lost her color. She did, indeed. A flash, like fear, vibrated across her figure and upraised face, then fell, and she had herself instantly. She held up both hands to him and drew him graciously into the bright warmth fo the room, led him to the lamp before she spoke, took off the yellow globe, and let the white radiance full on his face.

" You are well! " she said, exultantly. " You are a well man ! "

" As well as I ever was in my life, Doctor Zay. And stronger, by far. Do you see ? "

He squared his fine shoulders, and smiled.

" Yes, I see."

Her firm eyes lifted, looked at him piercingly, then wandered, wavered. A beautiful mistiness overswept them; her will, like a drowning thing, seemed to struggle with it; she regarded him through it fixedly ; then her dark lashes dropped. She turned away, not without embarrassment, and motioned him to a chair.

He forgot to take it, but stood looking at her dizzily. She wore something brown, a dress of heavy cloth, and it was trimmed with leopard fur, like that he saw in the sleigh. She did not recover her composure. She was like a beautiful wild creature. Her splendid color and fire mocked him. Who was he that he should think to tame her ? Yet, should a man let go his hold on a moment like this ? By the beating of his own heart, he knew that life itself might never yield him such another. He flung his whole soul into one swift venture.

"Dear," he said, "I am too strong, now, to be denied. I have come back for you."

"Oh, hush!" she cried. She had a tone of fathomless entreaty. She turned from him passionately, and began to pace the room.

He saw how she tried to regain her poise, and he saw with exultance how she failed.

"No, no," he said, with a low laugh. "That is not what I have traveled three hundred miles for. Oh, how glad I am I surprised you, — that I took you off your guard! Don't mind it! Why should you care? Why should you battle so? Why should you fight me? Tell me why."

He followed her with an imperious step. She came to a halt, midway in the bright room. She lowered her head and craned her neck, looking from him to the door, as if she would take flight, like a caged thing. He stretched his hand before her.

"Why do you fear me so?"

"I fear you because you love me."

"No, that is not it," he said, firmly. "You fear me because *you* love *me*."

He thought, for the moment, that he had lost

her forever by this bold *détour*. She seemed to double and wheel, and elude him. She drew herself up in her old way.

" It is impossible ! " she said, haughtily.

" It is natural," he said, gently.

" You do not understand how to talk to a woman ! " blazed Doctor Zay. " It is presumptuous. It is unpardonable. You torture her. You are rough. You have no right " —

He advanced a step nearer to her.

" How beautiful you are ! " he said, deliriously.

She turned from him, and walked to the other end of the room. He looked across the warm, bright width. A high fire was flashing in the open hearth. She stopped, and held out her hands before it ; he could see that they shook. She stood with her back to him. He could hear the storm beating on the windows, as if it were mad to enter this sacred, sheltered place, where fate had thrown them together, — they two out of the wintry world, — for that one hour, alone.

He advanced towards her, with resolute reverence, and spoke her name. She looked over her shoulder. He felt that she defied him, soul and body.

" I have assumed a great deal, I know," he said, in a tone from which the last cadence of self assertion had died; " it is in your power to correct my folly and deny my affirmation."

She turned her face towards the fire again, before which her averted figure stood out like a splendid silhouette. This silent gesture was her only answer.

" I am not so conceited a fellow as to insist that a woman loves me, against her denial," proceeded Yorke, with a manly timidity that well became him ; " and I have been rough, I know, coming upon you so suddenly, and taking advantage of your natural emotion. I do not wish to be ungenerous; no, nor unfair. I will not urge you any more to-night, if you would rather not. Shall I go away ? "

" Yes, please," she said in a whisper.

He turned to obey her, but, half across the room, looked hungrily back.

Then he saw that she had clasped her hands upon the mantel-piece, and that her strong face had sunk till it was buried in them. She started as he turned, as if his gaze had been a blow, and shrank before him, a shaken creature.

Even at that moment, he felt more a sense of awe than of transport, at the sight of her royal overthrow. He was beside her in a moment, and gently putting his own hand upon her cold, clenched fingers said, —

"Dear, is it true ? "

" Oh, I am afraid — it is — true."

" And why should you be afraid of the truth ? "

" Oh, it is a fearful thing — for a woman to —
love — a man " . . .

"It does n't frighten me." He held out his
arms, with his low, glad laugh. " Come, and see
how dreadful it is ! Come ! "

But she shook her head, and both her firm hands
warned him off.

" I have lost my self-possession," she pleaded.
" I have lost — myself. Let me alone. I cannot
talk to you to-night. Go, and don't — I cannot
bear to have you expect anything. I entreat you
not to hope for anything. It will be so hard to
make you understand " . . .

" It will, indeed," cried the lover joyously, " be
hard to make me understand anything but Eden,
now ! "

But he spared her for that time, and, drunken
with hope, went out, the maddest, gladdest, most
ignorant man that faced the storm that night.

He waded across the piazza, where the snow
was now drifting high. The dead stalk of a honeysuckle clutched at him feebly, as he went by.
He presented himself at Mrs. Butterwell's door,
and bore dreamily the little domestic whirl which

followed. The only coherent thought he had was
a passionate desire to be alone. Mrs. Butterwell
hastened to call the doctor, but he said he had
spoken to her as he came along. Mr. Butterwell
began at once to give him the particulars relative
to the last hours of the sorrel. Mrs. Butterwell
bustled about blankets, and fires, and *things*. She
looked a great way off, to Yorke, and small; he
heard her imperfectly, and had to ask her to re-
peat what she said. He seemed to be floating, a
being of another race, from another planet, high
above the heads of these old married people; in a
blinding light, at a perilous height, from which
he regarded them with a beautiful scorn.

He hastened to his room, under plea of fatigue, at
the first pardonable moment. It was warm there,
and still. The bed had been moved into a new
place, and the framed certificate was gone. The
hair-cloth sofa was there, and the little three-legged
table where the medicine used to stand. There was
a great fire in a fat, air-tight stove. He wheeled
up the black sofa, and sat down, and watched
the red oblong blocks of light made by the open
damper in the side of the stove. He sat there a
long time. Sleep seemed as impossible as pain,
and connected thought as foreign as fear. He
drifted in his delirium. He had no future, he

knew no past. She loved him. He reeled before the knowledge of it. Possession seemed profanity. Where was her peer in all the world ? And she chose *him !* With closed eyes he repeated the three words, *She loves me*, as he might have dashed down a dangerous wine, of which he had already more than man could bear. He was intoxicated with her.

He got through the next day as best he might. His host and hostess brought a first mortgage upon him, and Doctor Zay was hard at work. She was early at breakfast, late at dinner, and apparently took no tea. He saw her once struggling through the snow to give an order to Handy, who seemed to have added a number at his hatter's for each degree of severity in the thermometer. Handy had private views, which no man could fathom, relative to Mr. Yorke's unexpected appearance; but they were not of a nature which improved his temper, and, under the present climatic conditions he was denied the resources of the sawdust heap. Handy wore blue mittens and a red tippet tied over his ears. He drove with the doctor that day, to watch the pony, who was uneasy from the cold, in her extended " waits." Doctor Zay was wrapped in her furs, and had long, seal-skin gloves. She looked a trifle pale. Yorke watched the brave girl ride away into the deadly weather. She drove slowly, battling with the unbroken road. She carried a shovel to cut their way through drifts.

In the evening, as soon as might decently be, he went to her rooms. She was alone, and welcomed him with unexpected self-possession. She had a feverish flush on her cheeks. She began to talk as if nothing had happened. She inquired about his health, and the medical items of his recovery. She spoke of his mother, and his life in Boston.

Indulgently, he let her go on. He experienced an exquisite delight in all this little parrying and playing with fate, and in the haughty consciousness that he could put an end to it when he chose. He occupied himself in noticing that she wore a woolen dress of a ruby color, with a plush jacket and white lace.

"I have been at work myself, this winter," he ventured to say. " Did I tell you ? "

" No. What have you done ? "

" Sat in my office and prayed for clients."

"I approve of that. Did n't you get any ? "

" Oh yes ; some wills and leases, and that kind of thing. Greatness is not thrust upon me. But I 've *sat* there."

" Go on sitting there," said Doctor Zay, with a little nod.

" Thank you. I propose to."

She colored, and was silent.

" I wish you could have heard the Christmas oratorio," began Yorke again; " and Salvini, and the Damnation of Faust, — it was given twice. I used to think there was nobody in Boston who enjoyed Salvini as you would. Then we 've had unusually good opera. I must tell you about the pictures some time ; there have been one or two really excellent exhibitions."

" Tell me now," said she hungrily, leaning her head back in her chair and closing her eyes.

" No, not now. I have other things to say. You must come and see and hear for yourself."

" I don't know but I shall," she said simply.

" Confess you are starving in this snowdrift ! "

" A little hungry, sometimes ; it is worse in the winter. It would rest me to hear one fine orchestral concert. Do you remember what Irma said ? "

" Irma who ? "

" Why, in ' On the Heights.' ' I want nothing of the world without, but some good music, with a full orchestra.' "

" You shall hear a hundred," murmured he.

" It is fatuity to imprison yourself here, — it is cruel. I can't bear it. It must come to an end as soon as possible. It has infuriated me all winter to think of you. I had to drive you out of my mind, like the evil one. You must come down from your heights to the earth, like other peeple."

" Perhaps," said Doctor Zay, " when some of my poor women here are better. I have a few cases it would be disloyal to leave now. But perhaps, before I am old, I may move. I have thought that I should like to settle in Boston, if I were sure of a footing. I know the women there, in our school. Some of them are excellent ; one of them is eminent. But there are none now (there was one, but she died) working on precisely my basis. Indeed, there are very few men who stand just where I do, and they would not help me any. I should be rather alone."

It was impossible to mistake the fine unconsciousness of these words. Yorke looked at her with amazement, which deepened into a vague distress.

" We are not thinking of the same things at all ! " he said suddenly.

" What *could* you think I was thinking of ? ' she cried hotly.

" And what could you think *I* was thinking of ?

What does a man think of when he loves a woman ? "

" Oh, you 've come back to that again," said Doctor Zay, with an unnatural because feeble effort at lightness. But she pushed back her chair, and her manner instantaneously underwent a change. Yorke watched her for some moments in guarded silence.

" I have returned," he said at length, " to where we left off, last night. Why do you wish to make it hard for me ? "

" I was insane," she said, " to let you get to that point. I ought to have prevented — a woman should control such things. I do not know what I was thinking of."

" You were thinking that you loved me," he said gravely.

She was silent.

" Do you want to take that back ? "

" I wish I had never said it."

" Do you wish to take it back ? "

" Alas," she said, below her quickening breath, " I cannot! It is too late."

" You admit as much as that ? It was not a mood, nor a — but you are not capable of caprice. Then you have admitted everything," he said ecstatically, " and all the rest is clear."

She smiled drearily. "Nothing is clear, Mr. Yorke, except that we must separate. We have both of us lived long enough to know that a man and woman who love each other and cannot marry, have no choice but to turn short round, and follow different roads. You and I are such a man and woman. Let us bring our good sense to the thing, at the outset."

"I am desitute of power to see why we should not marry," said Yorke, with a sudden faint sinking at the heart. She was without the tinseled tissue of coquetry. He knew that he had to deal not with a disguise, but a conviction. She had not that indigence of nature which could have offered irreverence either to his feeling or her own. "I told you long ago," he went on, "that you should not be expected to surrender your profession. I should be ashamed of myself if I could ask it of you. I am proud of you. I feel my heart leap over everything you achieve. It is as if I had done it myself, only that it makes me happier, it makes me prouder. I want you just as you are, — the bravest woman I ever knew, the strongest woman and the sweetest. Do you think I would take your sweetness without your strength? I want it *all*. I want *you*. There is nothing I will not do to make you feel this, to make it easy, to

help you along. I could help you a very little in
Boston. That has been a comfort to me. Why,
what kind of a fellow should I be, if I could approach a woman like you, and propose to drink
down her power and preciousness into my one little thirsty life, — absorb her, annihilate her, —
and offer her nothing but myself in exchange for
a freedom so fine, an influence so important, as
yours? I shall never be a great man, but I am
not small enough for that!"

She had listened to him attentively, and now
lifted her eyes, which seemed again to retreat from
him with that sacred timidity.

"I never heard a man talk like that before,"
she said softly. "It is something even to say it.
I thank you, Mr. Yorke. Your manliness and no-
bleness only make it — harder — for me " — Her
voice sank.

"Everything should be done to make the sacrifice as light as it can be made," urged Yorke. "I
have thought it all over and all through. I know
what I am saying. This is not the rhapsody of a
lover who cannot see beyond his momentary ec-
stasy. I offer you the devotion of a man who has
belief in the great objects of your life; in whom
you have created that belief; to whom you have
become — Oh, you are so dear to me!" he added

brokenly, " I cannot think of life without you. I
never knew what love was like before. I never
understood that a woman could be to any man
what you are, must be, to me."

While he spoke she had grown very pale, and it
was with difficult composure that she said, —

" Listen to me, Mr. Yorke! This is only —
hurting — us both, you and me too, to no whole-
some end. Hear what I have to say, and then we
must stop. I appreciate — oh, believe me! —
your generosity, and the loyalty you have to your
own feeling for me. I never expected to find it.
I did not suppose you were capable of it. I grant
you that. I have never thought but that you
would desire the woman you loved to be like other
women, to give up everything. I have trained
myself to think so, all along. You have taken me
by surprise, I admit. You are more of a man than
I thought you were " —

" It is your own work, if I am," he interrupted,
smiling hopefully.

" But you do not know," she proceeded hastily,
" what it is that you are saying. I do. You and
I are dreaming a dream. It has a waking, and
that is marriage. Few young men and women
know anything more of the process of adjusting
love to marriage than they do of the architecture

of Kubla Khan's palace. I have had, as you will
see, exceptional opportunities to study the subject.
I have profited by them. Mr. Yorke, I never knew
but three marriages in my life that were *real !*"

"So you told me once before," he said. "I
never forgot it. Ours would be the fourth."

She shook her head with a melancholy smile.
"You do not understand. You have not had my
chances to see how it is. I do not think lightly
of these things. Next to the love between man
and his Creator (if there is such a thing, and I
believe we must admit that there is), the love of
one man and one woman is the loftiest and the
most illusive ideal that has been set before the
world. A perfect marriage is like a pure heart :
those who have it are fit to see God. Any other
is profanity to me ; it is a desecration to think of.
I should be tortured. It would kill me to miss it.
It is a matter in which I cannot risk anything, or
I must reduce the risk to a minimum. Oh, women
of my sort are thought not to reverence marriage,
to undervalue it, to substitute our little personal
ambitions for all that blessedness ! I never spoke
of these things before. I am not ashamed to tell
you. Oh, it is we who know the worth of it ! —
we who look on out of our solitary lives, perhaps
through our instructed experience and trained

emotion.   We will not — I will not *have* any happiness that is not the most perfect this world can give me.   I will not stoop to anything I can fathom and measure.   Love should be like a mighty sea. It should overflow everything.   Nothing should be able to stand before it.   Love is a miracle.   All laws yield to it.   I should scorn to take anything that I feared for, or guarded, — to look on and say, At such a time, such a consequence will follow such a cause.   Then he will feel so and so.   And then I shall suffer this and that, — and to know, by all the knowledge my life's work has brought me, that it would all come as I foresaw, — that we should ever look at one another like the married people I have known.   Oh, I have watched that bitterness too often !   I know all the steps, — I have had their confidences.   You don't know what things people tell their doctors.   I have heard too much.   Years ago, I said, I will never suffer that descent."

"Do you mean," asked Yorke trying to speak with a courage which he did not feel, " that you took a vow never to marry at all ? "

"Oh no," she said, with her ready candor. " I am not one of those women.   It is not honest to assume that there is any perfect life without happiness.   It is idle to pretend that happiness and loneliness are not contradictory terms. I have always known that I should marry if the miracle happened. I never expected it to happen. I put it out of my mind. I have known I should be a solitary woman. I am prepared for it. I would rather live twenty lonely lives than to suffer that desecration, — to see you look some morning as if it wearied you. I have seen them! I know the look. It would murder me."

"The miracle has happened!" He approached her with a passionate movement. "Trust it."

She shook her head.

"We love each other," he urged, — "we love each other!"

"We think so," she said sadly. "*You* think so. But you do not know what it all means. If I had been like the other women — Oh, I am sorry you have wasted all this feeling on me. If it had been some lovely girl, who had nothing to do but to adore you, — who could give you everything" —

"I should have tired of her in six weeks," said Yorke.

"And I will give you sixteen to tire of me!" she said quickly. But when she saw how this wounded him she was sorry she had said it, and hastened to add more calmly, "You see, Mr.

Yorke, you have been so unfortunate as to become
interested in a new kind of woman. The trouble
is that a happy marriage with such a woman demands a new type of man. By and by you would
chafe under this transitional position. You would
come home, some evening, when I should not be
there (but I should feel worse not to be there than
you would to miss me). You would need me
when I was called somewhere urgently. You
would reflect, and react, and waver, and then it
would seem to you that you were neglected, that
you were wronged. You would think of the other
men, whose wives were always punctual at dinner
in long dresses, and could play to them evenings,
and accept invitations, and always be on hand,
like the kitten. I should not blame you. Some
of the loveliest women in the world are like that.
I should like somebody myself to come home to,
to be always there to purr about me ; it is very
natural to me to accept the devotion of such
women. There was one who wanted to come down
here and stay with me. I would n't let her ; but I
wanted her. With you it is more : it is an inherited instinct. Generations of your fathers have
bred it in you. You would not know how to cul-
tivate happiness with a woman who had diverged
from her hereditary type. Happiness must be

cultivated. It is like character. It is not a thing
to be safely let alone for a moment, or it will run
to weeds. It would slip out of our hands like
thistle-down, and I should be made to feel — you
would feel, and your mother and all the people
you had been taught to care for — that I was to
blame ; that it was a life-long mistake for you to
have married a woman with a career, who had anything else to do but be your wife " —

" My mother, of all women I know, would be
the first to uphold you," interrupted Yorke.
" She believes in all that sort of thing about
women. I never thought of it till this minute.
It used to mortify me when I was a boy ; then it
only bored me. I shall kiss her for it when I get
home ! You need not give a second thought to
my mother. She has never got over what you
did for me last summer, and she 's dying to see
you, in any capacity. If you came to her in that
of a daughter, she would set you on a pinnacle,
and fall down and worship you."

" It has been very manly in you," said Doctor
Zay musingly, " never once to ask me to give up
my work. I shall not forget it."

" I never *thought* of asking it," said Yorke.
" It 's not because I have any particular theories,
and I should be ashamed to let you credit me with

any sort of nobility about it. I don't *want* it any other way. It would undo everything. It would make another woman of you. I want you just as you are. Come ! " he said, with a different tone. He leaned above her. She had never seen such wells of tenderness in any man's eyes. She tried to look into them, but her own fell.

" You make it so hard for me ! " she cried, in a quick, anguished tone.

Then Yorke drew back. " You do not trust me," he said hoarsely. " You do not believe that I love you."

She stretched out her hands to him in a mute appeal.

" I have waited on your caution and protest long enough," he went on excitedly. " I went home last summer, as you bade me. I let you think I thought you might be right. I let you treat my love like a fit of the measles. You supposed I was going away to convalesce like a boy, and establish your theory. I never believed it for one moment ! I knew all the time that what you call the miracle had got me. It has got you, too, thank Heaven ! You can't escape it. You can't help it. Try, if you want to. I 'll leave you to work it out. A man can stand a good deal, but there comes a point beyond which he must retreat in self-defense. I have reached that point."

He turned from her, glowing with swift wrath. His face looked as if it were carved out of hot white lava; it seemed to her as if it would cool off in that color and expression, and remain by her forever, like a medallion. The rare tears sprang to her burning eyes. She felt how desolate she was to be.

At the door he paused, and looked, relenting, back.

"How tired you are!" he said, with infinite tenderness. "I would have rested you, poor girl!"

"Oh, don't!" she cried piteously. He approached her; she motioned with her warning hands. He stood hesitating, and she saw how perplexed and tossed he was.

"If you had truly loved me," he said savagely, "we should not have parted in this way. It would not have been possible to you. You could not have tortured me so. You would have trusted me. You would have risked *any*thing. We should have taken hold of our problem together. Our love would have carried us through all these — little things — you talk of. I have over-estimated the miracle, — that is all."

Before he had finished speaking she glided up to him; her deep-colored dress and waving feminine motions gave her the look of some tall velvet rose, blown by the wind. She put both her hands in his, threw her head back, and looked at him. For that one moment she gave her soul the freedom of her eyes.

" You shall know," she whispered. " You shall know, for this once ! . . . Do you see ? "

He drew away one hand, and covered his face.

" It is because I love you that I — hurt you so. It is because I love you that we must part in this way. It is for your sake that I will not let you make a life's mistake. Oh, how could I bear it ! I should waste myself in trying to make you happy. I could not live unless I made you the happiest man in all this world, — no, don't interrupt me; I know what you would say — but it would not be so. I will never marry a man unless I can make him *divinely* happy ! I will not wrong him so. I will not wrong myself. This is right that I am doing. I am accustomed to making difficult choices and abiding by decisions. It is hard at first, but I am trained to it; I know how to do it. Don't worry about me; I shall get along. Go, now, — go quickly ! I can't bear any more — of this." She drew back from him by a subtle movement, and gathered herself commandingly. He hesitated for a moment, opened his lips to speak, said nothing, obeyed her, and went.

XIII.

He decided not to see her again, and left by the morning stage.

When he had got back to Boston, he wrote to her what he thought a very deep letter. She answered it by a beautifully straightforward, simple note, in which there seemed to be nothing concealed, because there was nothing to conceal.

He wrote at intervals through the remainder of the winter; she answered him kindly. He tried to keep himself informed of the state of her health, and did not succeed in the least. She inquired minutely after his. Once she sent him a prescription marked *ars.* 2 *m.*, for an influenza. She exhibited the best of good *camaraderie*, and was rigorously destitute of tenderness. She seemed to have accepted a certain relation of kindliness and frank mutual interest, with that mysterious facility by which women substitute such things for a passion. He was far more disheartened than if she had intrenched herelf behind a significant silence.

In April Mr. Butterwell had occasion to write

concerning the purchase, in Boston, of a horse to replace the sorrel. Mrs. Butterwell added a postscript. She said that the doctor was growing very peakèd and had gone to Bangor on a week's vacation, visiting a college classmate. She said the doctor had done a terrible winter's work. She said she hoped the Lord knew how the small-pox got to Sherman, for she was sure she did n't. She said Dr. Penhallow had gone to Europe.

In May Mr. Butterwell wrote again to say that the new horse was satisfactory, but that the lawyer was drunk ; and if Mr. Yorke felt any uneasiness about his uncle's estate —

Mr. Yorke did experience great uneasiness about his uncle's estate. He took the first boat of the season, and steamed away promptly for Machias. He arrived there in the afternoon, and found a horse and boy, and started for Sherman. He reached the cross-roads at dusk, dismissed his driver, and, carrying his light bag, walked as briskly as the atrocious state of the roads permitted, towards the village.

In going by a little group of lumbermen's cottages, he noticed a covered buggy standing at a ragged gate.

He would have passed it without a second thought, but for a sudden consciousness that the

horse was an acquaintance whom he was likely to
cut. He perceived then that it was indeed Old
Oak. He looked into the buggy and recognized
the blankets and fox-robe ; for it was winter still
in the reluctant Maine May. Without a moment's
hesitation, he got into the buggy, and wrapped
himself up in the robes, and waited.

He had to wait a long time. It grew dark.
Several people passed, but no one noticed him.
Some men were hanging about the house, and a
woman or two; they seemed to be neighbors.
He could not make out what was the matter, but
inferred that these good people had some source
of serious excitement connected with the lumberman's cottage. He asked no questions, not wishing to be seen. Now and then, he thought he
heard cries in the cottage.

It might have been half an hour, it might have
been more; but she came out at last. She had on
a brown felt hat, with a long feather. She walked
fast, nodding to the loafers, and speaking curtly ;
and, coming up, swung herself into the buggy, in
her supple way. She had sat down beside him,
and begun to tug at the robes, before she saw that
she was not alone in the dark carriage.

" Don't let me startle you," said Yorke.

She sat quite still, half leaning forward, for an

instant; then sank back. She did not speak, **nor** take the reins. He perceived that she trembled from head to foot.

" I have done wrong!" he cried remorsefully.

" I did not — expect — to see you," she panted. "I was not quite myself. I have been going through a terrible scene. Where are the reins?"

" I have them. I shall keep them, by your leave." He touched Old Oak, and they started off slowly, plunging through the deep spring mud.

" You will upset us in this quagmire," she complained. " I know every stone and hole. Give me the reins."

He did so, without comment. She drove steadily, but feebly. She began to talk at once.

" There 's a man in that house in delirium tremens. It is the worst case I ever had. They called me at three o'clock. I 've just got him quiet. He was firing a revolver all over the house when I went."

Yorke uttered a smothered cry.

" At everything and everybody," said Doctor Zay. " Ball after ball, as fast as he could pull the trigger. They were all frightened. Nobody could do anything. I — He is all right now. Nobody has been hurt. I got it away from him. He is asleep. I — Mr. Yorke — will you please — to take — the reins?" She sank backwards, and slowly leaned and fell against the buggy's side. " Don't be disturbed," she gasped. "I shall not faint. I never did — in my life. I am only — out of breath. I shall be — all right — soon."

He resolutely put his arm about her, and got her into a more comfortable position. She panted, and was very pale, but had herself under soldierly control. He saw that she was right; she would not faint.

" Either, alone, would not have been — too much," she said apologetically. " But both together — to find you — and then I was up all night with a patient who suffered horribly. And I have n't — eaten very much to-day. I am ashamed of myself!" she added, in a stronger voice.

"I'm glad you had a buggy," observed Yorke maliciously.

" Oh, I had to," she said innocently. " Since the diphtheria my throat has been a little troublesome — and these cold spring winds — Thank you, Mr. Yorke, I am quite myself, now. I can sit up alone."

" I don't think you can," he said decidedly.

" Mr. Yorke " —

" Dear ? "

" Oh, hush ! "

" I have overtaken Atalanta this time. She stopped for a leaden apple, — for a revolver ball, — and I got the start. Do you suppose I am going to forego my advantage so soon ? Do you think you are going to send me off again, after all we have gone through ? Do you think I will give you up to your pistols, and your diphtheria, and small-pox, — you — *you*, — my darling, my poor, brave lonely girl ? Do you think I will ever leave this accursed State of Maine again without you ? You don't know what kind of a man you 're dealing with, then, that 's all," he added, by way of anti-climax. But his heart bounded to see that she did not protest and battle ; nor, indeed, did she answer him just then, at all. She was worn out, poor girl.

He did not disturb her silence, which he felt stealing upon himself deliriously, as if it were the first fumes from the incense of her surrender. How should he breathe when the censer swung close ?

" Mr. Yorke," at last, " are you *sure ?* "

" As I am of my life."

" That it is *me* you want, — a strong-minded doctor ? "

" A sweet-hearted woman ! It is only you."

" How do you know I sha'n't make a — what was it ? — ' cold,' ' unnatural,' ' unwomanly' wife? How can you expect anything else, sir ? "

" I never saw a woman in my life who would do as much, give as much, to make a man happy as you would, — as you will."

" I wonder how you dare ! " she whispered.

She turned her neck, with a reluctant movement, to look at him, as if he had been some object of fear.

" Oh, I dare more than that."

" How long have you — cared — for me ? "

" From the very first."

She sighed. " I wish I could say as much ! I can't. It took me some time. I cared most about the case, till you got better. And then I was so busy ! But " —

" But what ? "

" Oh, I could make up for that. I would n't be " —

" Don't stop," rapturously. " What would n't you be ? "

" I would n't be outdone in any *such* way. If we ran the risk, I mean, — if it seemed to be best for you. I don't believe it is ! I think it would be the worst thing that could happen to you. Why don't you get out of the buggy, and go back to Boston ? What did you come here for ? "

" To look after my uncle's estate, to be sure."

" Oh ! . . . You must be very anxious about it ? "

" I am very anxious."

The buggy lurched and lunged remorselessly over the dark and swampy road. She sat erect and white. She did not lean against anything. She did not speak, nor turn her face towards him. He dimly felt that only another woman could understand her at that moment, and had a vague jealousy of the strong withdrawal which nature had set between her strength and his tenderness, as if he found a rival in it.

" Dear," he said once more, with that lingering accent on the word which gave to his urgency more the force and calm of an assured, long-married love than of a crude young passion, " you told me that love was like a mighty sea. It has overflowed everything. Nothing has been able to stand before it. It is a miracle, — like eternal life. Dear, are you ready to believe in the miracle ? "

" Be patient with me," said Doctor Zay. " I have a scientific mind. The supernatural does n't come easily to it. How shall I begin ? "

" Say after me, ' I believe in the life everlasting,' — that means my love, you know. I want to hear you say it, first of all."

" I believe — in — *you*. Will that do ? "

" I will try to make it do," said Yorke.

" But I don't believe in your driving," observed the doctor. " There is a ditch four feet and a half deep, with a well in it, off the right, here. You are making straight for it. Give me the reins ! If you don't mind — please."

"I don't care who has the reins," he cried, with a boyish laugh, " as long as I have the driver ! "

They had got home, by this, though neither perceived it, till Old Oak stopped in the delaying spring twilight, and sighed the long sigh of the virtuous horse, who rests from his labors, aware that his oats shall follow him. Yorke accompanied the doctor, without hesitation, to her own rooms. She experienced some surprise at this, and vaguely resented his manner, which was that of a man who belonged there, and who intended to be where he belonged. He held the office door open for her to pass through, and then shut it resolutely. All the scent and warmth that he remembered were in the rooms. In the uncertain light she looked tall and far from him. He felt that all her nature receded from him at that moment, with the accelerated force of a gathering wave.

" It is not too late," she panted. " You can save yourself from this great risk. You can go.

I wish you would go! This is not like simple happiness, such as comes to other people. It is a problem that we have undertaken, — so hard, so long! No light feeling can solve it; no caprice or selfishness can live before it. If we fail, we shall be the most miserable people that ever mistook a little attraction for a great love."

"And if we succeed" — he began, unabashed by this alarming picture.

She gave him one blinding look.

"Come," said Yorke, passing his hand over his eyes. "You have had your way long enough. My turn has come. Has n't it? Tell me!"

"What do you want?" she asked humbly.

"I don't want to feel as if I were taking a sort of — advantage. If you put me off one minute longer, I — shall. I shall take all I can get. I shall like to remember, all my life, that you came to me first, of your own accord; that you loved me so much, you would grant me this — little proof."

He held out his arms.

"Is *that* all?" she whispered. With a swift and splendid motion she glided across the little distance that lay between them.

AFTERWORD

Regarded by her nineteenth-century contemporaries as one of the preeminent writers in America, only to slip in the early twentieth century into critical neglect, in recent years Elizabeth Stuart Phelps (1844–1911) has recovered much of her literary reputation and an appreciation for the significance of her writing. The response to her work of Vernon Parrington in his *Main Currents in American Thought* exemplifies the ambivalence of critics prior to the 1960s. On the one hand, he acknowledged that Phelps (whom he placed in the company of Stowe, Freeman and other "female writers"), while not a "great" writer, was one of those authors who "essayed to be faithful recorders of what came under their eyes." On the other hand, Parrington felt that Phelps's was a limited perspective at best, profoundly hindered by her being "an Andover Brahmin, highly sensitive, whose deeply religious nature was ruffled by every vagrant wind."[1]

Phelps's reputation, however, has undergone a

significant revitalization since the reissuing of
her novel *The Gates Ajar* in 1964. Feminist critics particularly have been responsible for detail-
ing Phelps's importance as a novelist whose
works offer enormous insight into the social and
cultural history of the late nineteenth-century
United States, especially into issues of the nature
of the family, gender roles, and the changing position of women in middle-class U.S. society.[2] Perhaps Phelps's greatest accomplishment is her elu-
cidation of the conflict confronting middle-class
women struggling to choose between marriage
and a profession.

Doctor Zay, Elizabeth Stuart Phelps's 1882
novel about a female physician wrestling with the
choice between matrimony and medicine, reveals
the same interesting thematic treatment of gender and class roles coupled with a concern for social history which characterized her earlier novels, *The Silent Partner* (1871) and *The Story of
Avis* (1877). The major thematic tension in *Doctor Zay* is created in the reversal of the traditional
gender roles between the intellectual professional, the physician, Dr. Zaidee Atalanta Lloyd,
and her male patient, the emotional egoist, Waldo
Yorke. Phelps's contextualizing of the drama
within the social history of late-nineteenth-
century New England is similar to her use of testimony before the Massachusetts Bureau of Labor Statistics in *The Silent Partner.* The realism
of both novels is established by her deliberate
documentation of the rise of the culture of profes-

sionalism among the middle and mercantile classes, especially the entrance of women into the professions.

In this respect Phelps's novel was part of the school of U.S. realism which flourished during this period and was championed by William Dean Howells. A prolific novelist himself, Howells's major impact on U.S. literature was accomplished through his positions as editor, first of *The Atlantic* and later of *Harper's* magazines. From these pulpits of influence, Howells defended the cause of realism, a school of literature whose major tenet was verisimilitude, actively encouraging and supporting the careers of such writers as Mark Twain, Henry James, Sarah Orne Jewett, Stephen Crane, and a host of others, among them Elizabeth Stuart Phelps. Though Howells personally was far less sensitive than Phelps about the working conditions facing women in New England, his observations are revealing about the social attitudes and social history of the period and provide a context in which to view Phelps's novels. Typifying Howells's perception of the condition of many women of the middle and upper classes of the period, Helen Harkness, his protagonist in *A Woman's Reason*, is oblivious to the realities of the economic world in which she lives:

> for her life, like that of most American girls of prosperous parentage, had been almost as much set apart from the hard realities of breadwinning

> as the life of a princess ... she knew that the
> money was from her father's business, but she
> never really asked herself how it was earned.[3]

Women such as Helen Harkness and Dr. Zay were
expected by society to confine their attentions to
the domestic sphere circumscribed by matrimony. This would be in keeping with the "cult of
motherhood" popularly espoused by many men
and women, but challenged by a burgeoning
women's rights movement.[4]

Howells's rendering of male characters in his
own novels reinforces Phelps's sense of the quandary of young men such as Yorke in late-
nineteenth-century New England and serves as
an exemplary expression of the social and economic insecurity of the middle class during this
period of U.S. history, an insecurity heightened
by the ravages of the depression of 1873:

> There seemed to be no such place for them; the
> world in which their sires had prospered did not
> want them, did not know what to do with them.
> Through the strange blight which had fallen
> upon a land where there should be work for ev-
> eryone willing to work, there seemed to be noth-
> ing but idleness and defeat for these young men
> in the city of their ancestry and birth ... Per-
> haps there was some error in the training of
> these young gentlemen which had not quite fit-
> ted them to solve the simple yet exacting prob-
> lem of making a living.[5]

Doctor Zay is a novel thoroughly defined by the social and cultural context in which it was written. As the two contending protagonists are a physician, and, in the case of Yorke, a lawyer, it is evident that Phelps was very much aware of and imaginatively confronting the social history of the middle class. The gender roles of women generally and the position of women in the medical profession in particular occupy center stage in the novel. While on the surface the narrative is governed by a conventional love story, at its richest levels, *Doctor Zay* is a foray into the middle-class ideology of the late-nineteenth-century United States, an ideology centered on certain assumptions about class and gender.

THE CULTURE OF PROFESSIONALISM

The decades following the Civil War until the turn of the century witnessed the most dramatic growth in U.S. history and also its most radical social transformation, a transformation occasioned by intense immigration, urbanization, industrialization, and the rise of the women's rights movement. For middle-class writers such as Elizabeth Stuart Phelps, the changes wrought by these phenomena challenged the old verities of the social structure and gave rise to what historian Burton J. Bledstein calls a "culture of professionalism." In other words, the middle class was attempting to secure its social position in the face of what it perceived as the dual threats of immigration from below and the consolidation of the nation's wealth by the industrialists and later the finance capitalists from above.[6]

The middle class in the United States in the mid-nineteenth century—consisting of shopkeepers, tradespeople, merchants, small manufacturers, and a modest group of professionals such as lawyers and doctors—was a social feature of a nation of small towns and modest cities. With the advent of massive immigration and industrialization, the middle class found itself compelled to consolidate its social position and turned to professionalization to make itself indispensible to the new social and economic order. Professionalism and its corollary devices of certification, licensure, and degrees both validated the skills and education of professionals and also conferred upon them social and political power by virtue of exclusivity and authority. Professionalization as a social and cultural phenomenon was, in the words of one historian, "a struggle for cultural authority as well as for social mobility," amounting virtually to "a cultural revolution."[7]

One index of the extent of this movement was the founding of professional schools or associations:

The law established its first national professional association in 1878, librarianship in 1876, and social work in 1874. Dentistry founded its first university school (in contrast to a training school) in 1867, architecture and pharmacy in 1868, schoolteaching and veterinary medicine in 1879, and accounting in 1881. The Wharton School of finance and economy was founded in 1881, a prelude to the declaration that business was a profession. The first state license law for dentistry appeared in 1868, for pharmacy in 1874, for veterinary medicine in 1886, for accounting in 1896, and for architecture in 1897.[8]

Of all the professions, medicine in particular made major strides during this period to consolidate its position. The number of medical schools increased from forty-two in 1850 to one hundred thirty-one in 1890.[9] Specialization within the medical profession, a sign of increasing professionalization, was evidenced by the founding between 1864 and 1888 of ten national professional societies ranging from the American Ophthalmological Society in 1864 to the American Gynecological Society in 1876 to the American Pediatric Society in 1888.[10] Most social historians are in agreement that the success of the medical profession in attaining social prestige and consequently power was in fact virtually unrivalled by any other. "The professional appeared in the role of a magician casting his spell over the client and requiring complete confidence; and the client listened to words that often sounded metaphysical and even mystical. 'Once the priests were physicians,' a speaker told the American Public Health Association in 1874, 'now the physicians are becoming, in their own way, priests, and giving laws not only to their own patients, but to society.""[11]

Professions existed in the United States, of course, long before the Civil War. The professionalization of medicine, for example, can arguably be dated to the mid-eighteenth century when Dr. William Shippen delivered his first lectures on midwifery in Philadelphia.[12] "America's 'first wave of professionalism' began around 1750 as the usages and forms of the British professions were adopted by Americans of lower rank. The movement towards professionalism in medicine found expression in the creation of the first medical schools and medical societies and agitation for protective medical legislation. These developments all began to occur at the same time. The first medical school was chartered in Philadelphia in 1765."[13] By 1850, there were ten law schools, two schools of dentistry, six schools of pharmacy, and forty-two medical schools in the United States at a time when there were three in all of France.[14] Nonetheless, the period of professionalism's true flourishing was in the decades following the Civil War, the period in the midst of which *Doctor Zay* is set. By the turn of the century, well over three hundred professional schools existed in the United States.

WOMEN AND PROFESSIONALIZATION

While the professionalization of medicine contributed to securing the social position of the middle class as a whole, there are serious questions about its adverse impact on the position of women in U.S. society. Many historians view the professionalization of medicine as a representative case illustrating the gradual narrowing in the nineteenth century of women's political rights and social roles. Barbara Ehrenreich and Deirdre English, for example, perceive it to be part of the process of oppression of a patriarchal system which relegated women to secondary positions. They saw it as "the end of the gynocentric order" in which women, especially in the capacity of midwives, traditionally dominated the healing arts in colonial times.[15] It was during the colonial period that "lay practitioners, using native herbs and folk remedies, flourished in the countryside and the towns, scorning the therapies and arcane learning of regular physicians and claiming the right to practice medicine as an inalienable liberty comparable to religious freedom."[16]

It appears that women had the freedom to act as medical practitioners, especially as midwives, so long as such activities were defined as domestic functions. This was especially the case with attendance during pregnancy and childbearing which comprised the major medical activity in an era in which surgery was a rarity and herbal lore acquired through lay practice accounted for most pharmacology. Once professionalization redefined such activities as services to be rendered by trained and licensed physicians in exchange for fees, they perforce fell outside the province of women's activity. Nonetheless, until the early nineteenth century women dominated both midwifery and the lay practice of medicine, serving remote communities, plantations, and even acting as surgeons in the Revolutionary War.[17] Conflict between men and women over the rights to practice medicine were evident even during the colonial period. In one instance in seventeenth-century Maine, a man was prosecuted for acting as a midwife.[18] The conflict generally was the consequence of pervasive and passionately held cultural definitions of gender roles. As Mary Jacobi observed in 1891:

> There is an exact parallelism between the relations of men to midwifery and of women to medicine. The limitation of sex in each case was decided by a tradition so immense, as to be mistaken for a divinely implanted instinct, intended by Providence as one of the fundamental safeguards of society and of morals. In each case, the invasion by one sex of a "sphere" hitherto monopolized by the other, aroused the coarsest antagonism of offended delicacy.[19]

Women's participation in the practice of medicine began to erode significantly in the early nineteenth century for reasons which were economic, social, and ideological. Though professionalization in general did not flourish until the latter third of the century, some professions had already begun to formalize themselves in the early decades, instituting the legal device of licensure. State legislatures were persuaded by physicians to permit the state medical associations to issue licenses which certified the professional skill and training of the physicians who possessed them. Primarily an attempt to raise the social status of the medical profession and to increase the professional power of the regular physicians as represented by the state medical associations, licensure actually conferred few legal rights on the physicians; in fact the possession of a license was not required for the practice of medicine. Though apparently an attempt to bring other physicians under the control of the medical associations, it seems that licensure, by raising the social status of physicians, at least indirectly contributed to a decline in the number of midwives or lay practitioners. It succeeded to this extent even though during this period it was in direct ideological conflict with the anti-elitist tenets of Jacksonian democracy.[20] It is important to note that this initial attempt to professionalize the practice of medicine was only partially successful and that by 1850 most of the licensure laws fell into decline; licensure did not reassert itself as an actual force until the last decades of the nineteenth century when professionalism finally prevailed as a major cultural force.[21]

While some historians emphasize the chilling effect the licensing of physicians had on midwifery, others see the two activities as affected by different conditions, noting that female midwives and lay practitioners tended to flourish primarily in areas where regular physicians were not available, especially at a time when the actual skills of the two groups were not dissimilar. Mary Walsh notes that from 1700 until 1835 no women were listed as physicians in histories of Boston and maintains that the professionalization of medicine was not necessarily the cause of the decline of midwifery, because midwifery itself did not obtain the necessary social or professional status, even before licensure. She argues that the social position of the midwives was a more important consideration than the status of midwifery itself. "Women in colonial society derived their social position from their kinship attachments to men: a father or a husband. Current research gives no support to the notion that midwives acted as if their social status was equal to that of a physician."[22]

As U.S. society evolved in the early nineteenth century, cities grew, and class hierarchies, especially in the cities, became more defined, in turn changing how physicians were regarded. Interestingly, the first significant shift in patronage from midwives to physicians occurred among upper-class urban women in the early decades of the nineteenth century even without the pressure of licensure, due either to the increased social prestige of the medical profession or to acceptance of its claims to greater skill.[23]

Walsh's perception of licensing in Boston as a

largely honorific practice which had no legal status and which was intended primarily to elevate
the social status of doctors is a very interesting,
but fairly conservative, assessment of women's
options, placing much of the blame for women's
failing to enter the profession on the women
themselves. She notes that the impact of licensing on female physicians was minimal, first as
there were no female physicians when licensing
first was instituted in 1781, and second, especially as licensing itself gave the physician virtually no significant rights. Walsh argues, on the
one hand, that "professionalization, with its carefully delineated medical prerequisites, spelled out
in detail the requirements for becoming a doctor.
If one must acquire a medical degree, interested
women could apply to medical colleges and if re-
buffed could then go on to establish their own."
On the other hand, Walsh does acknowledge that
women were limited by the prevailing ideology:
"The problem, of course, with professionalization
is that it did not develop in an ideological vac-
uum. Rather, its evolution was shaped by the sexual biases within American society. The colonies
were established on a strong patriarchal foundation, and female opportunities outside the home
and family have been circumscribed ever since."[24]
These ideological differences, of course, were rein-
forced by male control of property and wealth.

Ehrenreich and English see the issue in much
more fundamental terms than the device of licen-

sure itself, concentrating instead on the underlying gender politics of the professionalization of medicine.

> The female healer in North America was defeated in a struggle which was, at bottom, economic. Medicine in the nineteenth century was being drawn into the marketplace, becoming—as were needles, or ribbons, or salt already—a thing to be bought and sold. Healing was female when it was a neighborly service, based in stable communities, where skills could be passed on for generations and where the healer knew her patients and their families. When the attempt to heal is detached from personal relationships to become a commodity and a source of wealth in itself—then does the business of healing become a male enterprise.[25]

In other words, the very development of the middle-class culture characterized by professionalism led to a corresponding decline in the social and especially the economic prerogatives available to women.

This position is supported by evidence that the licensing laws gradually were rescinded by the mid-nineteenth century without any corresponding increase in the number of regular female physicians. In theory, women were free to practice medicine, though access to state medical associations and regular medical schools continued to be restricted. Nearly all of the forty-two regular medical schools in existence in 1850 excluded women from admission, obliging women who wished to practice medicine either to found their own medical schools or take recourse to seeking their training at alternative Eclectic schools or through apprenticeship with homeopathic physicians.[26]

At bottom, the exclusion of women from the practice of medicine was due to the expanding economic and social power of the regular physicians as the middle class moved to secure its position, coupled with the prevailing patriarchal ideology which drastically circumscribed the role of women. Whatever the benefits of professionalization to the middle class, professionalization of the medical profession systematically institutionalized the exclusion of women.[27]

Encouraged by the women's rights movement, the first medical college exclusively for women in the world, the New England Female Medical College, was founded by Samuel Gregory in Boston in 1848.[28] One of the ironies of the social history of medicine at this time was that the stronger the resistance on the part of the regular physicians to women or to the alternative sects, the more they thrived; this was especially true in Boston where one of the principal attacks against women's abilities, on the grounds of "menstrual difficulties," was launched by gynecologist Dr. Horatio Storer, the only male physician on staff at the New England Female Medical College in the nineteenth century.[29] In regard to this conflict, Mary Putnam Jacobi remarked on the great similarity of arguments advanced against the "intrusion of men into midwifery, and those which were subsequently urged against the admission of women into medicine."[30]

Homeopathy was the school of medicine especially popular among the urban upper classes, and not coincidentally, the school in which Dr. Zay was trained and to which the Yorkes subscribed. Founded by Samuel Hahnemann (1755–1843), a German physician, homeopathy

> saw disease fundamentally as a matter of spirit; what occurred inside the body did not follow physical laws. The homeopaths had three central doctrines. They maintained first that diseases could be cured by drugs which produced the same symptoms when given to a healthy person. This was the homeopathic "law of similars"—like cures like. Second, the effects of drugs could be heightened by administering them in minute doses. The more diluted the dose, the greater the "dynamic" effect. And third, nearly all diseases were the result of a suppressed itch, or "psora." The rationale for homeopathic treatment was that a patient's natural disease was somehow displaced after taking a homeopathic medicine by a weaker, but similar, artificial disease that the body could more easily overcome.[31]

The popularity enjoyed by homeopathy among the urban upper classes may be attributed to its similarity with aristocratic eighteenth century notions of medicine in which symptoms were also stressed and the doctor's primary role was to lend a sympathetic ear to his aristocratic patrons. Homeopathy centers on a very personal and nurturing approach to the practice of medicine, paying a great deal of attention to the individual patient.[32]

Though there was a major purge of homeopaths from the Massachusetts Medical Society in 1876, homeopathy itself continued to flourish for the remainder of the century, reaching its peak in the 1880s and 1890s.[33] "The myth persists today that homeopaths and herbal doctors were suppressed by the dominant allopathic profession. Yet the sequence of events suggests otherwise. Both the homeopaths and Eclectics won a share in the legal privileges of the profession. Only afterward did they lose their popularity. When homeopathic and Eclectic doctors were shunned and denounced by the regular profession, they thrived. But the more they gained in access to the privileges of regular physicians, the more their numbers declined."[34]

The decline in the alternative sects was also due to tangible advances in the scientific underpinning of regular medicine itself. By 1876, Pasteur and Koch had proved that micro-organisms caused specific diseases, giving to medicine a scientific basis which had been perhaps its most glaring omission and would prove to be its greatest strength in securing the profession. Mary Jacobi, writing in 1891, also felt that the perceived competence of male physicians led to their dominance: "But when the necessity for knowledge was recognized, when men became skilled while midwives remained ignorant,—the choice was no longer possible; the greater decorum of female midwifery was obliged to yield to the greater safety of enlightened male practice."[35] One measure of medicine's improvement was the decline in the rate of infant mortality from 273 per thousand in 1885 to a third of that by 1915.[36] This improvement in the scientific basis of medicine was crucial not only to medicine as a profession, but to the middle class itself, because medicine was considered by many to be the foremost profession in the social hierarchy and its fortunes and validity as a scientific enterprise would largely determine the fortunes of the middle class itself.

During the decades immediately following the Civil War, the medical profession in general expanded greatly, and at first the number of women entering the profession increased. Seventeen medical colleges for women were founded in the United States. The number of female physicians during this period increased dramatically from an estimated 200 (.4 percent) in 1860 to 2,432 (2.8 percent) in 1880 to 7,387 (5.6 percent) in 1900.[37] After resisting the applications of women for more than thirty years, by the 1880s and 1890s both the state medical societies and the regular medical schools such as Johns Hopkins and Tufts began to admit women.[38] It should be noted, however, that the gains of women in securing admission to the medical profession did not develop in a straight progression.

Even as medicine as a profession improved, it closed its ranks ever more tightly against women. For example, the percentage of female doctors in Boston (which led the nation), reached its peak in 1900 at 18.2 percent but declined by 1930 to 8.7 percent. In the general "reform" of the medical profession in the early twentieth century, exemplified by the 1910 Flexner Report (commissioned by the American Medical Association to investigate the quality of the nation's medical programs), ninety-two medical schools closed or merged, including seven of the ten medical colleges exclusively for women. By 1909, the number of female medical students had declined by 35 percent compared to 1894, and between 1909 and 1912 the proportion of women graduating from medical schools declined from 4.3 percent to 3.2 percent, reflecting a general decline nationwide in the percentage of female physicians.[39] Starr accounts for these declines as matters of both social morality and ideology:

> The growing number of women doctors in the late nineteenth century may have been partly a product of Victorian concerns about the propriety of male physicians examining women's bodies. Conversely, the fall in their numbers may have stemmed partly from the waning of the Victorian sensibility. In his 1910 report, Flexner thought the declining numbers of women reflected declining demand for women doctors or declining interest among women in becoming physicians. Others, however, have since pointed

to the active hostility of men in the profession
... Administrators justified outright discrimina-
tion against qualified women candidates on the
grounds that they would not continue to practice
after marriage.[40]

This decline would seem to indicate that the period in the late nineteenth century which witnessed the growing involvement of women in the
practice of medicine was a temporary social phenomenon which was able to exist because of the
immature state of the institutionalization of the
medical profession. Once that institutionalization
become more formalized, as evidenced by the
Flexner Report and its consequences, women
were once more excluded by the profession as it
came under the sway of the same patriarchal ideology which had always prevailed in the United
States, but had not yet found the structural
means to assert itself in the medical sphere. It
must be understood that *Doctor Zay* documents
a historical moment in which women were becoming increasingly involved in the medical profession and asserting their rights more generally in
society.

THE PATH TO REALISM

Looking back on her youth in her autobiography, *Chapters From a Life,* Phelps reflected on
her own traditional values as a woman and a

writer in the United States in the 1860s:

> At this time, be it said, I had no interest at all in any especial movement for the peculiar needs of women as a class. I was reared in circles which did not concern themselves with those whom we should probably have called agitators. I was taught the old ideas of womanhood, in the old way, and had not to any important extent begun to resent them.[41]

Though Phelps herself does not say so explicitly, it is clear that she became very much aware of how signally she rebelled against the conventional ideology in which she was reared at Andover, that bastion of New England traditionalism and a source for her Puritan "zeal to reform," as Van Wyck Brooks calls it.[42] Andover was, after all, in Phelps's own view, "a heavily masculine place,"[43] one against which she was provoked to rebel intellectually, much as the suffering of the workers at the nearby Pemberton Mills fire moved her to write what Parrington himself regarded as perhaps the first industrial novel in New England, *The Silent Partner.*[44] And rebel she did, authoring before she was twenty-five a pair of articles in *Harper's New Monthly Magazine* urging women to apply themselves to a broad range of professions, regardless of how much they were considered socially inappropriate for women.[45] Significantly, it was in one of these articles that she first wrote about what would be one of the most dominant themes in the rest of her career, the matrimonial dilemma facing female professionals, especially writers, saying "As a general thing, it is next to impossible for a woman with the care of a family on her hands to be a successful writer."[46] As regards *Doctor Zay,* it is also interesting to note that among the professions she urged women to consider was medicine.[47]

By 1869, according to her own account, Phelps had begun to experience a deeply felt change in her social views, one which brought her into sharp conflict with her society. "It is almost impossible to understand, now, what it meant when I was twenty-five, for a young lady reared as I was, on Andover Hill, to announce that she should forthwith approve and further the enfranchisement and elevation of her own sex."[48] Two years later, in an essay called "The True Woman," she directly challenged the conventional, limiting conception of woman's place and role in society, mostly circumscribed by marriage, saying, "The 'true woman' of popular speech is the gauntest scarecrow ever posted in the rich fields of truth to frighten timid birds away."[49]

Perhaps the best index of the prevailing patriarchal ideology with which Elizabeth Stuart Phelps had to contend may be found in her own father's essays. Austin Phelps, the president of Andover Theological Seminary, wrote two essays on women's rights which were "a blend of misogyny and idolization of women."[50] In the first essay, which is fraught with racist sentiments,

"Woman-Suffrage as Judged by the Working of Negro-Suffrage" (1878), Austin Phelps is vehemently critical of "Negro-suffrage," arguing that it is "a tampering with the franchise which is *against nature* [his emphasis]."[51] In essence, he holds that blacks have not reached the necessary "stage of civilization" to be worthy of the franchise.

Though in his view white women are far more qualified than black people to hold the franchise, on the grounds of education and culture, Austin Phelps disqualifies them for not having the "physical power to defend it" which he regards as an essential principal of government: "Liberty, such as is involved in the gift of suffrage, is impossible, on any large scale, to a race, or nation, or tribe, or class, which has not power to *take* the right, if it is a right, and to hold it against all aggressors."[52] Concluding that women could never enforce their own legislation over men's opposition, he admonishes condescendingly that "A war of races would be a tragedy. A war of sexes would be a farce."[53]

Austin Phelps enlarges his reasons for maintaining the disenfranchisement of women in "Reform in the Political Status of Woman" (1881), arguing women are inherently inferior and that their demand for equal rights generates gender conflict. Resting his case for the status quo on the documents and principles which he believes have informed Christian civilization in general and U.S. civilization in particular, Austin Phelps grounds the subordination of woman in the "very act of her creation," as related in the Bible, and considers as "animus" those arguments which question the absoluteness of the Biblical characterization of the sexes. Further, he is concerned about the increasing incidence of divorce in New England, blaming it on a lack of respect for the sanctity of marriage and the "dignity of maternity."[54] He even takes a backhanded swipe at his daughter for considering authorship, public speaking, and political activity as more noble than her traditional roles as daughter, wife or mother.[55]

Austin Phelps's summation of his argument against political rights for women resounds with sentiments in defense of patriarchy and the status quo at the expense of women which are still shockingly familiar to us today, and absolutely crucial to understanding the ideological context in which his daughter composed *Doctor Zay*. As he writes:

> The absurdity of thrusting upon one-half of the human race a privilege which they have never asked for, and their desire of which is a thing not proved; the absurdity of imposing upon one-half of the race a duty the gravest that organized society creates, but which they have no power to defend in an emergency; the absurdity of holding woman to military service, as she must be held if she is to stand on any fair terms of equality with man in the possession of this "natural right"; the absurdity of the intermingling of the gravest du-

ties of the court-room and the senate-chamber
with those of the nursery,—these, and other like
things involved in the proposed revolution and
its sequences, we claim have the look of absurd-
ity to the average sense of mankind.[56]

Elizabeth Stuart Phelps's response to this con-
descending patriarchal ideology is manifested in
her novels where she grapples directly with the
role of women in U.S. society.[57] Though often ac-
cused of indulging in sentimental fiction,[58] like
many middle-class writers of the late nineteenth
century in the United States, she was swept up in
the midst of a major reconsideration of the role of
literature spearheaded by William Dean Howells,
with whom she was in active correspondence.[59]

Phelps's own literary theory largely parallels
Howells's idea that "realism is nothing more and
nothing less than the truthful treatment of material."[60] Phelps wrote, "In a word, I believe it to be
the province of the literary artist to tell the truth
about the world he lives in, and I suggest that, in
so far as he fails to be an accurate truth-teller, he
fails to be an artist."[61] But she diverges from him
in a very important respect, taking issue with
Howells' concern that the New England novelists
had failed because "it was her [New England's]
instinct and her conscience to be true to an ideal
of life rather that to life itself." Phelps countered
in turn that "since art implies the truthful and
conscientious study of life as it is, we contend
that to be a radically defective view of art which

would preclude from it the ruling constituents of life. Moral character is to human life what air is to the natural world;—it is elemental.''[62] Thus she argues the necessity of including moral injunctions in literature, answering Howells's concerns that the novel ought not to involve itself in didactic moralizing and that the novel ought to portray life accurately, even where life is sordid and mean. Phelps summarizes her idea of the proper role of literature by saying:

> The last thirty years in America have pulsated with moral struggle. No phase of society has escaped it. It has ranged from social experiment to religious cataclysm, and to national upheaval. I suggest that even moral reforms, even civic renovations, might have their proper position in the artistic representation of a given age or stage of life.''[63]

Once referred to as "a stenographer for divinity," Phelps was too often dismissed as the author of romantic religious novels, such as her best-selling *The Gates Ajar,* by critics who failed to acknowledge her contribution to U.S. realism in those novels which confronted and analyzed the social history and gender politics of the late nineteenth-century United States, especially as regarded women.[64] Most important among these were *The Silent Partner, The Story of Avis,* and *Doctor Zay.*

Nonetheless, despite a literary career which spanned more than four decades, Phelps's commitment to women's issues did not develop linearly, and the fluctuations also need to be carefully considered. On the issue of marriage, for example, *The Silent Partner* (1871) strikes a much more unconventional stance, espousing autonomy and career at the expense of matrimony, than does *Doctor Zay* a decade later. Among realist novelists who wrote about female physicians, Phelps in *Doctor Zay* occupies a middle ground on the issues of matrimony and professionalism. Her Dr. Zay, while much more a feminist protagonist, for example, than Howells's physician Dr. Breen, the major figure in his novel *Dr. Breen's Practice* (1881), still represents something of a regression from a feminist perspective compared to Sarah Orne Jewett's *A Country Doctor* (1884).

THE SILENT PARTNER AND *THE STORY OF AVIS*

Deeply concerned about the social effects of industrialization which she found evident around her, Phelps wrote *The Silent Partner*, the story of a New England mill and its impact on the lives of women, basing the novel in part on the testimony of observers and the Reports of the Massachusetts Bureau of Labor Statistics.[65] In this novel, Phelps wrote perceptively and sympathetically about the working, economic, and domestic conditions of the working class, writing through the perspective of both Perley Kelso, a wealthy partner of the mill, and Sip Garth, the worker who endures the working conditions directly. Together Perley and Sip present a broad view of the lives of women who work both inside and outside the home. Coming home from her usual eleven and a half hours at her loom in the mill, Sip explains succinctly that she must then go to work: "Washing. Ironing. Baking. Sweeping. Dusting. Sewing. Marketing. Pumping. Scrubbing. Scouring."[66] Like Phelps herself, Perley crossed the blind gap between the classes to observe the conditions directly: "but I have in fact come out, and come out alone as you see me, to see with my own eyes how people live who work in these mills."[67]

Perhaps most significantly, in *The Silent Partner* Phelps has both her female protagonists reject matrimony, noting the restrictions which confront women, in Perley's case largely social and legal restrictions, and in Sip's case economic and class restrictions. Perley Kelso not only rejects the socially conventional matrimony offered her by one of the other partners; she also rejects a romantic marriage with the radical worker with whom she has worked to better conditions at the mill. This compounded doubling of the rejection of matrimony is not only remarkably emphatic; it also ran counter to all literary as well as social conventions of the period.

While the major female characters in *The Silent Partner* reject matrimony, in *The Story of Avis* (1877) the protagonist, artist Avis Dobell, accepts it after her initial refusal, though much to her ultimate regret, representing a distinct ambivalence in Phelps's feminist position about marriage, an attitude possibly influenced by her own declining health and consequent declining independence in the years following the composition of *The Silent Partner*.[68] Nonetheless, Phelps's concern that marriage and any other career are mutually exclusive for women is reiterated strongly. Again and again, Phelps observes that a married woman's profession is her husband and that the prospects are limited for a woman simultaneously pursuing a career outside the home and marriage. In considering the subject, Phelps depicts Avis as thinking that kitchen work is for servants, translating gender roles into class roles, though eventually she finds that such domestic tasks prove to be the responsibility of all married women.[69] Phelps sees the problem as being in the essential nature of women themselves as they have been wrought:

> Success—for a woman—means absolute surrender, in whatever direction. Whether she paints a picture, or loves a man, there is no division of labor possible in her economy. To the attainment of any end worth living for, a symmetrical sacrifice of her nature is compulsory upon her. I do not say that this was meant to be so. I do not think that we know what was meant for women. It is enough that it *is* so. God may have been in a just mood, but he was not in a merciful one, when, knowing that they were to be in the same world with men, he made women.[70]

As in *The Silent Partner*, Phelps's realism continued to manifest itself in *The Story of Avis*, though after her initial foray industrialism ceased by then to be a subject of her fiction, a concern she imbedded metatextually into the novel itself:

> When she raised her eyes, they fell upon forms and faces grown gaunt with toil,—an old man sowing sparse seed in a chill place; the lantern-flash on a miner's stooping face; the brow and smile of a starving child; sailors abandoned in a frozen sea; a group of factory women huddling in the wind; the poisoned face of a lead-worker suddenly uplifted like a curse; two huge hands knotted with labor, and haggard with famine, thrust groping out upon the dark.
>
> But her heart cried out, "I am yet too happy, too young, too sheltered, to understand. How dare I be the apostle of want and woe."[71]

Philip Ostrander, Avis's husband, was initially unsuccessful in his wooing, a struggle which Phelps cast in mythic terms: "The young man's nature had leaped to entrap her, as the hero in the old mythology crossed the ring of fire that surrounded the daughter of the gods. When he had made the plunge, he found indeed a woman sleeping; but it was a woman armed."[72] Eventually, however, Ostrander is successful, less because of his own merits than because of his subsequent invalidism stemming from an injury in the Civil War.[73] Similarly, invalidism figures prominently in *Doctor Zay.* Eventually the marriage fails, in part because of Ostrander's flaws—insensitivity and infidelity—and in part because of the intrinsic demands of marriage and motherhood on Avis who is frustrated in the pursuit of her art.

It is important to note that Phelps, as in *The Silent Partner,* does not reject marriage per se, but only for certain women, such as Avis. She is perfectly happy to allow other characters, such as John Rose and Coy Bishop, to marry and symbolically represent the potential success of matrimony. She is most adamant in *The Story of Avis,* however, that the matrimonial alternative should not be expected of all women. Ostrander dies in the midst of the recovery of their love after his second illness, but Phelps apparently was doubtful that the relationship could be sustained and resorted to his romantic death to affirm love without subjecting it to the burden of proof of being sustained by an actual relationship.[74]

DOCTOR ZAY

Moving from the comparatively remote world of the artist in *The Story of Avis* to the more economically and socially engaged world of middle-class professionals in *Doctor Zay,* Phelps developed her major theme of women's dilemma of having to choose between marriage and another occupation. Intimately related to this theme, too, is the general issue of socially defined gender

roles and the conflict between the sexes which ensued. It is notable that both the male and female
protagonists of the novel are middle-class professionals, perhaps the first instance of this in U.S.
literature.

Herself the daughter of a physician, Doctor
Zaidee Atalanta Lloyd took on her father's profession and, as did Phelps herself, the name of her
deceased mother.[75] A Vassar graduate, Zay became a homeopathic physician as the result of
three years of rigorous medical school training as
well as a year of study abroad, a typical course of
training for a physician at that time.[76] Specializ-
ing in a practice largely devoted to women and
children, Zay is vested with a consciousness of
the symbolic importance of her role in the social
history of women: "There are new questions constantly arising," she went on, "for a woman in
my position. One ceases to be an individual. One
acts for the whole,—for the sex, for a cause, for a
future." (122) Paraphrasing sentiments which
Phelps herself expressed in her essay "What
Shall They Do," Zay went on to comment on the
price a woman was obliged to pay in pursuing a
profession: "I suppose everything is this world
renders its cost, but nothing so heavily, nothing
so relentlessly, as an unusual purpose in a
woman." (123)

Like the entire class of gentlemen of whose
eroded social and economic fortunes Howells
wrote in *A Woman's Reason*, Waldo Yorke is a
lawyer by education, if not quite by profession, in

that he did not practice it. As such, he appears to be Phelps's male counterpart to Howells's stereotyped Dr. Breen, the wealthy young female physician whose commitment to her profession is tenuous at best. Most importantly, Yorke is a young man essentially displaced in his own society and time. "Distinguished-looking," "well-born," and "well-bred," Yorke nonetheless is educated but without a profession, is impotent of action, and is of a generation of New Englanders which has ceased to play an active part in its own, its region's, or its nation's destiny. Lamenting at one point, "If I had to work for a living, I might have been worth something" (78), he represents not only a gender alternative to the professional Doctor Zay, but also is representative of a social group at a particular moment in U.S. history. Yorke's profession is the first concession of a hereditary monied class to the occupational necessity obliged by the new economic and social system characterized by the rise of professionalism among the middle-classes.

Framed on the surface by a conventional love story of pursuit, wooing, and marriage, *Doctor Zay* contains all the hackneyed devices of the sentimental romance: the elusive woman, the lovelorn, wealthy young suitor pursuing the object of his affections through virginal forests, her resistence, his insistence, her surrender, their matrimony. Beneath this familiar surface, however, *Doctor Zay* tends towards a radical inversion of the conventional values of Phelps's society, one which calls into question the social imperative of matrimony. Yorke, for example, is introduced early in the novel as he rides to claim his inheritance, dreaming of "a woman who would be Life and Light to him." (12) All thought of his traditional inheritance, however, is quickly lost in his encounter with the young woman who "spoke as simply as one gentleman might have spoken to another," one of the first signs that things were no longer as once they were. (20) For matrimony now had to take into account the social transformations which had taken and were taking place. Dr. Zay herself articulates the change: "Yorke, you have been so unfortunate as to become interested in a new kind of woman. The trouble is that a happy marriage with such a woman demands a new type of man." (244)

In many respects Phelps casts Yorke as a straw man whose shallowness and weakness highlight the strength and virtues of Dr. Zay. Knowing "nothing of the natural history of doctresses," he is representative of Phelps's audience and with them is the object of her instruction. Nonetheless, she grants him a partially redeeming measure of self-consciousness, especially late in the novel as he struggles towards being worthy of his quest after having been rendered somewhat "feminine" as a result of his physical injuries. His own self-characterization in a moment of frustration provoked by Dr. Zay's professional imperturbability defines quite accurately his own and his class's nature:

> Inherited inertia. Succumbed to his environ-
> ment. Corrosion of Beacon Street upon what
> might, in a machine-shop, for instance, or a fac-
> tory, have been called his brain. Native indo-
> lence, developed by acquired habit. Hopeless cor-
> relation of predestined forces. Atrophied
> ambition. Paralyzed aspiration. No struggle for
> existence. (166)

Unfortunately, Phelps is quite ambivalent about
Yorke and his occasional moments of self-
illumination are usually submerged within his
male character as he regains his health. Having
gained Dr. Zay's concession of her love for him as
the novel nears its conclusion, he reasserts his
primal maleness and asserts his possessiveness:
"I don't care who has the reins," he cried, with a
boyish laugh, "as long as I have the driver." (257)
Then he strides into Zay's room, causing her to
vaguely resent "his manner, which was that of a
man who belonged there, and who intended to be
where he belonged." (257) It is about as ambivalent an embrace of matrimony as one can find.[77]
In the final analysis, the reader must conclude
that in this instance Dr. Zay's profession is far
more compelling an alternative than her impending marriage.

Though the novel does end with an impending
marriage, and in that sense was a retreat from
the position Phelps held in *The Silent Partner,*
there is good reason to question just how optimistic Phelps was about its prospects. Phelps is

careful to protect the marriage itself from being
subject to the scrutiny of the reader by consign-
ing it out of the frame of the novel, much as she
did at the end of *The Story of Avis.* The real problem is that a state of equality between the two
protagonists does not exist. In conventional social terms, Dr. Zay, by virtue of being a woman,
should defer to Yorke. Yet ironically, Phelps as-
signs Yorke a near-parodic role, investing him as
she does with all the classic traits of neurotic hys-
teria usually attributed to women by male com-
mentators in the nineteenth century.[78] Yorke, in
Phelps's terms the quintessential "unoccupied
man," is drawn as deficient in several key respects, most significantly, from a New England
point of view, as lacking in moral purpose. Dr.
Zay, on the other hand, is a paradigm of moral
and social commitment and is invested with both
spiritual and physical energy. Consequently, the
reader must wrestle with the illogic of Dr. Zay
succumbing to Yorke's importunings to submit
to matrimony. On the surface the novel offers the
superficial explanation that Yorke has reconciled
himself to her career, but this is emphatically out-
weighed by his characterization and Phelps's re-
luctance to extend the plot to see if this ideal relationship can be realized. Though concluding
conventionally with matrimony, the novel simultaneously subverts it.

As in *The Story of Avis,* however, Phelps is
careful in *Doctor Zay* not to reject matrimony as
an alternative for all women. In some instances,

especially for working-class women, Phelps
seems to feel that marriage is in fact the appro-
priate course to follow. The relationship of the
character Molly and her recalcitrant lover Jim
Paisley is the converse of that of Dr. Zay and
Yorke. Dr. Zay recognizes that for the pregnant
and economically dependent Molly marriage is an
absolute necessity and she bends her will upon
Paisley to compel him to meet his obligations to
the woman he has impregnated. While in
Phelps's view matrimony is not a necessity for
middle-class professional women such as Dr. Zay,
economically and socially independent as she is,
she does acknowledge that for the mass of
women matrimony is still a viable and even necessary social and economic alternative. This
marks a departure from the position she em-
bodied in *The Silent Partner* in the character of
Sip Garth. In keeping with her literary theory,
Phelps imbeds in the novel the moral instruction
which she deems as so essential to literature.[79]

Invalidism is a special issue for Phelps, too, especially given her own history of poor health
which may partially serve to explain the recur-
ring relationship between invalidism and matrimony in both *Doctor Zay* and *The Story of Avis*.
At one point, she says of Zay "Her splendid
health was like a god to her." (110) In contrast,
Yorke later observes: "The terrible leisure of invalidism gaped, a gulf, and filled itself with her. If
he could have arisen like a man, and bridged it, or
like a hero, and leaped into it, she would never, he

said to himself doggedly, have this exquisite advantage over him. He lay there like *a woman* , reduced from activity to endurance, from resolve to patience, while she amassed her importance to him." (119) More telling than Phelps's own illness and increased dependency during this period is the fact that by 1880 there were in New England nearly 75,000 more women than men; this fact also contributed to women's relative disadvantage, vis à vis men, in courtship and matrimony.

At the thematic heart of the novel and one of its essential devices is inversion. "Put yourself in my place for a moment. Reverse our positions," insists Dr. Zay, at one point, simultaneously urging Yorke and the reader to examine gender roles, matrimony, and professionalism from a new perspective. Despite casting the novel in the form of a sentimental romance, Phelps is in fact challenging some of the most cherished assumptions about women's proper social role. By her lights marriage had ceased to be the sole object of a woman's life, especially in the context of the rise of professionalism and the radical transformation the United States itself was experiencing during the last quarter of the nineteenth century.

ATALANTA: THE MYTH OF PURSUIT AND MARRIAGE

Central to *Doctor Zay*'s concern with gender roles and conflict, as emblemized by Zay's middle name, is the story of Atalanta, the primal myth of pursuit and marriage. Atalanta is best known as the virgin warrior who would consent to marry only if her suitor could best her in a foot race. The penalty for losing was death. Eventually, she was beaten by Melanion who was assisted by Aphrodite, the goddess of love. Aphrodite gave him three rare golden apples which during the course of the race he rolled before Atalanta each time she began to get ahead of him. His stratagem worked; Atalanta lost, having been slowed by stooping to pick up the apples. Referred to directly several times in the course of the novel, the story of Atalanta serves Phelps as the mythic paradigm, not only for Yorke's pursuit of Zay, but for man's pursuit of woman generally. At the heart of the myth are two essential elements: first, the autonomy, elusiveness, and superiority of the woman, and second, the man's dependence on both stratagem and the complicity of love to obligate the woman to him in marriage.

Less well known are other aspects of the Atalanta myth, as related by Robert Graves, which also actively inform the gender conflict so crucial to the novel. Atalanta's father, Iasus, wanting a male heir, left her exposed to die on a hillside. Suckled by a bear and eventually rescued by a clan of hunters who raised her, she remained a virgin and always carried arms. Invited to participate in a hunt for the Calydonian Boar, she was sexually attacked by two Centaurs whom she killed in self-defence with arrows from her bow.

When the boar confounded the hunting party,
killing several and setting the others in disarray,
Atalanta drew first blood with an arrow. Another
hunter, Ancaeus, who sneered at her effort, was
next struck by the charging boar which castrated
and disembowelled him. As a daughter born of a
father desiring a son, and later as a young woman
subject to constant sexual attack against which
she was obliged to defend herself, Atalanta epito-
mizes an ideal feminist protagonist asserting herself in a patriarchal world.[80]

Phelps's general familiarity with Greek myth is
evident in many of her works, and *Doctor Zay*
from its commencement resonates with such allu-
sions.[81] For example, Mrs. Yorke is very pointedly
described, at first apparently irrelevantly, as being "lame." But Phelps's allusion is to the lame
Olympian, Hephaestus, the husband of the goddess Aphrodite who assisted Melanion in besting
Atalanta in order to marry her. The inversion in
gender, giving the mother the limp, is in keeping
with those which follow in the novel, and in fact
serves as a foreshadowing of such gender inver-
sions.

The myth of Atalanta itself is referred to on
three occasions, more and more explicitly as the
pursuit heightens. (71, 131, 254) From the first
page, Phelps sets her male protagonist, Waldo
Yorke, on an "arduous pursuit for uncertain privilege," a foreshadowing of the essential male
quest for possession and dominance which informs the novel. The first description of Zay, just

before she agrees to guide Yorke, is that she has the step of "a person in habitual haste," a reference to her namesake Atalanta. The myth, however, is inverted as Zay in her swift phaeton proceeds to beat Yorke to the town of Sherman, he being delayed, at least in part by stooping to pick up the apple-blossom she dropped in his path, albeit to guide him. In the final reference to the myth, Yorke acknowledges that he has captured his matrimonial quarry because, in this nineteenth-century adaptation of the myth, she has exhausted herself through fulfilling her professional obligations, in this instance tending an overwrought patient wielding a pistol: "I have overtaken Atalanta this time. She stopped for a leaden apple,—for a revolver ball,—and I got the start." (254)

OTHER FICTIONAL PHYSICIANS: HOWELLS, JEWETT, MEYER

Their attention demanded by the social changes in flux about them, other novelists besides Elizabeth Stuart Phelps were writing about female physicians. The four novels about female physicians written during this period represent a spectrum of responses to the social dilemma confronting them: In William Dean Howells's *Doctor Breen's Practice* (1881), the doctor sacrifices her career to marry; in Phelps's *Doctor Zay* (1882), the doctor submits to matrimony but continues her career; in Sarah Orne Jewett's *A Country Doctor* (1884), the doctor rejects marriage and pursues her career; and in Annie Nathan Meyer's *Helen Brent, M.D.: A Social Study* (1892) the doctor pursues her career but forgoes marriage, though desiring it, for the lack of a suitable partner. In all these novels about professionalism, it is interesting to note that the female physician is depicted as being outside normative family structures, usually losing one or both parents at an early age. The novels are all consistent in the absence of a father, as if collectively to imply that an autonomous professional woman was the consequence of familial insecurity, or conversely, of liberation from paternal authority. In fact, in virtually all nineteenth-century novels in which women pursue careers they do so only in the absence of or upon the death of a father.

William Dean Howells's *Doctor Breen's Practice* was already being serialized when he received a letter from Phelps informing him of her intention to also publish a novel about a female physician, an enterprise which he then encouraged. Apart from being a middle-class woman and a homeopath, Howells's Grace Breen has virtually nothing else in common with Phelps's Zay, and represents in many respects the negative stereotyping to which female physicians were subject. Breen's motives for pursuing medicine are solely due to a thwarted love affair. In the novel, Breen never actually practices medicine, and Howells makes it clear that she was "rich enough to have no need of her profession as a means of support."[82] This is an important class consideration as Breen is free to make choices as a result of the economic independence in a way that Dr. Mulbridge, the male allopath in the novel, is not. In this sense her wealth renders her ahistorical as she is removed from the historical and social imperatives facing others. Dr. Breen's choice stems not from economic or social or even moral necessity, but from a form of psychological self-excoriation as the result of thwarted love: a romantic convention.[83] In contrast, Dr. Mulbridge, the male physician, is described as having been born to his profession. Howells, whose subsequent novels so often assayed to cleave rigorously to the tenets of realism, dealt with social history but superficially in this instance. He sacrificed his radical choice of protagonist to the conventional demands of romance by resolving the novel with matrimony.

Doctor Breen's Practice ends with her marrying a wealthy young manufacturer and surrendering her practice except to minister informally to the children of her husband's mill workers. In his conclusion, Howells ruminates over the significance of Breen's act and considers the assumption of Miss Gleason, his parody of a woman's rights advocate, that "when it is felt that she ought to have done for the sake of woman what she could not do for herself, she is regarded as having been sacrificed in her marriage." But Howells rejects this interpretation, even though by his own evidence "the conditions under which she now exercises her skill certainly amount to begging the whole question of woman's fitness for the career she had chosen."[84] In other words, though the novel itself testifies to Breen having sacrificed her career for her marriage and having been diminished by that act, Howells concludes ambivalently, and demurs from deciding whether Dr. Breen's marriage was for better or worse.

In depicting characters realistically, and not idealizing them, Howells often alienated readers who wanted his work to be more morally didactic, a position Phelps shared. For example, Elizabeth Cady Stanton found "a remarkable want of common sense in all his women." She admitted that "they may be true to nature, but as it is nature under false conditions, I should rather have some pen portray the ideal woman, and paint a type worthy of our imitation."[85] It is unfortunate that Howells, himself a strong supporter of women's suffrage, could not transcend his own gender biases. It is significant that Howells has a woman, Mrs. Maynard, who is also Breen's friend, doubt her abilities and reject her as a physician, while Phelps has a man do the doubting, and eventually the accepting. In Phelps, too, the female physician continues her professional practice after matrimony while in Howells she does not.

The most autonomous of the three female physicians depicted by these novels is Nan Prince of Sarah Orne Jewett's *A Country Doctor* (1884), the only woman of the three to reject matrimony in order to pursue her profession. Jewett, like Phelps, is careful to be explicit that she does not reject matrimony per se; rather, she wants society to allow that the option of pursuing a professional career ought to be open to all individuals regardless of gender.

> I won't attempt to say that the study of medicine is a proper vocation for women, only that I believe more and more every year that it is the proper study for me. It certainly cannot be the proper vocation of all women to bring up children, so many of them are dead failures at it; and I don't see why all girls should be thought failures who do not marry.[86]

Jewett grounds her view of woman's social role in her own analysis of how society itself has changed, an important insight during a period when U.S. society and culture was in the midst of such dramatic flux: "The preservation of the race is no longer the only important question; the welfare of the individual will be considered more and more. The simple fact that there is a majority of women in any centre of civilization means that some are set apart by nature for other uses and conditions than marriage."[87]

Like Phelps, Jewett holds that pursuing a professional career is one of the greatest struggles for a woman of her day. Expressing the prevailing male ideology through Dr. Leslie, Nan's mentor, Jewett echoes Phelps's perception in her earlier novel, *The Story of Avis,* that unlike a man, a woman cannot sustain both a career and a marriage: "He tried to assure himself that while a man's life is strengthened by his domestic happiness, a woman's must either surrender itself wholly, or relinquish entirely the claims of such duties, if she would achieve distinction or satisfaction elsewhere. The two cannot be taken together in a woman's life as in a man's."[88] But whereas in 1884 Jewett concluded from this that the proper course for her protagonist was to eschew marriage in favor of her career, Phelps had retreated from that position in an unconvincing effort to accommodate the two poles of the dilemma.

Occupying the middle ground somewhere between Phelps's and Jewett's physician protagonists, Annie Nathan Meyer's Helen Brent does not regard matrimony and a profession as mutually exclusive, but she fails to find a "new man" capable of rising to her enlightened level. Her lover, Harold Skidmore, like Yorke, is a lawyer, a man who laments in metaphors quite expressive of the gender politics of the time, "why were women either dolls or steam engines?"[89] In this she was captive of what Meyer terms "a man's idea of what a woman's love ought to be."[90]

Herself more of an advocate of meritocracy than the other novelists, Meyer set *Helen Brent, M.D.: A Social Study* during the period of women's entrance into the medical professions: "The time was past when women had to struggle for the legal right to practice, or for recognition from

the medical organizations; but the present problem was to enable women to obtain the best possible training for the profession."[91] Dr. Brent is
described as having "a contempt for that sort of
sexual rivalry" which would favor women over
men, even in the hiring of female physicians at
the Root Memorial Hospital and College for
Women which Dr. Brent directs.[92]

> She still cared more for the development of hu-
> manity than for the development of women,
> more for the progress of civilization than for the
> progress of a certain portion of it. She believed
> that every real and earnest advance made by
> women must mean real advance made by the en-
> tire world, but it must *be real* advance.[93]

Nonetheless, Brent is connected to the culture
of women, seeking stimulation and reaffirmation
by reading works by such women as Dorothea
Dix, Mary Somerville, and Margaret Fuller. "She
required these moments to bring back her dam-
aged faith in womanhood."[94] Also, like Phelps,
Meyer cast her female physician in terms of
mythic conflicts and symbols. Attending a Wag-
nerian opera towards the close of the novel Helen
identifies with the heroine. Brünnhilde serves in
this instance not as "a woman armed," as she did
in Phelps's *The Story of Avis,* but as the figure of
the woman cursed by the patriarchal god Wotan
for daring to "separate herself from her sisters"
and "speed on to tracks that have been forbidden
thee."[95]

FOR THE STATUS QUO, BUT . . .

Taken on the surface in the terms of the sentimental romance in which it presents itself, *Doctor Zay* leaves the reader with an uncomfortable feeling that something is awry, because something indeed is, for Phelps shares with many of the other middle-class reformers of her day a paradoxical stance towards their society that both confirmed and denied the status quo. The middle-class reformers—counting among their number such persons as Henry George, Jane Addams, Edward Bellamy, Elizabeth Cady Stanton, and Henry Demarest Lloyd—were simultaneously committed to preserving the essential structure of their society, especially the middle class and its culture, while also urging its social, economic, political, and moral reform. In some respects they were motivated by a sincere desire to redress injustice, but they also recognized that if the middle-class did not initiate these reforms, they would be inviting more radical solutions initiated by those whom society oppressed. As Henry Demarest Lloyd counselled his readers in *Wealth Against Commonwealth*, "With reform it [change] may come to us. If with force, perhaps not to us. But it will come."[96] Consequently, much of the literature of this period of American history expresses itself as does *Doctor Zay*, at one and the same time affirming the conventions of society, but also challenging its most cherished beliefs and assumptions.

It was in this context—historical, literary, and ideological—that Elizabeth Stuart Phelps wrote *Doctor Zay*, a novel intimately participating in the major issues of its day: gender roles, matrimony, and professionalism. Phelps herself was quite modest about her role in this reform movement, though at the same time she acknowledges her participation in it.

> A maker of books with any tendency towards moral reform may be at some peculiar disadvantage. As I look back upon the last twenty-five years of my own life, I seem to myself to have achieved little or nothing in the stir of the great movements for improving the condition of society which have distinguished our day; yet I am conscious that these have often thrust in my study door and dragged me out into their forays, if not upon their battlefields.[97]

Doctor Zay remains for us today an important artifact of a society in transition at an historical moment when women were struggling successfully to redefine their role within that society. Though admittedly Phelps reveals in it some of her own ambivalence about marriage, by imbedding feminist politics within the conventional form of the sentimental romance, she provides us with a novel which encapsulates the very contradictions of her society. Truly, in her own words, "a woman armed," Phelps invites her readers into the embrace of a comfortable romantic tale, only to gracefully invert the prevailing conventional social assumptions about the roles of men and women, matrimony and professions, Atalanta and her suitor. Though Yorke may have captured the driver, Phelps implies quite clearly who is likely really to win the race.

MICHAEL SARTISKY
Louisiana Endowment for the Humanities

NOTES

1. Vernon Louis Parrington, *Main Currents in American Thought, Volume III: The Beginnings of Critical Realism in America* (New York: Harcourt, Brace & World, 1958), 61–62.

2. Carol Farley Kessler, *Elizabeth Stuart Phelps* (Boston: Twayne Publishers, 1982), especially 128–34. See also two recent reprints of novels by Elizabeth Stuart Phelps (Ward): *The Silent Partner* (Old Westbury, NY: The Feminist Press, 1983; reprint of 1871 edition), afterword by Mary Jo Buhle and Florence Howe; and Carol Farley Kessler, ed., *The Story of Avis,* (New Brunswick, NJ: Rutgers University Press, 1985; reprint of 1877 edition). Phelps herself once characterized her principal causes as: "Heaven, homeopathy, and women's rights." Cited in Mary Angela Bennett, *Elizabeth Stuart Phelps* (Philadelphia: University of Pennsylvania Press, 1939), 1. *The Gates Ajar* was the first of a trilogy of novels depicting a utopian heaven.

3. William Dean Howells, *A Woman's Reason* (Boston: Houghton Mifflin, 1982; reprint of 1883 edition), 7–8.

4. The extreme of this attitude was expressed by

such men as Dr. Charles Meigs, a Boston obstetrician who observed in his textbook that woman "has a head almost too small for intellect, but just large enough for love." Cited in Mary Roth Walsh, *Doctors Wanted: No Women Need Apply* (New Haven, CT: Yale University Press, 1977), 111.

5. Howells, *A Woman's Reason,* 132–133.

6. From 1870 until 1900, the population of the United States doubled from 38.5 million people to 76.1 million, largely due to foreign immigration. By 1900, 14 percent of the population was foreign born; in the major cities over 100,000, which increased in number during this period from fourteen to thirty-eight, these immigrants comprised 35 percent of the total population. The urban population itself increased proportionally from 26 to 40 percent from 1870 to 1900. During this same period, the number of banks and their assets multiplied sixfold and the nation witnessed the concentration of capital and production in the rise of the trusts. The miles of main railroad track increased from 46,800 in 1869 to 190,000 in 1899. See Charles A. Beard and Mary R. Beard, *A Basic History of the United States* (Philadelphia: Blakiston, 1944), 292–311, and Burton J. Bledstein, *The Culture of Professionalism* (New York: W. W. Norton, 1976), 46.

7. Paul Starr, *The Social Transformation of American Medicine* (New York: Basic Books, 1982), 17. It should be noted that as *Doctor Zay* is concerned with a female physician in New England, the discussion here of the history of the medical profession is largely confined to that region, except where otherwise indicated. See also Robert H. Wiebe, *The Search for Order: 1870–1920* (New York: Hill and Wang, 1967), 111–132.

8. Bledstein, 84.

9. Starr, 99.

10. Bledstein, 85.

11. Ibid., 94–95.

12. Gerda Lerner, *The Majority Finds Its Past: Placing Women in History* (New York: Oxford University Press, 1979), 19.

13. Starr, 40.

14. See Bledstein, 84, and Starr, 42.

15. Barbara Ehrenreich and Deirdre English, *For Her Own Good: 150 Years of the Experts' Advice to Women* (Garden City, NY: Anchor Books, 1979), 11. Ehrenreich and English's analysis of the professionalization of the medical profession is part of their larger analysis of the place of women in society. They perceive an essential conflict between the nurturing, natural role of women and what they perceive as an essentially male trait of reifying all human activity into economic terms ruled by capitalistic values. In this they assert a fundamental association between male nature and capitalism itself, assuming that political and economic values are gender-specific:

> Biologically and psychologically, she [woman] seems to contradict the basic principles of the Market. The Market transforms human activities and needs into dead things—commodities—woman can, and does, create life. Economic man is an individual, and monad, connected to others only through a network of impersonal economic relationships; woman is embedded in the family, permitted no individual identity apart from her biological relationships to others. Economic man acts in perfect, self-interest; a woman cannot base her relationships within the family on the principle of *quid pro quo:* she gives. (19)

16. Starr, 31.

17. Kate Campbell Hurd-Mead, *Women in Medicine* (Haddam, CT: Haddam Press, 1938), 482–90, contains one of the most interesting accounts of the range of

women's medical activity during the colonial period. See also: Joseph Kett, *The Formation of the American Medical Profession: The Role of Institutions, 1780–1860* (New Haven, CT: Yale University Press, 1968), 108. Another interesting, if brief, discussion of the practice of medicine by women in the colonial and Revolutionary War period is to be found in Mary Putnam Jacobi, "Women in Medicine" in *Woman's Work in America*, ed. Annie Nathan Meyer (New York: Henry Holt, 1891), 141–42. Also see Lerner: " When Dr. Shippen announced his pioneering lectures on midwifery, he did it to combat 'the widespread popular prejudice against the man-midwife' and because he regarded most midwives ignorant and improperly trained." (19–21.17.)

18. Hurd-Mead, 486.

19. Jacobi, 140.

20. Other issues of importance to women, including abortion, became tangled in the movement towards professionalism. See James C. Mohr, *Abortion in America: The Origins and Evolution of National Policy, 1800–1900* (New York: Oxford University Press, 1978):

> Many regular doctors believed strongly that their future depended upon rigorous professionalization. But professionalization, the creation of a self-regulated guild with privileged status, depended in large part upon the ability of the group as a whole to enforce standards of behavior upon all of the individuals who wanted to be part of the profession. Since any healer who wanted to practice medicine could do so, the punishment of expulsion from a formally organized medical society was no particular threat. As a result, codes of ethics were largely unenforceable. Under these circumstances many professional-minded physicians looked to the state for help. An anti-abortion law would lend public sanction to the professionals' efforts at disciplining

their own organizations. Put somewhat differently, the
anti-abortion crusade became at least in part a manifes-
tation of the fact that many physicians wanted to pro-
mote, indeed to force where necessary, a sense of professionalism, as they defined it, upon their own colleagues.
(161–62)

21. Walsh, 10–15. The whole issue of professionalism
necessarily involved ideological conflicts between dem-
ocratic and elitist camps. Starr notes that "The professions offended Jacksonian ideology primarily because
of their attempts to establish exclusive privileges. In
the demands of insurgent parties, the abolition of 'licensed monopolies' had a high priority, and though
this referred mainly to business corporations with special privileges, the professions were included. The number of states and territories requiring professional
study to practice law fell from three quarters in 1800
to a third in 1830 and then to one quarter by 1860. The
decline in medicine was even more dramatic." (57)
(Starr cites these statistics from Arthur M. Schle-
singer, Jr., *Age of Jackson*, [Boston: Little, Brown,
1945], 134 and James Willard Hurst, *The Growth of
American Law: The Law Makers* [Boston: Little,
Brown, 1950], 280.) This remained true for the next
three decades when a reversal in the trend then manifested itself.

22. Walsh, 10. It should be noted that as social historians Walsh on the one hand and Ehrenreich and English on the other hold opposing ideological positions
on the difference between women's public and private
power. Where Walsh tends to emphasize the public di-
mension, often defined by society at large, of women's
power and position, Ehrenerich and English concen-
trate on the actual power wielded by women in the private sphere.

23. Catherine M. Scholten, "'On the Importance of

the Obstetrick Art': Changing Customs of Childbirth in America, 1760–1825," *William and Mary Quarterly* (Summer, 1977), 427–45, cited in Starr, 49–50.

24. Walsh, 11–15.

25. Ehrenreich and English, 41.

26. Lerner, 20.

27. "The point here is not so much that any one aspect of the process of professionalization excluded women, but that the process, which took place over the span of almost a century, proceeded in such a way as to institutionalize an exclusion of women, which had earlier been accomplished irregularly, inconsistently, and mostly by means of social pressure. The end result was an *absolute* lowering of the status for all women in the medical profession and a *relative* loss. As the professional status of all physicians advanced, the status differential between male and female practitioners was more obviously disadvantageous and underscored women's marginality." (Lerner, 20.)

28. Graduates of the New England Female Medical College went on to play significant roles in the history of medicine: "Dr. Rebecca Lee, in 1864 the first black woman to receive a medical degree in the United States, established a successful practice in post-Civil War Richmond. Dr. Mary Harris Thompson, who graduated the year before, founded the first hospital for women and children west of the Allegheny Mountains in Chicago in 1865 and in 1870 founded the Women's Hospital Medical College of Chicago, which was absorbed by Northwestern University in 1892." (Walsh, 61.)

29. Walsh, xv and 109.

30. Jacobi, 142–44. On the one hand: "The employment of men in midwifery practice is always grossly indelicate, often immoral, and always constitutes a se-

rious temptation to immorality." (Summary of Mr. Gregory's argument in "Man-Midwifery Exposed," 1848). On the other hand: "If I were to plan with malicious hate the greatest curse I could conceive for women, if I would estrange them from the protection of women, and make them as far as possible loathsome and disgusting to man, I would favor the so-called reform which proposed to make doctors of them." (Editorial Buffalo Medical Journal, 1869, 191).

31. Starr, 96–97.

32. Starr, 97–99. See also Ehrenreich and English, 59.

33. Walsh, 195.

34. Starr, 107.

35. Jacobi, 140. It should be noted that male physicians often refused to train midwives.

36. Wiebe, 114–16.

37. Walsh, 186. "In 1880 the regulars conducted seventy-six medical schools, the homeopaths fourteen, and the Eclectics eight. Ten years later, the respective totals were 106, 16, and 9." (Starr, 99.)

38. Beginning in 1852, when Dr. Nancy Talbot Clark was the first woman to seek certification from a state medical society, through the 1870s and 1880s, women brought constant pressure to bear on the state medical societies to admit women. Finally in 1884 the tide turned and the Massachusetts Medical Society by a vote of 209 to 123 voted to accept both men and women as candidates for admission into the society. Dr. Emma Call of the New England Hospital became the first female member. (Walsh, 151–62.) Johns Hopkins did not admit its first female medical students until 1893. "In 1893, three of Boston's four medical schools were open to women students: two regular medical schools, Tufts Medical School and the College

of Physicians and Surgeons and one homeopathic school, Boston University." (Walsh, 182.)

39. While there is a general consensus among historians as to this decline, their figures vary somewhat, in part depending on whether they are counting the number of female medical students or physicians. See Starr, 124, Ehrenreich and English, 88, and Walsh, 185–86.

40. Starr, 124. Even as late as 1976, the percentage of female physicians in Boston was only 11.7 percent. It should be noted, however, that the national average demonstrates a gradual increase over the last century, increasing from 2.8 percent in 1880 to 8.6 percent in 1976. (Walsh, 185–86.)

41. Elizabeth Stuart Phelps, *Chapters From a Life* (Boston: Houghton Mifflin, 1896), 99.

42. Van Wyck Brooks, *New England: Indian Summer* (New York: E.P. Dutton & Co., 1940), 80.

43. Phelps, *Chapters,* 133.

44. Parrington, 61. This novel was preceded by an earlier short story about the fire called "The Tenth of January." Phelps has also been called "the first American novelist to treat the social problems of the Machine Age seriously and at length." (Walter Fuller Taylor, *The Economic Novel in America* [Chapel Hill: University of North Carolina Press, 1942], 58.)

45. Elizabeth Stuart Phelps, "What Shall They Do," *Harper's New Monthly Magazine,* September 1867, 519–23 and "Why Shall They Do It," *Harper's New Monthly Magazine,* January 1868, 218–23.

46. Phelps, "What Shall They Do," 519.

47. "Be a doctor? and be sure that you could be few things more womanly or more noble." (Phelps, "What Shall They Do," 523.) This is particularly interesting given the observation of Mary Angela Bennett, her bi-

ographer, that "the only career really open to women at that time was marriage. Women doctors were just beginning to be heard of—with shudders." (Bennett, 25–26.)

48. Phelps, *Chapters,* 249–50.

49. Elizabeth Stuart Phelps, "The True Woman," *The Independent* 23, No. 1193 (12 October 1871):I, reprinted in Phelps, *The Story of Avis,* 269.

50. Kessler, *Elizabeth Stuart Phelps,* 71.

51. Austin Phelps, *My Portfolio* (New York: Charles Scribner's Sons, 1882), 97.

52. Ibid., 98.

53. Ibid., 101.

54. "Teach woman that marriage under existing conditions is vassalage, and then divorce for 'incompatibility of temper,' or any other 'skeleton in the house,' becomes another of her 'natural rights.'" (Austin Phelps, 109.) "The same passionate reasoning is seen in the recklessness with which the dignity of maternity is often flouted in the service of this social revolution." (Ibid., 110.)

55. Ibid., 110.

56. Ibid., 113.

57. In addition to her three novels, Phelps's fiction provides other instances of women successfully entering a variety of careers. "The Girl Who Could Not Write a Composition," *Our Young Folks,* August–September 1871, is an early work on the theme of a woman going into business upon the death of her father. There also are the female preacher of "A Woman's Pulpit," in *The Atlantic Monthly,* July 1870, and the protagonist of "The Chief Operator," *Harper's New Monthly Magazine,* July, 1909. (cited in Bennett, 39 and 59–60.)

58. "The realistic content of her fiction is usually re-

served for background and minor characters; her plots are those of sentimental fiction." (Helen Sootin Smith, introduction to Elizabeth Stuart Phelps, *The Gates Ajar* [Cambridge, MA: Belknap Press, 1964; reprint of 1868 edition], xx.)

59. Shortly after completing his novel about a female physician, William Dean Howells encouraged Elizabeth Stuart Phelps to pursue her idea for a similar novel. See Jean Carwile Masteller, "The Women Doctors of Howells, Phelps, and Jewett: The Conflict of Marriage and Career," in Gwen L. Nagel, ed., *Critical Essays on Sarah Orne Jewett* (Boston: G.K. Hall, 1984), 135.

60. William Dean Howells, *Criticism and Fiction*, ed. Clara Kirk and Rudolph Kirk (New York: New York University Press, 1965; reprint of 1891 edition), 38. Howells's work in particular, and the genre of realism in general, constitute the major documents of middle-class ideology in both its conservative and radical forms. For an extended discussion of the role of realism in U.S. ideology and culture, see Michael J. Sartisky, "A Literature Bound by Ideology: William Dean Howells and the Limits of Realism" (dissertation, State University of New York at Buffalo, 1981).

61. Phelps, *Chapters*, 259.

62. Ibid., 261.

63. Ibid., 265.

64. James D. Hart, *The Popular Book: A History of America's Literary Taste* (Berkeley: University of California Press, 1963), 120. Phelps's *The Gates Ajar* was the object of parody on this score in Mark Twain's derisive short story, "Extract from Captain Stormfield's Visit to Heaven" (1907).

65. Elizabeth Stuart Phelps, *The Silent Partner* (Boston: James R. Osgood, 1871), vi.

66. Ibid., 90.

67. Ibid., 108.

68. Elizabeth Barrett Browning's poem *Aurora Leigh* served as the inspiration for Phelps's writing on women's quandary between marriage and domesticity or another career. (Bennett, 17 Phelps's own illness began around 1877 and became severe in the 1880s. She suffered from insomnia, a tendency towards tuberculosis, and bouts of partial blindness. She married Herbert Dickenson Ward, many years her junior, in 1888.

69. Phelps, *The Story of Avis,* 27.

70. Ibid., 69–70.

71. Ibid., 82.

72. Ibid., 63.

73. "It was his physical ruin and helplessness which appealed to the strength in her." (Phelps, *The Story of Avis,* 99.)

74. Ibid., 241.

75. Christened Mary Gray, Phelps adopted her deceased mother's name circa 1854.

76. Phelps is imposing autobiography on her character: "I am uncertain whether I ought to add that I believe in the homeopathic system of therapeutics. I am often told by skeptical friends that I hold this belief on a par with the Christian religion; and I am not altogether inclined to deny the sardonic impeachment! When our bodies cease to be drugged into disease and sin, it is my personal impression that our souls will begin to stand a fair chance; perhaps not much before." (Phelps, *Chapters From a Life,* 252.)

77. Curiously, both Phelps in *The Silent Partner* and Howells in his second novel, *A Chance Acquaintance* (1873), reject matrimony as the conventional resolution of their novels, but in the early 1880s both succumb to it. In Howells's case, this was due to the out-

rage of his readers when he failed to have his protagonists marry; this, incidentally, was a pattern from which he deviated only once in his career. Given the lack of any logical attraction between Zay and Yorke, Phelps'sresorting to this romantic convention in contradiction of the weight of evidence of Yorke's limitations serves to generate serious reservations on the part of the reader and thus undermines the convention itself.

78. Phelps comments on reversals of gender roles: "It was apt, he remembered, to be the woman whom nature or fate, God, *or at least man* [my emphasis] (the same thing doubtless, to her), had relegated to the minor note. It occurred to him that in this case he seemed to have struck it himself." (97) Note the other numerous instances in which Yorke is described as a woman: fainting in a "lady-like" (140) or submitting in a "feminine" (69) manner.

79. One suspects that Phelps, despite her Andover upbringing, or in rebellion from it, is capable even of the occasional risquéc observation. As Dr. Zay returns from discovering the identity of the young man who has impregnated young, unwed Molly, she informs Yorke of the fact. Phelps has him respond with an uncharacteristic and morally ambiguous double entendre: "Yorke uttered a sympathetic ejaculation as her meaning flashed upon him." (137)

80. Robert Graves, *The Greek Myths: Volume I* (New York: Viking Penguin, 1960), 264-68. Additional aspects of the myth of Atalanta are also germane to the novel, though as they refer to the period of Atalanta's marriage, they extend beyond the frame of the novel itself. Reconciled to her father by virtue of her exploits, she was commanded by him to marry. To this she consented, but only with the conditions stated pre-

viously. According to some versions of the myth, she continued to pretend to be a virgin even after her marriage, though she is reputed to have borne a son whose name, Parthenopaeus, meant "son of a pierced maidenhead." According to another version of the myth, Atalanta and Melanion, once married, defiled a temple of Zeus by making love in it. Zeus then punished them by transforming them into lions which meant, according to some mythographers, that they were thus prevented from ever again being lovers.

81. In *The Story of Avis,* the myth of the artistic virgin goddess Artemis and Ariadne, a woman and rival artist, is referred to several times. Other mythic pairs, such as Isis and Osiris and Siegfried and Brünnhilde, are also present. In *Doctor Zay,* Yorke's uncle's will is described as being vested with "Orphean power" (5), and on the next page there is a reference to "a myth of the Golden Age." "Myth" in reference to the uncle appears again three times on page eight. Still later, the Atalanta myth resonates when Phelps refers to the "virgin State of Maine" (11) and the apple blossom she dropped on the road before him. (25) Elsewhere are strewn references to Lachesis, "the measurer," one of the three Fates (126), and caryatids, or columns shaped like women. (22)

82. William Dean Howells, *Doctor Breen's Practice* (Boston: James R. Osgood, 1881), 12.

83. Ibid., 43.

84. Howells, *Doctor Breen's Practice,* 271.

85. Cited in Masteller, 144.

86. Sarah Orne Jewett, *A Country Doctor* (Boston: Houghton Mifflin, 1884), 283.

87. Ibid., 336.

88. Ibid., 335.

89. Annie Nathan Meyer, *Helen Brent, M.D.: A So-*

cial Study (New York: Cassell Publishing, 1892), 137.

90. Ibid., 26.

91. Ibid., 19.

92. Ibid, 49.

93. Ibid., 49–50.

94. Ibid., 93–94.

95. Ibid., 143.

96. Henry Demarest Lloyd, *Wealth Against Commonwealth* (New York: Harper & Brothers, 1894), 521.

97. Phelps, *Chapters,* 249.

The Feminist Press at The City University of New York offers
alternatives in education and in literature. Founded in 1970,
this nonprofit, tax-exempt educational and publishing organi-
zation works to eliminate sexual stereotypes in books and
schools and to provide literature with a broad vision of human
potential. The publishing program includes reprints of important works by women, feminist biographies of women, and
nonsexist children's books. Curricular materials, bibliogra-
phies, directories, and a quarterly journal provide information
and support for students and teachers of women's studies. In-
service projects help to transform teaching methods and cur-
ricula. Through publications and projects, The Feminist Press
contributes to the rediscovery of the history of women and the
emergence of a more humane society.

NEW AND FORTHCOMING BOOKS

Carrie Chapman Catt: A Public Life, by Jacqueline Van
Voris. $24.95 cloth.

Competition: A Feminist Forum, edited by Helen E.
Longino and Valerie Miner. Foreword by Nell Irvin
Painter. $29.95 cloth, $12.95 paper.

The Cross-Cultural Study of Women, edited by Margot I.
Duley and Mary I. Edwards. $29.95 cloth, $12.95 paper.

Daughter of Earth, a novel by Agnes Smedley. Foreword by
Alice Walker. Afterword by Nancy Hoffman. $8.95 paper.

*Daughter of the Hills: A Woman's Part in the Coal Miners'
Struggle,* a novel of the thirties, by Myra Page.
Introduction by Alice Kessler-Harris and Paul Lauter and
afterword by Deborah S. Rosenfelt. $8.95 paper.

*The Defiant Muse: French Feminist Poems from the Middle
Ages to the Present,* a bilingual anthology edited and
with an introduction by Domna C. Stanton. $29.95 cloth,
$11.95 paper.

*The Defiant Muse: German Feminist Poems from the
Middle Ages to the Present,* a bilingual anthology edited
and with an introduction by Susan L. Cocalis. $29.95
cloth, $11.95 paper.

*The Defiant Muse: Hispanic Feminist Poems from the
Middle Ages to the Present,* a bilingual anthology edited
and with an introduction by Angel Flores and Kate
Flores. $29.95 cloth, $11.95 paper.

The Defiant Muse: Italian Feminist Poems from the Middle

Ages to the Present, a bilingual anthology edited by Beverly Allen, Muriel Kittel, and Keala Jane Jewell, and with an introduction by Beverly Allen. $29.95 cloth, $11.95 paper.

An Estate of Memory, a novel by Ilona Karmel. Afterword by Ruth K. Angress. $11.95 paper.

Feminist Resources for Schools and Colleges: A Guide to Curricular Materials, 3rd edition, compiled and edited by Anne Chapman. $12.95 paper.

Harem Years: The Memoirs of an Egyptian Feminist, 1879–1924, by Huda Shaarawi. Translated and edited by Margot Badran. $29.95 cloth, $9.95 paper.

Leaving Home, a novel by Elizabeth Janeway. Afterword by Rachel Brownstein. $8.95 paper.

The Parish and the Hill, a novel by Mary Doyle Curran. Afterword by Anne Halley. $8.95 paper.

Rights and Wrongs: Women's Struggle for Legal Equality, 2nd edition, by Susan Cary Nichols, Alice M. Price, and Rachel Rubin. $7.95 paper.

This Child's Gonna Live, a novel by Sarah E. Wright. Appreciation by John Oliver Killens. $9.95 paper.

Turning the World Upside Down: The Anti-Slavery Convention of American Women Held in New York City, May 9–12, 1837. Introduction by Dorothy Sterling. $2.95 paper.

The Wide, Wide World, a novel by Susan Warner. Afterword by Jane Tompkins. $29.95 cloth, $11.95 paper.

With Wings: An Anthology of Literature by and about Women with Disabilities, edited by Marsha Saxton and Florence Howe. $29.95 cloth, $12.95 paper.

Writing Red: An Anthology of American Women Writers, 1930–1940, edited by Charlotte L. Nekola and Paula Rabinowitz. Foreword by Toni Morrison. $29.95 cloth, $12.95 paper.

FICTION CLASSICS

Between Mothers and Daughters: Stories across a Generation, edited by Susan Koppelman. $9.95 paper.

Brown Girl, Brownstones, a novel by Paule Marshall. Afterword by Mary Helen Washington. $8.95 paper.

Call Home the Heart, a novel of the thirties, by Fielding Burke. Introduction by Alice Kessler-Harris and Paul

Lauter and afterwords by Sylvia J. Cook and Anna W. Shannon. $9.95 paper.

Cassandra, by Florence Nightingale. Introduction by Myra Stark. Epilogue by Cynthia MacDonald. $4.50 paper.

The Changelings, a novel by Jo Sinclair. Afterwords by Nellie McKay, and Johnnetta B. Cole and Elizabeth H. Oakes; biographical note by Elisabeth Sandberg. $8.95 paper.

The Convert, a novel by Elizabeth Robins. Introduction by Jane Marcus. $8.95 paper.

Daddy Was a Number Runner, a novel by Louise Meriwether. Foreword by James Baldwin and afterword by Nellie McKay. $8.95 paper.

Guardian Angel and Other Stories, by Margery Latimer. Afterwords by Nancy Loughridge, Meridel Le Sueur, and Louis Kampf. $8.95 paper.

I Love Myself when I Am Laughing . . . And Then Again when I Am Looking Mean and Impressive: A Zora Neale Hurston Reader, edited by Alice Walker. Introduction by Mary Helen Washington. $9.95 paper.

Life in the Iron Mills and Other Stories, by Rebecca Harding Davis. Biographical interpretation by Tillie Olsen. $7.95 paper.

The Living Is Easy, a novel by Dorothy West. Afterword by Adelaide M. Cromwell. $9.95 paper.

The Other Woman: Stories of Two Women and a Man, edited by Susan Koppelman. $9.95 paper.

Reena and Other Stories, selected short stories by Paule Marshall. $8.95 paper.

Ripening: Selected Work, 1927–1980, 2nd edition, by Meridel Le Sueur. Edited with an introduction by Elaine Hedges. $9.95 paper.

Rope of Gold, a novel of the thirties, by Josephine Herbst. Introduction by Alice Kessler-Harris and Paul Lauter and afterword by Elinor Langer. $9.95 paper.

The Silent Partner, a novel by Elizabeth Stuart Phelps. Afterword by Mari Jo Buhle and Florence Howe. $8.95 paper.

Swastika Night, a novel by Katharine Burdekin. Introduction by Daphne Patai. $8.95 paper.

The Unpossessed, a novel of the thirties, by Tess Slesinger. Introduction by Alice Kessler-Harris and Paul Lauter and afterword by Janet Sharistanian. $9.95 paper.

Weeds, a novel by Edith Summers Kelley. Afterword by

Charlotte Goodman. $8.95 paper.

A Woman of Genius, a novel by Mary Austin. Afterword by
Nancy Porter. $9.95 paper.

Women and Appletrees, a novel by Moa Martinson.
Translated from the Swedish and with an afterword by
Margaret S. Lacy. $8.95 paper.

Women Working: An Anthology of Stories and Poems,
edited and with an introduction by Nancy Hoffman and
Florence Howe. $9.95 paper.

The Yellow Wallpaper, by Charlotte Perkins Gilman.
Afterword by Elaine Hedges. $4.50 paper.

OTHER TITLES

Antoinette Brown Blackwell: A Biography, by Elizabeth
Cazden. $24.95 cloth, $9.95 paper.

*All the Women Are White, All the Blacks Are Men, but
Some of Us Are Brave: Black Women's Studies,* edited by
Gloria T. Hull, Patricia Bell Scott, and Barbara Smith.
$12.95 paper.

Black Foremothers: Three Lives, by Dorothy Sterling. $9.9
paper.

Complaints and Disorders: The Sexual Politics of Sickness,
by Barbara Ehrenreich and Deirdre English. $3.95 paper.

*A Day at a Time: The Diary Literature of American Women
from 1764 to the Present,* edited and with an introduction
by Margo Culley. $29.95 cloth, $12.95 paper.

Household and Kin: Families in Flux, by Amy Swerdlow,
Renate Bridenthal, Joan Kelly, and Phyllis Vine. $9.95
paper.

How to Get Money for Research, by Mary Rubin and the
Business and Professional Women's Foundation. Foreword
by Mariam Chamberlain. $6.95 paper.

In Her Own Image: Women Working in the Arts, edited and
with an introduction by Elaine Hedges and Ingrid Wendt.
$9.95 paper.

*Integrating Women's Studies into the Curriculum: A Guide
and Bibliography,* by Betty Schmitz. $9.95 paper.

Käthe Kollwitz: Woman and Artist, by Martha Kearns,
$9.95 paper.

Las Mujeres: Conversations from a Hispanic Community,
by Nan Elsasser, Kyle MacKenzie, and Yvonne Tixier y
Vigil. $9.95 paper.

Lesbian Studies: Present and Future, edited by Margaret Cruikshank. $9.95 paper.

Mother to Daughter, Daughter to Mother: A Daybook and Reader, selected and shaped by Tillie Olsen. $9.95 paper.

Moving the Mountain: Women Working for Social Change, by Ellen Cantarow with Susan Gushee O'Malley and Sharon Hartman Strom. $9.95 paper.

Out of the Bleachers: Writings on Women and Sport, edited and with an introduction by Stephanie L. Twin. $10.95 paper.

Portraits of Chinese Women in Revolution, by Agnes Smedley. Edited and with an introduction by Jan MacKinnon and Steve MacKinnon and an afterword by Florence Howe. $10.95 paper.

Reconstructing American Literature: Courses, Syllabi, Issues, edited by Paul Lauter. $10.95 paper.

Salt of the Earth, screenplay by Michael Wilson with historical commentary by Deborah Silverton Rosenfelt. $10.95 paper.

These Modern Women: Autobiographical Essays from the Twenties, edited with an introduction by Elaine Showalter. $8.95 paper.

Witches, Midwives, and Nurses: A History of Women Healers, by Barbara Ehrenreich and Deirdre English. $3.95 paper.

With These Hands: Women Working on the Land, edited with an introduction by Joan M. Jensen. $9.95 paper.

The Woman and the Myth: Margaret Fuller's Life and Writings, by Bell Gale Chevigny. $8.95 paper.

Woman's "True" Profession: Voices from the History of Teaching, edited with an introduction by Nancy Hoffman. $9.95 paper.

Women Have Always Worked: A Historical Overview, by Alice Kessler-Harris. $9.95 paper.

For a free catalog, write to The Feminist Press at The City University of New York, 311 East 94 Street, New York, NY 10128. Send individual book orders to The Feminist Press, P.O. Box 1654, Hagerstown, MD 21741. Include $1.75 postage and handling for one book and 75¢ for each additional book. To order using MasterCard or Visa, call: (800) 638–3030.